KJ MCQUADE

# Fathoms

*A Seaside Monster Mystery Novel*

*First published by ELK Publishing 2025*

*Copyright © 2025 by KJ McQuade*

*Library of Congress Control Number: 2025908341*

*First edition*

*ISBN: 979-8-9987495-1-3*

*This book was professionally typeset on Reedsy.
Find out more at reedsy.com*

# Contents

## V   Monday

## VI   Tuesday

## VII   Wednesday

## VIII   Thursday

## IX   Friday

*To Victoria & Emrick*

# Prologue

The boat's top-mounted lamp started flickering less than an hour into the deputy harbormaster's shift. He had noticed the bulb needed to be replaced two nights before, even left a note about it at the station. But there he was, motoring through the fog cast in an alien, quivering orange glow, for the second straight night. A few hours later, he was almost used to it.

The Lincoln Head beacon to the east only registered as a dull white flash, like faraway lightning timed to strike every four seconds. The regular lazy tones of the foghorn were more a comfort than a guide. Anyone who made their business on East Hook Bay could find their way through the fog.

He swung the boat around to port and pulled back on the throttle, easing into his wind-down. Puttering back and forth across the bay like a farmer tilling the calm black water with the propellers on his twin engines, he methodically swept the lamp back and forth as he progressed. For the last year, he had ended all his night shifts this way. Better not to guess what the harbor may have claimed in the night and better he find it than some loudmouth lobsterman. Still, his pulse quickened and his grip on the wheel tightened every time something other than buoys or seaweed coalesced into focus. After his fifth clear straightaway, the deputy harbormaster took a long sip from his thermos; the coffee had long since gone cold, which would have been more annoying if it weren't mostly whiskey. He looked at his watch and saw that it was 4:42. On a clear day he would start seeing a glow at the east horizon, but they weren't expecting clear days for some time.

The usual crew at the Porpoise usually asked him about the sunrise when he came in for breakfast after his shift and what conditions it portended. If he saw tourists or strangers around during the season he would usually reply, "What do you mean? The sun doesn't rise here 'til June fifteenth." Tourists almost always ruefully laughed, wishing they'd had that information before they booked their getaway.

The deputy harbormaster tried to focus on breakfast to keep the boredom, and nervousness, at bay as he scanned the water. His cholesterol was too high. The last doctor he saw told him to try having oatmeal for breakfast, as if that were something he could look forward to while shivering out in purgatory. No sir, he was having sausage and eggs at the Porpoise, drenched in ketchup, with a scalding cup of coffee. If his doctor was so good then he'd have already figured out how to get rid of the matching rashes on the insides of his biceps.

The lamp's flickering grew more insistent. He banged on the hard plastic roof under the light with the side of his fist a few times and the beam steadied somewhat. He picked out a buoy a hundred yards ahead he'd use to make his turn and rechecked the compass for his heading. The harbormaster had been putting about twenty feet between each straightaway, the lamp couldn't pierce the fog much more than that. But he sensed a change to the air; the wind was picking up and dissipating the heavy nightly fog into the lighter daily mist. He wiped off his glasses, closed the windows, zipped up his jacket to the throat, flicked on the wipers and reversed his heading thirty feet closer to the bridge, trying his luck with fewer rows. And an earlier breakfast.

His gamble would have paid off. The lamp was able to bore a little further into the fog before it stopped flickering and went out entirely only halfway through the straightaway. The deputy harbormaster cursed out loud, his voice echoing off the rocks and water he could no longer see. As he cut the engines and zoomed in on the GPS display he uttered a silent curse at the harbormaster and his fellow deputies for their laziness and for putting him into the situation. Distracted, thinking about what regulations and codes they all broke sending him out at night with faulty equipment, he felt the bobbing boat shudder as it drifted into a buoy. He sighed and un-velcroed the flashlight from beneath the dash. "Let's see if they forgot about you too," he murmured as he pointed it off starboard and thumbed the switch forward. The beam shot out into the marine layer, whiter than the lamplight and weaker, unable to penetrate the gray wool beyond a few yards.

He pursed his lips and let out his breath, too slow for a whistle. He couldn't sweep the harbor with the flashlight. The tide had just started to come back in and without good light he was likely to scrape some of the shallower rocks by the shoreline. His only choice was a slow, straight shot through the middle of the bay back downtown to the Harbor Patrol pier. He restarted the engine, pushed the throttle one click forward and spun the wheel with his right hand as he pointed the weak white beam on his heading home.

As he puttered through the dark water, he had to keep his eyes moving between all the buoys, moorings, boats and rocks he had to steer around and the GPS, while periodically checking to make sure he re-corrected his course after every

3

maneuver. The display showed him going down the center of the bay, refreshing almost in time with each foghorn blare, showing his triangle's slow progress towards the warm, dry station and the hot, wet coffee at the Porpoise.

After a few minutes of uneventful navigation, the flashlight beam hit a rusting metal wall ten feet directly in front of him. Startled, the deputy harbormaster's instincts, dulled as they were by whiskey, fatigue and age, took over and he pulled back the throttle and spun the wheel hard to port, ending up safely parallel to the wall with two and a half feet to spare. Up close, he recognized the wall as the hull of the *Edna Millay*, a half sunken commercial fishing vessel the new scrap-metal-collecting owner hadn't bothered to raise and tow. Confused, he checked the GPS again. The *Edna Millay* had been resting on the east side of the harbor for five years and he was in the center. The screen showed him right in the middle, heading 255 degrees southwest by west, 1.5 knots from the pier.

He throttled back his concern about the appearing ghost ship, understanding things always move on the water, almost always with sensible explanations. He figured the new owner may have started towing it; it did look like it was sitting higher in the water. His heart still pounding from the surprise, he gave the *Edna Millay* a wider berth, turning further to port. As he cleared the bow he paused before turning back to starboard, towards home, to check the GPS screen again. 255 degrees southwest by west, 1.5 knots from the pier. It hadn't refreshed. He tapped it with his hand and the screen went black then re-illuminated with a blank blue kills screen. He grabbed it, was tempted to rip it off the dashboard and throw it in the fog, but instead let go and looked at the magnetic compass above the dash. 130, he was going southeast.

He put the boat in idle and finished his coffee while formulating a plan. The sun was on its way up and the prudent thing would have been to drop anchor and wait until visibility improved. He could also radio the station and get towed or guided in. Both options involved a cold, wet wait in the fog that was starting to suffocate him. He knew he could get back, if he took it very slow and through some miracle the flashlight's batteries didn't go dead. He grabbed his empty thermos and leaned over the side of the boat to clean it off in the salt water, just in case someone else did need to come on board that morning. He stood back up and waved the light until it found the *Edna Millay*.

Knowing the pier was Northwest of the rusted ship, which had apparently not yet been towed, the deputy harbormaster spun the wheel to set his new heading through gritted teeth. He wondered how long one of the other deputies would have kept going in the wrong direction in his situation. They all relied way too much on GPS. He thought he remembered hearing about some necessary software update in a team safety meeting the month before, but he would find out for sure when he got back. Right after breakfast he'd march back into the station and give the harbormaster holy hell for putting his life in danger. A lot can go wrong on the water in the dark in the best circumstances. He was sent out there with no lamp and no GPS, in fucking East Hook. He tried to remember where he kept the union contact info card, they would probably need to step in for something like that.

A few cold minutes of slow going after getting back on the right heading, he started to recognize boats and familiar rock outcroppings that assured him at least the old compass still worked. He was going the right way. The deputy harbormaster kept his flashlight moving in front of him, not wanting any surprise bumps or scrapes when he was so close to home. Having passed into the inner harbor, he had a lot more obstacles to dodge. Not that he wouldn't have an excuse if he did hit something.

Slowly it started to get lighter, and the mist was clearing a bit. Rays from the impending sunrise hitting what was left of it seemed to shift everything a few shades left on the color-wheel from normal. Brown-gray rocks glowed orange, the water a light purple blue under his flashlight. He even caught some seaweed that flashed bright pink, the tendrils resembling a sort of geometric pattern. The pattern only struck him as odd after he'd moved the beam more starboard. He moved it back and upon closer inspection, saw that it wasn't seaweed, but cloth, and not really floating, but on a rock. The rock appeared a sickly pale white in the mixed light and looked to be bobbing with the tide, more likely a piece of Styrofoam or birch branch than a rock. As the boat glided forward, the beam caught something glinting a few feet in front of the cloth.

Even at five miles an hour, the deputy harbormaster was moving too fast to keep the light's beam steady. He stayed on his path for a few dozen heartbeats, his fatigue outweighing his curiosity. Something about that glint stuck with him though. There's plenty of metal in the water: chains, clasps, motors and hulls, but nothing gold.

He put the boat in reverse.

His angle wasn't perfect, and when he found the cloth again he was farther from it than on the first pass, but once he moved into idle, he was able to focus on what he was seeing.

He caught the glint again and felt something drop in his

stomach. He couldn't put his finger on it until he noticed the rhythm of how it bobbed. It moved not in time with, but lagging behind the bobbing of the cloth, like the tail of a snake following the head, connected, but in a jointed, independent way. In idle, the boat drifted closer, the pull it had on his attention manifested its own gravity. A gravity pulling the deputy harbormaster further into the depths, as he wished more and more every second he were on dry land.

The unsettled feeling in the pit of his stomach evolved into full on nausea as he recognized a small, sleek, pointing piece of flotsam now only a few feet from the hull. It was a shoe, a high-heeled, woman's shoe. He moved the flashlight beam with his now unsteady hands up from the shoe toward the cloth and the glint. Up close, the cloth was a waterlogged patterned pink blouse or dress, and the glint a gold charm bracelet. The objects were bobbing in time with one another because they were both connected to the same skinny, sickly pale arm.

# I

# Wednesday

# Academicism

"What draws your eye in this quadrant?"

Maya chimed in, "I like the way the outside is darker than the office, like it's tinted glass. How'd you get that effect Ellis?"

In general, I refused to defend my work during group defenses. If the piece didn't speak for itself, silence and a shrug was the only help it'll get. Maya's comment was more of a question though, in the neighborhood of praise.

"I added a brown, kind of burnt orange to a more normal outdoor palette and, uhh, deepened the shadows."

"And you added a brown glow to the plants on the sill and the top of the bookshelf." After Guardado pointed it out, most of the class leaned forward to see it and I heard what I hoped was a quiet ahh from one of them. "But why do you think Ellis spent so much time on a glass effect? Why draw the eye to the background?"

I stayed quiet and shrugged.

"Your tentacle businessman is striking and anonymous, menacing and bland. The office is fully realized, a place we've all been. So what are we feeling when we look at this?"

I did my impression of a blank canvas.

"One of the customers might be fidgeting, and one might be talking. What other movement are you trying to show? Looks like the monster banker is just taking it all in." Capturing movement in painting is all suggestion. Tensed muscles, impossible-to-sustain posture, references to famous photos, everything relies on the viewer's imagination. "Colors are cool, even if the orange suggests violent sunlight outside, the greens suggest powerful air conditioning. Maybe you could have some leaves of the plant by the wall be out of whack, suggesting air coming from the ceiling, but the place..." He paused, preparing to render his initial judgment, "...is real, I feel it, I've been there."

I stayed a statue. Guardado always started with the good. *Tread lightly*, I always said to myself in these situations, *for you tread upon my dreams.*

"Why? I can go to a bank and take an actual photo, more realistic than any painting, if I want to see that. It looks like an office in some desert suburb, where a monster banker is tricking an unsuspecting couple, but what is it?"

"If this were an intro class, I'd spend a whole day on the technique, and Ellis, I could. The level of detail in just the background astounds: the thin corded carpeting, the generic leadership posters, ergonomic keyboard pads and accounting binders in the bookshelf, the longer I look the more I see and recognize. But this piece is as soulless as the office you're showing." There it was. "Bankers are monsters? This is a political cartoon that took three weeks to make."

One.

"I don't mean to pick on you Ellis, but it's again represen- tative of the hole at the center of your Monsters series. The course asks you to look at how society treats the other, how the different and foreign are painted as monsters and how it colors everyone's opinions, consciously and subconsciously. And your response is to make painting after painting beating people over the head with the same message: be afraid of monsters." He stopped to hear from me.

I'd heard it before from Guardado, it was his little pet cause, one I could never agree with. I knew deep in the center of me, my heart tapping out a simple message in Morse code since I was very young: be afraid of monsters.

But there was less than a week left of classes and I'd at least learned what he wanted to hear. "What about a painting from the banker's perspective, with the desperate people coming in depicted as some lower caste swamp monsters or something?"

"Yes!" He pointed at me as I said it. "You have a soul!" He made a show of calming down, as if his earlier passion were just a performance. "Show it in your work. You have one more chance: your final piece. Is that the subject?" I didn't move, he shook his head. "I hope you've already started. It's due in a week." I had hoped to have a subject picked by then too. Whatever small crisis of inspiration I was going through, that defense wasn't likely to help.

"Just get the big thing right, because the small things, literally everything else..." He did a chef's kiss and a few students laughed. He moved on to the painting next to mine.

"Ok this one has kind of the opposite problem, I get what you're trying to say and I think it's an important and brave message, it just looks like a four year old scribbled it on my wall."

There wasn't much of Ivy showing beneath her hoodie and behind her laptop screen, but I picked her out in the corner booth. I had learned to push past her electrified fence aura and tossed my bag on the cushion next to her. She jumped, saw it was me and went back to glaring at her screen. "Greg doesn't look left in any of these goddamn takes."

"Yeah, but you can really see the pain in his eyes."

She laughed, but I doubt she heard me through her headphones. Her posture relaxed and she leaned back in her seat a bit, still looking at the footage. "He's actually doing good…" Bravo Greg. She pulled her right ear free. "How did your defense go?"

"I still don't get it. My monsters are too scary." I said it like I was mocking Guardado, even though I knew he was probably right.

"Your professor sucks, I loved it."

"So what are you trying to say, with your film? Hope it's not something everyone already knows."

Ivy looked up from her computer but not quite at me and spoke in a singsong voice: "Everyone already knows how most stories are going to end, you surprise them with the way you tell it. Friend."

I was pretty sure just the last part was hers. "What's that from?"

"Alexandrovic. He wrote it in his film criticism book he made us buy last semester." Ivy's youth was showing. I made it a point to not remember what my professors said.

"How much progress you hoping to make this weekend?"

"I want pretty good versions of scene fourteen and twenty-eight, then I can see what priority reshoots we need before people start going home."

"Oh god, will you need me as a stand in again?"

Ivy, with her eyes still on the screen, snorted a little at the thought. "That was a failed experiment. You can't even stand still normally. Even your back looks totally terrified." I never understood how actors can be comfortable looking so stupid. "What do you have to do?"

"I've got to start sketching tonight, like right now actually, but we should be able to squeeze some fun in."

Ivy and I had been dating for 8 months, a long 8 months of listening to her rave about the sunsets in Days of Heaven and the Dutch angles in Third Man. Sometimes I think Ivy's love of film grew from her Los Angeles upbringing, but it was probably due to her lonely upbringing. Working parents and no siblings have a habit of getting replaced by stand-ins, movies and television if the kid is lucky. Ivy's parents were an accountant and a doctor, which gave her a rare practicality at art school. I don't know if I was attracted to that or her passion. I also don't know what attracted her to me. Either way, we had been good together for a while. I usually sketched during movie night, and Dutch angles have worked their way into my compositions.

"Christie is hosting this wine and cheese party at her boyfriend's apartment tomorrow; we should at least show up."

I wasn't sure we at least had to do anything, but didn't have an alternative suggestion. "Doesn't she live near Antonio's? We can eat there first."

"I feel disgusting. I haven't worked out in like a week. I don't need Antonio's."

"What are we doing tonight?"

"I don't know." I could feel her laptop pulling her back.

"Like I mean should I get coffee?"

"Actually, if you want to stay get me a caramel honey latte.

15

I just really want to figure out this scene while I have it… Do you have something you can work on?"

I was standing in line and my phone started ringing. I was pretty sure it was Ivy giving me more instructions for her drink. I was hoping she'd get something without whipped cream so I could see the barista's technique for shaping the steamed milk. It wasn't from Ivy though, it was Rocco, from the sticks. I stepped out of line and answered.

"Rock!"

"Ellis Hook! How's it going?" He sounded tired.

"Usual man, painting. How's the early season?" I had a big smile on my face.

"Starting to get crowded. Only with dumb ones. We've had a marine layer every day for two weeks. All the tourists I've seen looked pissed."

"Yeah well you get what you pay for. You doing any tours?"

"Not this year, no one's getting out on the water." He cut off suddenly and took a deep breath. "So listen, got some bad news… Cadie O'Reilly died."

I stopped smiling. "What happened?"

"She drowned. One of the harbormasters found her in the downtown bay this morning."

"What?!"

"Yeah, in the middle of it though, not on the shore."

"Like she fell off a boat?"

"So I only know what people are telling me, but they said she was wearing a dress, like a summer dress."

I started sweating and felt something in my stomach start making its way up to my throat. "What are people saying?"

"So this just happened, it's not in any news or anything yet, but right now it's just a million questions. Some people think she might've been drunk or high."

"Oh my god. Had you seen her recently?"

Rocco sighed. "Not really, one or two times at the Gannett, but nothing longer than a quick hello." He paused again. "One of the twins saw her and said she was acting crazy, saying weird stuff, not making sense, but when I saw her she seemed normal."

"Didn't someone drown like a month ago?"

"Yeah, Jim Minonne, back in April, in the Headsman though."

I had a million more questions running through my head but caught myself and just asked the sympathetic one.

"So you have to call a bunch of people today?"

"I called Desmond and you so far. I'm probably gonna call Rick right after. Like I said, no one knows this yet, I just... I needed to talk to you guys about it."

"Yeah."

I wanted to say the right thing, but I just stayed quiet. Even over the phone, I could see the wheels turning in Rocco's head. When he talked, it sounded like he was looking at the water.

"You just... You always remember your first."

I wished I had some water to look at, instead of the courtyard, rhythmically obscured by the fog my shallow breaths were making on the glass.

"Yeah, buddy, you do. No one's made any plans for the funeral right?"

"No, nothing yet. It'll probably be Friday or Saturday though."

"Let me know. Thanks for calling me... This sucks."

"Yeah man... So I'm gonna call Rick, but you coming home

for the funeral?"

"Yeah, for sure."

"Ok, good. Take care man... stay alive."

"You too."

I put my phone back in my pocket and stood still, facing the window. Cadie O'Reilly, gone. Rocco was right, you never forget your first.

I refocused my eyes to catch my reflection in the glass, to confirm I was still there. My almost transparent outline was starting to form when I heard a bang above me and felt the vibration trough my fingertips on the on the window. I jumped back and looked around me to see what was going on, then looked back out the window and found the source. A pigeon had flown into the glass above my head, and now lay dead in a feathered puddle two feet in front of me on the other side of the window.

# II

# Friday

# Impressionism

The funeral was Saturday at the Harbor church, and we left Friday, after Ivy's last class. I told her she didn't have to come. I wasn't sure I wanted her to come, but she said she wanted to be there for me. I suspected she really wanted to see my hometown and stay in the house I grew up in, locking us into a more serious relationship just before I graduated. Either way, she had the car.

I could feel her becoming more nervous the closer we got to East Hook, and I found myself feeling the same way, even though I couldn't exactly explain why. As we crossed the state line I looked at the new bright red streaks she colored into the side of her hair with surprising annoyance, and hoped she'd opt for long sleeves to cover her Guy Fawkes tattoo all weekend. I knew it was stupid, I liked her hair, and liked her tattoo, I just wasn't sure East Hook would like them. I wondered if passing back into my home state reverted me back in some ways.

"So what was your high school mascot again?" She smiled slyly. "I'm going to ask the old timers about the local teams, to fit in."

"The Kraken."

Ivy burst out laughing, "I knew it was stupid, why not the

sharks or some real sea creature?"

I shook my head, thinking that better not be her go-to joke when we arrive. East Hook took its fake sea creatures pretty seriously.

"So you paint tentacles because of school spirit?" She was teasing, but she wasn't far off. It was more out of town pride, with a lot of commercial considerations. My tentacle paintings had so far netted me: no-charge upgrades to large pizzas at Harbor Pie, first drink on the house at the Porpoise, a ten percent friends of Renard discount at RNA Books, and one free round trip ticket to Haven Island every year on the Salt Cod. The going rate for seascapes wasn't nearly as high, not in that town.

"You're gonna get sick of seeing my tentacle paintings after this weekend." Not all of them had tentacles, but most did. All of them had monsters though, at least every one worth hanging in public.

"Great, I haven't seen enough of those."

She had some time before she had to see the latest one. I had made zero progress on my final painting in the days before we left. I sketched out a few monsters, some fearsome, and some more pathetic, but every time I started to add water detail, I pictured Cadie floating in it. I tried a few dryer settings, forests and deserts and cities, but the problem wasn't only Cadie. I couldn't understand what Guardado was asking for. I needed a painting where the monster was the good guy, or just misunderstood, but that would make the subject something other than a monster.

I never got blocked, especially not with monsters. I had noticed the specific course in the catalog the summer before

22

my first semester. I even called my high school art teacher, Mr. Sinclair, to tell him about it. We laughed together about how it was all meant to be. Semester after semester I kept putting off taking it, keeping it in my back pocket for when I needed an easy A. I waited until my final semester, and I was ready to settle for something way lower.

We had planned to return Sunday afternoon, leaving me time to hopefully put the finishing touches on my painting before the Monday due date. Two nights, one suit. Ivy kept calling me as she packed, asking if we were going to get out on the water, if we were going to have a fancy dinner, even jokingly asking if we were going to any parties in the woods. Apparently in most of the country, high-schoolers party in each other's houses.

She asked about Cadie a few times, wondering why I'd never mentioned her before, and wondered aloud how her death could have knocked me off my game so much. I mostly told her the truth, that she wasn't an ex-girlfriend, and that I hadn't seen her for a few years, but Ivy was still wary. It was another reason I agreed she could tag along.

She had passed the early highways-and-straight-lines part of the trip editing on her laptop with her headphones in, but when we turned onto the coastal route, she put her equipment away for some last-minute cramming.

"Which one did I meet?"

"Rocco."

"No I know that, the other one."

"Desmond."

"Yeah! What other friends will be there?"

"Who I'm still friends with?" I thought about it. "Nobody."

I could have told her about other people I typically see when I come back, but I was already tired of sharing. I may have owed her but wasn't looking forward to being her docent around town, explaining our weird customs, our weird people and our weird history. I was also going to have to explain weird Ivy to everyone back home.

It was never going to be a relaxing weekend, not quite *time to put off the world and go somewhere, and find my health again in the sea air*, but it would have been nice to have a short break from school and my life in the city. Instead I was colliding worlds, bringing an unfathomable creature back with me, infecting my hometown. The same stuff I did every week on canvas.


As we wound our way up the coast, I kept looking North and East until I saw some especially thick clouds in the distance, signaling East Hook. My mother had given the impression throughout the spring that the fog was basically constant, even claiming she hadn't seen one good sunset since March. I rolled down my window, to see if I could feel the telltale May chill, but it was still warm and sunny this far South.

The route was mostly gas stations and fast-food joints but went through a few charming fishing villages. As with every Friday afternoon in the summer, traffic stalled as tourists saw the sights instead of the crosswalks. The bigger towns were built on a few inlets and rivers, and the bridges across those rivers provided the best early views of the rocky, pine tree-reinforced coast. I heard Ivy say "Wow" slowly and just loud enough for me to hear as we went over the first one. I had planned to take her to see East Hook in late July, after the fog had burned off, so she could see East Hook in all its glory. I also had wanted to wait for the fog to burn off my immediate future, knowing where I'd be living, if I'd be making any money, and how Ivy fit into my post-grad plans.

If I were a better boyfriend, I would have wanted the mist to go away early, let her see my seaside town in all its glory. But I wanted the mist, we were there for a funeral.

When we turned off the coastal route towards East Hook, Ivy flipped down sun visor to check herself out in the mirror.

"So what are we having for dinner?"

"Leg of lamb." Ivy had been a vegetarian since she was eleven.

"Seriously?"

"She'll want something easy, like pasta."

She smiled. "Someone's gonna try and make me eat a lobster."

"They can try."

It wasn't even six pm when we got into East Hook proper, but it looked and felt much later. The clouds and fog filtered the sun into a meager light gray blob hanging just over the trees to the Southwest. My wish was apparently coming true, it was hard to imagine anything else happening there besides funerals. Home.

As we got closer, I started narrating the familiar landmarks. I showed her the gas station where we'd get drifters to buy us beer, and the mini golf place my father used to take me to. A few miles from home I started looking for the telltale section of twisted guardrail where my art teacher had a bad car accident two years before. I had seen Mr. Sinclair a few times since and he insisted he was fine, feeling better every day. His limp never improved, and he still needed a cane to walk around. I was hoping to see him that weekend, wondering if he'd be at Cadie's funeral. I wanted to check his progress, but really wanted to tap into his advice. Ever since noticing my talent, he'd never steered me wrong. I didn't mention it to Ivy as we drove past, and didn't mention the chills I felt on my neck for the rest of the ride. Good things didn't happen to people who believed in me. Good thing there were so few who did.

My mother was sitting at the table watching the tv and smoking a cigarette when we came through the door. It was never locked. She looked caught and immediately ashed it, stood up, smoothed out her shirt with her hands and walked towards us. "You made great time!" She gestured to the table and ashtray. "I didn't think you'd be here until seven." She started spiraling, smiling at Ivy, but pulsing with shame. "Hi darling, it's so nice to meet you. Sorry about the smell." She embraced Ivy, quickly, and held her at arm's length, pretending to examine her up and down, but while her head moved, her eyes stayed on her hair. "You're so beautiful! Ellis told me, but you never know." It was a trick I'd seen her do with the only other girl she met, not Cadie. It worked on Ivy, I could see her blushing.

She moved in to hug me, and held on a little longer, making sure I was really there. As she was pulling away she whispered. "I'm sorry." I tried to squeeze her arm to signal she shouldn't worry about it, but I was a little embarrassed, and surprised. As she pulled away, her voice got louder. "You could use a trim before the ceremony."

My mother had smoked exactly one cigarette a day for most days of my life. When she realized she was pregnant she quit and says she didn't smoke at all until I was a few months old, then moved to one a day. A few occasions called for more than one, like the weeks after my dad died, or the days after I set fire to my uncle's hammock, but for the most part she was disciplined. She said it kept her saner than any therapy. Results were inconclusive. I couldn't remember the last time I saw her smoke inside though.

"I don't normally do this." She said to Ivy, who I was trying to get a read on. She didn't seem too freaked out yet. She turned to me. "Things have been really weird here lately."

"Mist season." I offered. And a dead kid.

"No I used to love smoking out in the mist." She caught herself and turned back to Ivy, like an aside. "I smoke one a day, just one. And I haven't had more than that since I got pregnant. So what, twenty-two years." I didn't see a reason to call her out on it, and she continued her monologue. "But the last month things keep happening. That poor girl died."

"Cadie." I wanted to say her name. My mother didn't know about what we had, I made sure of it when I was in high school, but now I felt a little hurt by it, like she should have figured it out anyway. She could have been more of a help to me.

"Yeah, poor thing. And that family." She looked at Ivy and pouted, then went back to holding court. Her shame had evaporated quickly, it didn't linger like the mist. "But even besides that. Downtown, dead animals keep turning up." She saw our confusion. "In the roads, on the boardwalk, in front of shops."

"What animals?" I shuddered a little, remembering the pigeon back at school.

"All kinds. Birds, deer, a coyote, there was a porcupine in front of the bookstore at the start of the month. Last week I was driving and the traffic, right in front of the library, just stopped. There was a dead raccoon in the middle of the intersection."

"What's happening?" Ivy seemed worried.

"No one knows!" She sounded more excited than scared. She got my attention. "You know how it is here. Someone wrote in the paper one week saying it's some construction runoff poisoning them. Sure enough the next week someone else wrote that there was no evidence and the construction company was helping investigate." Of course they were.

My mother kept going. "So, two days ago. I didn't tell you this Ellis. I stepped out on the deck and heard a thump next to me. I can't see too far in the mist, so I have to look down and take a few steps, but I saw it. A squirrel fell from a tree stone dead onto the deck, like three feet from me."

"Oh my god!" Ivy loved animals; she spent the last few minutes increasing the pressure of her grip on my hand under the table. "What did you do?"

My mom's eyes widened as she took in the attention she was getting. "I screamed and ran inside and locked the door. I haven't been back out there." I looked out at the deck, thinking I'd need to sweep a dead squirrel into the bushes below. "But I checked the next morning, the wind blew it into the bushes."

"Are you sure?" I didn't want her surprised next time she was brave enough to go back out.

"Yeah. I saw it in the bushes, it's caught on one of the branches." She looked grossed out describing it. Ivy looked worse. My mother looked back at me like she had an idea. "Can you help me get it down? Maybe throw it into the woods? I don't want vultures on my deck."

After picking at the pasta salad my mother made us, Ivy

28

excused herself to go to the bathroom and found the shrine to my father. It had moved a few times in the years since he died, but the hall to the bathroom was a good permanent home. Everyone who came to the house and stayed at least an hour was bound to see it, but on their own terms, not in front of us. We didn't want anyone feeling like they had to say something, or worse, that we should.

"Ellis." I heard her while helping my mother switch her phone settings to night mode. I knew from the way she said it, loud enough so I could hear, but slow and breathy. She was calling me over softly and gently. My mom recognized it too and grabbed the phone out of my hand.

She was standing really close to it, looking up and scanning the details of his face for a resemblance to me.

"Eyebrows, lips, chin and hair." She turned to me then back to the picture.

"The whole face shape is the same. You could play him in a movie." I always thought his face sagged more than mine. Ivy was entranced by the picture, so I stepped behind her to take a look at Dad.

The police put the whole thing together for the funeral. It was a shield-shaped lacquered mahogany plaque with strip of silver across the top inlaid with East Hook's Hero. A glass protected eight-by-ten headshot of my father in full uniform took up most of it. His badge and honorary medal were arranged underneath. I knew I saw it every time I was home, but I couldn't remember the last time I looked at it.

He did look more like me than he had before. I was growing into his face, and maybe into his head.

"How old was he when this was taken?"

"Thirty-five." I said quickly. "Maybe thirty-four. I don't

know if they took those every year."

I kept my eyes on the picture. I could feel Ivy shaking her head. "That's so young. How many years ago was it?"

I was nine when he passed, and I did the math in my head, ill-equipped as any art student. "Twelve." June twenty-ninth. "Almost twelve. At the end of next month it'll be twelve."

Ivy reached to hold my hand, squeezed, then let go and put that arm around my shoulder. I could tell she was struggling to find something to say. This was why we liked it away from the crowd, we didn't need solace anymore.

Ivy found her voice. "What do you remember most about him?" She started rubbing my back.

It's never one thing. So much came to mind and I wanted to be careful what I projected, how honest I wanted to be with her right then. I studied the picture, almost a mirror image of myself, but for those deeper-set, darker eyes that even intimidated through the camera, protective glass and the grave. They shone through the dumb uniform he had to wear and stiff posture he affected just for the shoot. His eyes swam with intelligence, they could take in even the smallest detail at a glance and make immediate and complete sense of it. I see things for what they look like, he saw them for what they were.

When I first came into the house and looked out the window into blankness, one memory did jump out. "I remember he loved the mist. I'd catch him staring out at the wall of it, in the mornings with a coffee and at nights with a beer." Whatever he was looking for he kept to himself. I think he tried to share it with me once. He helped me up in front of a window and asked me what I thought was hiding amidst the gray. I don't remember what I said, but I do remember a sense of him not listening to me, just replying. That's the good thing about it, Ellis, we'll never have know.

Out of the corner of my eye, I noticed Ivy turn to me. "So he would have been happy now."

I kept looking at my Dad's eyes, trying to remember him being happy.

"Honestly, yeah I think he would be happy now. Happy he was dead."

Too honest.

# III

# Saturday

# Dadaism

T he mist had the decency to stick around for the funeral. I lay on my back in the familiar gray morning light looking up at the star stickers on the ceiling. I didn't notice them when I came down the night before because they don't glow anymore. I could hear my mother's muffled footsteps upstairs. Since I left home I started feeling guilty every time I slept late while I was back, like I was denying my mom time with me. I felt a little more guilty knowing Ivy was upstairs in the guestroom, thanks to local puritanical attitudes toward sharing a room before marriage, lying awake too. She was social, but not social enough to have coffee alone with my mother. Hopefully she was editing.

My father helped me put the stars up when I was seven or eight. The popcorn ceiling made it tough for the stars to stick, so we sanded a small patch smooth, I remember him holding me up, laughing and clenching his eyes closed as the ceiling plaster I sanded off rained down on his face.

I wondered why he didn't just wear goggles; he must have put them on me. It wasn't like him to start a job without thinking it through completely, thinking, out loud, all the reasons not to even start. Maybe that was why I hadn't started my final painting yet, every idea had too many drawbacks. I was looking more like him every day, it only made sense that I start thinking more like him. It petrified me.

My mother would never say anything bad about him to anyone but close family. Whatever faults he had, he more than paid for them that windy morning in the bay. There was nothing so bad about him either, I wondered how much I magnified his flaws to add some challenge to our relationship, to fit in better at art school. He wasn't loud, wasn't violent, wasn't petty, and everyone who knew him well called him a genius.

At his funeral they said he was the youngest detective any of them could remember, and the one the rest of the investigative team went to every time a nut was proving too hard to crack. It was the details, he noticed all of them, especially what was out of place. I noticed his eyes from his picture, but it was all his senses. He would just call out, "leaf-fire" to himself while sitting inside, the first one to smell the smoke, or "seaplane" when he recognized the rumble he felt through his feet. Never with any excitement, and he never went out to confirm or enjoy what he noticed, but he always noticed it. I could imagine how intense he must have come across to the other detectives at a crime scene or looking at photos with them.

I could imagine it because I lived my own version of it, when he'd bring me one of those puzzles from kid's magazines where you spot all the differences between two pictures. He'd stand in front of me, tracking my eyes scanning the document, the pit in my stomach growing every second that passed before I spotted something. More than half the time these fun puzzles ended in tears.

I rolled out of bed and stepped down on the floor carefully, out of habit, there weren't any paint tubes lying around anymore.

My mother didn't even say good morning when I came into view, just waved one hand at me, gesturing me to keep quiet. With her other hand she turned the volume up on the television. It was the local news, interviewing some Canadian tourist in a Mickey Mouse sweatshirt.

"It was like something out of a nightmare. I looked up and saw her back, then she was just gone." My mother anticipated my question and put one finger up to make me bite my words. The chyron running below the interview read "Girl missing off the coast of East Hook after jumping off Inbound Swift cruise."

I walked closer, somewhere I could sit down. It was too early for this. The details didn't seem to match all I'd heard the past few days. "Are they talking about Cadie?!"

"Ssshhh. No, another one." I stayed upright and kept walking to the TV to hear better.

The next quote was from a woman with a New England accent. "You never expect to see something like that." She looked down. "It's so sad, you never know what's going on in someone's head."

"Downeast Water Inc., owners and operators of the Swift, have no comment at this time. The Coast Guard is continuing their search just North of East Hook, the historic maritime town known for shipwrecks and drown…"

I turned the tv off manually at the set. I didn't need to hear about drownings in East Hook, not that day and not any day. My mother didn't either, which likely explained her muted reaction.

"It's so sad, this girl got on and just leapt off the side of the ship in full view of the other passengers. By the time it stopped steaming ahead, she was half a mile back." She looked down and shook her head. Then back up at me. A terrible way to go.

I couldn't convince my mother that I just wanted coffee, so I had a forkful of eggs in my hand when I heard the guest room door open, footsteps, then the bathroom door close. I snorted, laughing at myself for assuming Ivy would just stroll out of bed and hang out with a practical stranger. She brushed her teeth every time she left her apartment.

"What do you think Ivy wants?"

Ivy didn't need to worry about finding a vegetarian alternative at my house. My mother had more natural supplements, juices, seeds and grains than fit in her pantry. Above the sink in the window was a mini herb garden, supplementing the bigger, seasonal one outside. She was almost a vegetarian, but like her one cigarette a day habit, she would randomly order lobster rolls or fry herself a bacon cheeseburger when the mood hit.

"She'll be good with the oats and fruit, probably."

My mother was flipping through a fashion magazine, stopping sometimes to check her watch. She was taking a half day, to attend the funeral in the afternoon, but squeezed in four appointments before one, so everything needed to start on time. "Are you going to show her around this morning? Sorry I can't be with you, but it's so busy." All the locals try and get their hair cut before the summer people start to arrive, when prices go up, availability goes down, and the gossip under the dryers starts centering around lawn service providers and fundraisers.

"We're meeting Rocco for lunch."

She sighed. "Oh Rocco, how's he doing?"

I didn't know. When we'd made the plans he'd agreed in as few words as possible. I had called Desmond the day before to ask what he thought and he said the big guy was down, but that he was always kind of down, and now he had an excuse for it. Desmond couldn't meet us for lunch, but he was hosting a party after the funeral where we could all catch up. He was especially interested in seeing Ivy again, which made me uncomfortable, but I knew he was just trying to make me mad. Ivy hadn't even remembered his name.

I told my mother Rocco was down.

"So what else is new." She said and flipped another page on the magazine, taking her almost to the end. I started taking bigger bites to see if I could finish before she needed another distraction. I had too much food left. I heard her close the last page and saw her raise her head toward me.

"What are you learning these days?" Despite being a hair artist, my mother had little interest for the minutia of painting technique. She loved my work, and loved the opportunity it gave me, but she asked about school wanting only a surface-level sense of if she should be worried or not. I had struggled through high school, so she had a skepticism for any academic achievement I presented her with. Every semester I showed her my grades, and every semester she asked a version of the same question about if a good graphic designer could fake the screenshot she was looking at. I could always lie to her, so I pointed to the watermark and said it only showed on official pages. Of course someone could trick her with a fake website. The grades were real though. Art school was a different kind of challenge, one I had always felt much more capable of meeting.

I told her I had just one piece left before I graduated, but pushed back on giving her any details about what I was thinking to do for it, not in the least because I still had no idea, despite being two days away from the deadline. I hoped to do some sketching before we left for lunch. To keep my confidence up, I showed her a picture of the painting I had just done for Guardado's class, the monster banker with slicked back tentacle hair. I zoomed in on the hair, telling her my technique and how the bump in the back suggested more hair beneath.

Sufficiently distracted, she pointed to a spot on the back of the monster's head about three quarters of the way up, near the apogee of the rear skull curve and suggested lately bankers were shaving the back, so the tentacles could potentially stop there. I always welcomed her advice on hair.

The last year, after learning more about light and textures, I painted her a portrait of Medusa, with her oily snake hair managed into a tight, intricate braid. The gorgon wore bright red lipstick and deep rouge, to contrast the green tint of her skin. She had her cheeks sucked in, her eyebrows down and her lips puckered, as if she were making the cutest face she could while looking in the mirror. It hung behind the register, pointed toward the waiting area of my mom's shop. She says people ask to buy it once a month. I was planning on swinging by to show Ivy that one some time that weekend. I wasn't sure which other ones I'd want her to see.

Ivy and I found a spot right next to the restaurant. Downtown looked virtually deserted, a discouraging sign for a tourism-centered town in May. But it made sense, people may have started learning their lessons about the spring fog. We had no time to stop in any of the shops where one of my paintings hung, we were already twenty minutes late. My mother had peppered Ivy with questions while insisting on feeding her and Ivy was too polite to excuse herself. I promised we'd see one on our way out. We had plenty of time before the funeral started.

I watched her take in the downtown during our quick walk, it was small enough that she could see almost all of it with a slow pirouette. I didn't slow down to ask what she thought, and got halfway up the four steps to the restaurant entrance before I noticed she wasn't behind me. I didn't have to do a pirouette, she was only a few feet away, at the small public launch ramp next door, which, for the first time I could remember, was closed. A chain spanned the entrance, hanging between two posts, sagging a little too much in the middle with the weight of a plastic sign. I hopped down to see what it said, hoping it wasn't closed because the town was so deserted.

The sign didn't have much information, only six all-caps words in scarlet on a white background: DO NOT GO INTO THE WATER. I had to blink to make sure I was reading it right, and to steady the earth under my feet. The type-set looked official, but the language was too authoritarian to have been approved by any office. There wasn't even an explanation.

It was a warning. A familiar one for me, down to the exact wording my father used so often when I was little it may have been his mantra.

"Do you think it's because of Cadie?" Ivy's question helped nudge me back into the present, but I didn't cross over completely.

"I... I don't know."

Ivy leaned over the chain, looking into the murky water,

oblivious to the world spinning in front of me.

"People are direct here."

Not really, I thought, which made it so strange. "I guess so." I stepped closer to the sign and grabbed it. I wanted tactile proof I wasn't hallucinating, and I wanted to flip it over. The back was blank, the same white as the front.

I had to make sure the back didn't have the second part of my father's frequent warning:

You don't know what's down there.

Rocco was sitting alone at the last table, glaring out at the harbor, his drink reduced to only ice. His black suit was crumpled, and a few sizes too big. Some people just always look like they're in shambles. Before we sat down, he heard us coming and looked up, not smiling.

"Ellis hook."

"Rock. Sorry we're late".

He shrugged and gave Ivy a grim smile. "Hi Ivy, good to see you again."

Ivy's smile wasn't grim enough, she picked the wrong day to try out bubbly.

"Hi Rocco, good to see you too. So sorry about Cadie."

Rocco kept his expression. "Yeah it's the worst. Thanks for coming."

I worried I looked just like him, the sign had me so rattled I kept blinking to keep the world from melting. We both needed cheering up. "So what are you drinking? Let's get three more."

Rocco looked down, out of focus.

"It's just whiskey and ginger."

Ivy stepped forward and grabbed his glass.

"I'll get them."

I reached into my pocket to give her cash, but she was already on her way. I sat down across from Rocco. He made quick eye contact with me, then looked back down. Man dies several times between his two eternities, this was one of Rocco's deaths.

"How you doing?"

"Okay... They still don't know what happened. I don't know everything, but apparently she had wounds on her body, like bites."

I looked towards the bar, wanting that drink. "How long was she in the water? Do they know that?"

"I didn't hear, but apparently there's a question if the bites were before or after she... you know."

"What?" I started sweating again, I wasn't ready.

"It makes sense I guess, if she was in there for a while, for something to... take a bite."

"But that's so messed up."

"Yeah messed up for sure."

Rocco still had his head down, he looked out at the water, then looked at the table again.

"I heard two guys at the shack talking about her, they didn't know I was there, they were saying the deep got her, like it did Jim Minonne, the guy who drowned in April."

"And the girl who jumped off the Swift." I added as I looked out at the harbor.

Rocco hadn't heard, so I explained what my mother told me earlier. It didn't improve his mood. "The world is ending." He sighed into his drink, looking like someone should keep him away from high boats for a while.

I hoped her family wouldn't have to hear how she's just

another victim of the evil East Hook waters. "This fucking town tries to make a legend of everything." As I said it l looked out at the harbor. The gray water didn't look evil, but it did look like a terrifying place to die; cold, afraid and alone.

"Yeah. I wanted to say something, but like, what am I?"

I snapped out it and looked back at Rocco. "What?"

"Like I wasn't even her boyfriend when she died. I didn't even really talk to her the last few years."

"Yeah but you were with her for a long time."

"Yeah like 4 years ago."

I looked back, Ivy was standing with our drinks about 20 feet away, waiting for the right time to join. She saw me look at her and pretended she had stopped to look at something else. She came to the table and put two of the golden drinks down.

"One more." She said and turned around to go back to the bar for the third. Rocco finally looked at me. I tilted my glass towards him.

"To Cadie."

He clinked my glass without enthusiasm. "To the deep." I took a deep swallow, letting the burn of the liquor and the sting of the bubbles sit in my mouth for a while before swallowing. I needed sensations. Rocco took a much deeper swallow than I did, and it all went down quick. He was aiming for fewer sensations.

Ivy returned and we pretended we hadn't toasted yet. She gamely raised her glass. "To Cadie."

"To Cadie," We said at the same time, and both probably tried not to think: "To the deep."

Ivy kept bubbling, "So what's good here, besides sea food?"

Rocco was in no condition to get the joke.

"Ivy's a vegetarian. I told her we weren't known for the freshest greens up here. Good blueberries though."

He was slowly coming back, deadpanning. "Yeah and I think potatoes, up north."

"So basically get the fries." I said looking at him the whole time.

He was suppressing a grin. "And the blueberry ale."

I almost had him. "Desmond couldn't pull himself away, huh?"

"Nah, girlfriend duty. He'll be at the funeral though."

"How'd Mykayla lock him up."

"Mykenzy!"

"What? That's even worse!" Finally Rocco laughed. I was back in the East Hook I wanted to be in. Ivy looked confused. I turned to her to clarify.

"They're twins, a grade below us in school."

"Named Mykenzy and MyKayla? Why?"

"They spell 'em weird, too, all y's." Rocco jumped in laughing.

"Yeah and no one could tell them apart, ever. Do they still look the same?"

"No. One has longer hair I think. MyKayla. Once the first one introduces herself I'll be good for the night."

"I always pretend I can't spell their names, thank god for their parents. I'll walk up to one of them and say 'I was talking to someone about how you spell your name, it's one y or two? And they usually say 'two, then spell it!"

Rocco, still laughing, "Yeah, but the first like 5 letters are the same."

"No 3, so you go M...Y...K... then stop."

Ivy joined in. "Wait, MYK, how do they spell them?"

Talking about old times diverted us for a while. We were looking forward to Desmond's party, apparently everyone from high school who was still in town, temporarily or permanently, would be there.

Cadie would have wanted a party.

# Post Romanticism

The ride to the funeral was more of an adventure than Ivy or I would have preferred. Rocco was swerving, speeding and reacting too slowly to all the other cars on the road. I should have driven, but we didn't have far to go, and the car's airbags worked.

The church was on the East side of downtown, right on the water, and we passed the big crowd standing on the front lawn, taking the chance to greet each other and catch up before heading up to the much more somber scene inside. We found a spot at the back of the parking lot, with Rocco threading the needle between cars by sheer luck.

I saw my mother standing with one of her friends, looking at us. When we met eyes she sent vibes my way suggesting it looked like we drank too much. I ignored her and spotted Desmond near the edge of the lawn, like he'd barely got on the grass before someone stopped him, standing with the twins.

He looked good, tall and trim in a suit that looked expensive and fitted but almost certainly wasn't either. His job at a liquor distribution company, an industry that seemed to exclusively employ jocks, didn't pay that well. He was partway through a business degree at an online college, though. Growing up he had so much I envied, but seeing him then, it was his job stability and long-term career plan that made me want to trade places. My mother bought me the suit I was wearing when I was seventeen.

Rocco called out to Desmond, loud enough for everyone on the lawn to hear.

"Desmundo!" Desmond turned around and grinned when saw us. His eyebrows went up when he saw our condition, I even detected some of the same vibes my mother sent our way. When we reached him he looked me up and down and gave me a fist bump. He kissed Ivy on the cheek. Rocco got the same bump, but after examining him, Desmond just laughed. He looked back at me.

"Ellis Hook, what did you do to my boy?"

Ivy introduced herself to the twins and after receiving a compliment on her hair, closed ranks in a separate circle. I overheard her asking how they spell their names; she was so much better at new people than I was.

Rocco was promising Desmond he'd be fine, standing up straighter and making the fakest looking serious face for a few seconds. It had been nice getting him laughing at lunch, but we may have gone overboard. I knew he'd sober up fast though, it was his ex-girlfriend's funeral, and despite being on the water every day, he hadn't learned how to let it roll off his back.

Desmond had reason to be sober too. He had hooked up with Cadie when he was a freshman at a baseball party, and while they didn't stay together longer than a week, he lorded it over us literally every time we had a disagreement for the next six months. "Oh sorry I was too busy getting laid to know shit like that."

Apparently the spelling conversation was a short one, Ivy

came back to my side and looked at me. "What's the story behind Ellis Hook? You both called him that at school and I forgot to ask."

Desmond eyed me again, wondering how private this info was. He grinned back at her. "Ellis never told you about his criminal past?"

Ivy gave a surprised laugh. "No! He's ashamed of it I guess." She rubbed my back. "He doesn't seem like the type."

Desmond's smile got wider; I think he was much prouder of my criminal works around East Hook than all my commissioned ones.

"That's his tagging name. He spray-painted a shit-ton of walls around here." He craned his neck looking downtown. "Some are still up."

The playful look left Ivy's face and she looked at me, trying to ask a question with her face - why didn't you ever tell me about that. The answer was easy and not at all private, so I shared it with everyone without her having to ask out loud.

"It was so stupid, and I was terrible at it. I thought I was gonna do these wild, colorful tags, instead I just did two letters."

Desmond may have sensed the tension, because he started defending me.

"No we tried it." He wagged his finger between himself and Rocco. "That one night, remember. I sprayed outside the stencil and you got so pissed. Then Rocco did too."

I remembered. They brought the average quality of the tags way down that night. Whatever reputation my alter ego had was ruined. My other partner was much more precise.

"Who did it with you?" Rocco spoke up, at least not slurring his words.

49

"HK!" Desmond answered for me, and both twins guffawed while Rocco laughed. "Imagine those two together." He was done defending me, so I took over.

"He bribed me with weed. And he scouted locations." And he called me a pussy when I wanted to chuck the spray cans in the bay after seeing our first tag behind the bank.

"Who's HK?" Another surprise for Ivy. A secret painting partner I never told her about.

One of the twins, MyKenzy, I think, because she was standing closer to Desmond, answered. "This drug dealer we went to high school with. He's gross."

I couldn't argue with the description. I'd accidentally seen him over the winter break and not much had changed. "He had good stencil sense."

Ivy wasn't done with the interrogation. "You mean he held it still? It was just stenciled letters?"

The only colors we had were blue and yellow, cans Mr. Sinclair bought me when I had to paint a beach theme background for the prom. Blue for water, yellow for sand.

"The stencil was just two lines and a small curved triangle. The long line made the back of an E in blue and the sides of an H in yellow. The short lines made the horizontal parts of the E and the connector of the H. You had to turn it and get the angle, the distance and the meeting point right. The curved triangle went at the ends of the E lines, to make it look like a harpoon."

"EH - Ellis Hook."

It stood for East Hook, if artist intent meant anything. Almost all my art was civic-minded.

MyKayla, the other twin who had been watching Ivy and me closely since we arrived, spoke up for the first time, "Go downtown, a lot of your tags are still up there, seriously."

It was strange, I hadn't remembered painting that many downtown.

"I can't wait to see them." Ivy said, looking at me, not even feigning excitement. I put my arm around her to see what I could fix before the funeral started, and started steering her away from the circle.

"Hi Ellis, how's it going?" I heard a reedy voice behind me that I recognized. I turned around and saw Mr. Sinclair, who was both skinnier and shaggier than I'd ever seen him. The longer hair made him look younger than thirty-nine, or forty, but the lines on his face made him look older. He was wearing a dark suit, but with what looked like a short sleeve button-up flannel shirt underneath, and a skinny, cheap-looking tie. "How's the semester going?" His smile seemed bigger, so did his teeth. I noticed he didn't have his cane with him, so it was hard for me to tell how his recovery was going. Mr. Sinclair was the first adult I had ever considered a real live flawed person, and probably the first one I worried about, besides my mom.

The crowd we were in had moved on to other conversations. Only Ivy stayed by my side. I introduced her, making sure to heap praise on the film she's working on. Sinclair beamed at her but his eyes didn't focus and he didn't ask any follow-up questions. Instead he just generalized his first one. "So how are both your semesters going?" He was just looking at me. Ivy jumped in with a quick "Good. Just have to finish editing and I'm done. Sinclair nodded slowly, keeping that big grin, and looked back at me. Once again, I was the teacher's pet.

"I'm almost done. Just have to turn in a final project for one

51

class." I made a show of looking him up and down, taking him in. "How you feeling?"

"Good, good. Best I've felt in years." He was nodding while he talked, and kept nodding for a few seconds after, gradually slowing to a stop, with those bright choppers out the whole time. "What's the class?"

I returned his smile, actually excited to share it with him. "It's called Monsters! We saw it in the catalog before I went!" I heard myself getting louder and saw some people turn my way. Ivy looked down, briefly, and I immediately felt self-conscious. Of course I was enthusiastically yelling about monsters at a funeral. As if everyone here who knew who I was could expect anything less. I hated being a caricature of myself.

While Mr. Sinclair did not seem to recall seeing the course catalog with me, his enthusiasm matched my own, and he was a lot less self-conscious, booming a laugh that turned more heads than I did, and sent Ivy's eyes again to the ground. I glanced around and it seemed people were making a point to not look in our direction, and move farther away. "Sounds like a good fit!"

Even with the disapproving crowd I caught myself still smiling. Ivy wasn't, and that helped me stop. The Monsters class wasn't all that funny anyway. "You'd think, but the professor is kind of a fascist."

Mr. Sinclair's eyebrows went up, like he didn't understand, but his grin was still there. "Is he some comic book guy who says your monsters aren't good enough? It's the nerds who give everyone the hardest time." He turned to Ivy and winked. "Trust me, I'm one of them."

It was good to talk to him about this, as strange a vibe as I was getting. I knew it was kind of rude to Ivy, but she wanted to come here and observe me in my element. I figured I'd make it up to her when I was bored out of my mind on some red carpet in the future. Ivy stayed with it. "No, he likes his technique, his problem is like, philosophical."

Sinclair took this in, his nod returned, almost like a tick. He finally stopped smiling, pursed his lips like he was deep in thought, and shrugged. After consideration, he leaned forward to share his advice. I leaned in toward him, ready to absorb more wisdom from my true art mentor.

"Fuck him!" Sinclair started laughing again after he said it, still way too loud. It ended quickly, and he put his arm on my shoulder. "I mean it. You know monsters." He looked at Ivy. "I was sitting under one of yours the other day, the uhh, one with tentacles, and let me tell you, it's great. I knew it was great when you painted it and it's still great now." I was about to ask him to narrow it down a little further, but he didn't give me a big enough opening before continuing. "You know, like really know, what things look like, down to the mundane details. It's brilliant." Like the muted colors seen through tinted Southwestern bank windows on a late spring afternoon. He looked far away. "I could never do it."

My senior year, Mr. Sinclair painted a lobsterman pulling up his trap and seeing a tentacle on the line. He showed me before he was going to give it to a lobsterman friend, probably hoping to get some free bugs. It didn't have mist, had some strange perspective issues, like the lobster trap was bigger than the boat or something, and was pretty derivative of a painting I did for the Yacht Club called "Got One." I told him I liked it, and asked some question about how he made the bubbles look like spheres instead of circles. A month or two later, I went into his supply closet looking for a smaller brush and saw it leaning against the back wall. Apparently his friend agreed with me.

"Cadie came out of the womb wanting to make friends. I remember when she was a baby, she was always reaching her little hand out to strangers and family members when they came close. Other kids were shy and always wanted to be close to their mother, but not Cadie, she wanted the whole world. She had this innate understanding of how big the world was, and how there were so many people outside of her family, outside of East Hook, that she wanted to meet."

Sophomore year, Mr. Sinclair sat me next to Cadie in art class, I think as a favor to me.

"When Cadie was five, we were picking up my sister from the airport and we were early, so we pulled over near the runway and watched the planes take off. The first few scared her, with the loud noise, but soon she started asking questions. 'Where is this one going?' 'Why do they need to go so far away?' 'What's the farthest place you can go from here? I told her that the planes were flying to other airports that could take people anywhere on the planet. I guess wanted to get into a discussion about geography, get her interested in world travel. Instead she took in what I said, thought for a minute and asked, 'Do you think they've already met everyone here?" There were a few acknowledging chuckles, but I was just thinking about how Cadie might have never left East Hook.

After a month of seeing my work and hearing Sinclair's praise, Cadie asked me if I could paint her dog, Shasta.

"She saw the infinite in the small, the universe in the atom, more than anyone I ever knew. Why fly around the world

54

to meet new people, see new cultures, when there was so much left undiscovered in our own town, even in our own house. I admired that about her, her ability to find mystery in everyday occurrences. I think Cadie would rather know everything about one person, than a little bit about a lot of people."

She gave me a Polaroid of him sitting and looking up, but I drew him lying by her feet. I looked up pictures of sleeping dogs for reference, tried a couple different ways to capture light shining through the fur, and handed her my seventeenth draft two sleepless nights later.

"As she got older this focus on the now sometimes made her mother and I kind of crazy. 'Why worry about homework when I can hang out more with my friends?' 'Why would I rather ride to school with you when some older boys will drive me?" Mr. Reilly choked out a sob that sounded like a burst of laughter. The crowd laughed politely along with him. "But that was her, she loved us like she loved everybody."

She was so pleased with it she made sure I was going to some party in the woods that weekend. She found me as soon as we got there, and we kissed with my back against a tree. I felt electromagnetically bonded to her, physically unable to separate. I offered to paint Shasta in person at her house sometime.

"It was wonderful watching her grow up and start to share this love with the world. And while it's terrible, just terrible she was taken from us while she still had so much more love to give, I must admit she gave her fair share in the limited time she had. And that we can all act more like her, make the world more like her, and keep sharing her love with each other."

It was awkward and fast, and I think I kept my lips locked on hers the whole time, breathing in and out directly into her mouth. She scratched my back with her nails on my left side. I have never been prouder of myself and so grateful to someone else since.

"When she was younger I tried to get her to read, to get her interested in the world of her imagination, a world sadly, where her future exists now."

I thought about finding him after and saying how much I liked his speech, but Rocco's words echoed in my head. "Who was I?" I was just the guy who screwed his daughter once. This speech wasn't for me. He took a long pause and started to wrap up.

"She didn't take to reading like I did, but she liked when I would read her poetry before tucking her in. I had a few go-to poems, but she seemed to fall asleep most peacefully to the rhythms of Yeats."

Of course he picked Yeats. I thought about the stolen musty brown book hidden in my room, blushing in shame and glad any eyes coming in our direction would be drawn to Rocco's giant blubbering and convulsing frame. I wondered if that book could have provided Mr. Sinclair comfort these last few days.

I was too inward focused to hear how he set it up, but familiar words pulled me back into the church. To the funeral in the church, and I mouthed the words along with him as he spoke and had the same tears in my eyes as he did in his.

*Go ask the springing flowers,*
*and the flowing air above,*
*what are the twinborn waters?*
*They'll answer death and love*

# Baroque

We rode with Rocco to Desmond's, though I wasn't too excited about it, he kind of embarrassed himself at the service. Sitting next to me, shaking and whimpering, occasionally sniffling. The big guy felt things hard. We tried to keep it light on the short drive, focusing on the turnout and the eulogy, gossiping about the old familiar faces we saw. But when we turned a bend and the road opened up to the bay Rocco and I got quiet and stared at the water through the fog, I was thinking I was glad I wasn't out there floating, Rocco might have wished he was.

We stopped at the grocery store to pick up beer and white wine for Ivy. The plan was to order pizza at some point. I'd see if my discount at Harbor Pie still applied. I was expecting a smaller group, five or six of us: the car crew, Desmond, and one or both twins, and was looking forward to a smaller group after the big funeral crowd. Plus, Desmond's relationship with Cadie was a lot more like mine than Rocco's was, so I figured it would be good to see how he was feeling. Hopefully, he felt like me: numb, like I have been treading water off the Stains in May, but scared, like something big and scaly just brushed my foot. I hoped that's how I was supposed to feel, but knew it wasn't.

Pulling onto Desmond's street I could tell this wasn't an intimate gathering. At least fifteen cars, spilling out of the driveway of his white Cape, lined the curbs on both sides. When I opened the door after we parked, I could hear music coming from what sounded like his backyard, Country. I opened the door for Ivy, and she winced as she heard it. Rocco looked unfazed and started walking to the house after he grabbed the beer and wine from the back seat.

"Did you know this many people would be here?" I called after him.

He spun around, keeping his momentum going towards the house and walking backwards. He looked at all the cars like he was noticing them for the first time. Rocco shrugged, "It's always like this at Desmond's." He spun back and started walking a little faster. Like he didn't want to walk in with us. At least he carried in the beer.

Desmond's yard was a little overgrown but not by much. The edging was still sharp on the path. I knew he had moved in during the winter, probably just not in the habit of regular mowing after the snow melted no more than two months before. The house walls muffled the music a little and I couldn't hear the telltale murmur of conversation that typically bleed out of the house during a party. Ivy and I were holding hands and I paused and gave her arm a quick tug to stop her.

"I'm not sure how long I want to stay."

She looked up at me and raised her eyebrows. "I think Rocco might need you."

He needed something. I looked towards the front door and didn't see him. I thought I would have heard him open it at least. I checked the bushes under the window for a giant having a panic attack. "Rocco's a big boy." I was tired of his moping, and it made me a little sick. My grieving best friend was annoying me, how noble. Ivy kept looking at me. "Sorry, yeah we should stay a while."

"I'll have fun. I can't wait to see what else I'll find out." She didn't seem too put off by the tagging story.

We walked up the front steps. She stopped me at the door. "I thought all your parties were in the woods."

Just the fun ones, I thought to myself, glad she was back in a joking mood. "If Desmond didn't have a house, we'd be under the bridge, in the dugouts at the little league field, or behind the..." cemetery. I went to grab the doorknob and in we went.

The front door must have been lined with lead based on the wave of sound that crashed into us when we opened it. Four guys I didn't recognize were playing some video game with furious electronic music and whooshing sword slashes. Staccato laughter was swirling around with the pot smoke, I could track it making its rounds over the din of more serious conversations coming from all angles. We walked in and as I shut the door I put my hand on the wall next to the frame and felt the whole house vibrating to the rhythm of sub-woofers downstairs and dancing footfalls upstairs. It was about twenty degrees warmer inside and three times as humid. More groups were gathered around the TV than just the gamers, but I couldn't get a count because everyone seemed to be moving. People were walking towards us and away from us and just leaning against walls in the hall. No one looked up when we came in, probably because they couldn't hear the door open. It wouldn't have mattered if they had, I didn't recognize anyone.

We noticed a wide age range as we walked deeper into the house, towards what I was fairly sure was the kitchen. We passed one group that couldn't have been more than high school sophomores chugging from the same cheap rum bottle. Two women who might have been fifty passed us going in the other direction, both puffing on lit cigarettes. We stepped into the kitchen, under a speaker pulsing and thrashing out speed metal. I looked out at a window on the back wall, almost longingly, toward the chill country music backyard hoedown I thought I was going to.

Ivy could tell from my posture that it wasn't a normal East Hook party, and she stayed close. Girls were sitting on the island surrounded by booze, though not much more than would be at a high school party, not nearly enough for that crowd size and certainly not enough for me to just grab a beer. I'd been drinking all day, but my senses would need to be further dulled to survive in that environment. I wondered where Rocco went to with the case I bought, he should have been easy to spot. We'd seen no sign of Desmond or the twins or anyone from high school either. I turned to Ivy, and saw her squinting in the distance toward the staircase. I followed her gaze to a big dark guy standing at the base of the stairs with his arms crossed. He looked like he was chewing on two twizzlers, or just holding them in his mouth like a cowboy with a thistle. The other partygoers seemed to be giving him a wide berth, as tough as that was to do with all of us packed in so tight. Ivy turned back to me and saw that we were looking at the same thing. She furrowed her brow and opened her mouth but before she said anything she just smiled and shook her head, dumbfounded. I did the same thing.

We walked towards the stairs, not to strike up a conversation with sweet-tooth John Wayne, but because we saw the back door off the dining room. It was hard to spot at first because a thin girl was leaning back against it with her head down, like she was sleeping standing up. As we got closer it seemed like she wasn't even breathing. I looked around to see if anyone was watching out for her and when I did I got a closer look at the stair bodyguard and almost had a heart attack. He didn't have twizzlers coming out of his mouth, it was a pair of red shiny jointed pincers, like on a spider. Part of me knew they couldn't be real, but most of me just felt way too close to him. Plus he caught my eye during part two of my double take and I wasn't gonna look back again.

"What. The. Fuck." I heard Ivy whisper slowly under her breath, and start pulling me towards the door. I'd never needed fresh air more in my life. A few steps away from the space cadet on the door, I started stomping to get her attention, as if she could hear it through the roar and shake of the party. Ivy was more direct, less patient, and tapped her on the shoulder.

"Excuse me." The girl shuddered sleepily, like she knew what she would wake up into. "Excuse me!"

The girl started awake, and her head darted up. Her newly opened eyes scanned back and forth quickly and when they focused on us so close to her, they widened. She shrank and twisted into herself against the door in alarm. I put my arms out palms raised. "We just…" I slowly moved my hand to the doorknob as she twisted her hips away from its approach. When I got my hand around it and started to turn the knob the wheels in her head started to turn as well. She languidly drifted out of our way, keeping the wild, wide-eyed stare on us while backing into the dining room until I swung the door open to block her view. She was on track to back up into the bug man, I almost wanted to stay to see if her eyes would eject from her head when she got a look at him. Nothing was worth spending an extra second inside that place, so Ivy and I slipped out the door and slammed it shut behind us.

Out back was like a different world, or like the normal one we had briefly left. I could taste the mist on my tongue again, and hear the familiar twangs of guitar, or banjo, whatever country musicians play. We stepped down onto to a deck covered with an extended awning. Far fewer people were out there, and I recognized almost all of them. The music from inside sounded so faint. I must have gotten too used to thin city walls.

"Hook Hoss!" I heard from just off the side of the deck. Desmond was just below us wearing a cowboy hat with a horseshoe in one hand and a beer in the other, lazily playing some throwing/drinking game I'm sure he was winning. Seeing him was like a blood transfusion. "You make it through the bug's nest?"

As he said it he brought both hands to his face and stuck his two index fingers out of his mouth and wiggled them around, keeping his grip on the horseshoe and beer.

"Yeah what the fuck was that?" I was glad we weren't the only ones not used to it.

"The Quebecois" Rocco piped up from deeper in the mist, with a horseshoe and beer of his own. "Weird French fuckers here for the summer." Thanks for warning us ahead of time, big guy.

"There's more than one freaky spider-person?"

Everyone on the deck laughed. Desmond put down the

horseshoe. "I think it's supposed to be like a shrimp. They're obsessed with sea monsters, it's the whole reason they're here. I told them about you and your paintings." We must have stepped into the light because his face changed like he saw how scared we looked. "They're plastic Ellis, they attach to like a mouthguard."

Today I wasn't feeling whimsical about sea monsters. "Can we spray some Raid or something to keep them from coming back here?"

Desmond laughed, but the rest of the deck didn't join in. "They're friends with Josh, my…" he circled his ear with his finger, the crazy gesture, "roommate. They stay inside. A couple are pretty cool, have cool stories. I've only seen them wearing the pincers for the last few days." He looked at Rocco. "They're not just here for the summer, they've been here all winter. And they were all pretty close with Cadie." I saw Rocco put his head down through the mist. "Besides, they always fully stock the party when they come over." He saw we were empty handed. "You want anything?"

I didn't want something, I needed something to help me recover from our *dalliance with a demon thing*. I nodded so hard I might have sprained the top of my neck.

Rocco jumped in, "You want wine Ivy? I put it in the cooler with the beer in the corner, Ellis." I found the cooler and we walked there and opened it.

"Do you have any cups?" Ivy asked.

"Yeah inside" Desmond said, his attention returned to whatever game he was playing.

Ivy looked up at me, "Beer's good."

# Neo Classicism

Desmond's voice got low. "It used to be cool, but everyone's made it so weird now." Most people sitting around the bonfire nodded.

"Like pretending to be shrimp?" I joked. The mandible men were funny to me instead of scary now that they were out of sight. Desmond laughed politely, but quickly. He was trying to make a point. MyKayla was beaming up at him. I turned to see if Ivy was looking at me the same way, but she was looking at Desmond too. Not beaming but studying him, probably framing him in front of the trees and with firelight flickering under his jaw.

"No, it's like with the Cadie stuff, but even before Cadie, there are people squealing with delight that we're dying in the water. Saying it's sad, but you know, monsters are coming back…"

"Who said that?" Rocco spoke up. I was worried he drank so much he was starting to fold in on himself, but he was still sharp enough to not miss an opportunity to be the white knight.

"Some guy at the E Mart, jumped in when I was talking to the assistant manager."

"What'd you say?" MyKayla sat forward expectantly, she's

probably heard this story before and was setting him up for a cool line. Desmond waved her off, intent to reach whatever point he was making.

"I probably said something about it not being funny, but you seriously hear this shit all the time." He paused, seeming to arrive at his point. "Visitors, tourists - summer people, especially - want messed up things happening here, for a story. But the messed-up things are only happening to us, and we have to live with them all year." People around the fire nodded, and the flame felt hotter, combined with the heat flash of shame I felt as a non-year-round resident, one with an easily apparent connection to the local monsters. I thought I should either make some comment about not all visitors being bad for Ivy's benefit, or to silently and immediately finish the remaining three quarters of my beer. Desmond picked back up just after the can reached my lips. "Perfect example. Either yesterday or the day before, someone broke into four different lighthouses, you hear about this?" More nodding, not from Rocco though, who suddenly looked really concerned. "Yeah kids or someone climbed up to the lamps in four different houses and smashed the bulbs."

"Which ones?" Rocco asked with a sense of urgency. I had never asked him if he was working in the morning.

"Stainshead, Wilson Point, Buck Island, and Hornlight. It all happened over the course of like 2 hours, at night too."

"That's like, really bad." MyKayla judged. "People need those."

"Exactly! It's not just vandalism, like people could have been hurt." Desmond shook his head, incredulous. I felt nauseous, from more than the beer. That didn't stop me from signaling Desmond to throw me another one. Rocco, who had been following the conversation with a weird smirk, signaled Desmond too. Ivy was too focused on the story to see any of it, at least I hoped.

"Don't they have keepers?" She asked the group.

A few people shook their head, Rocco looked at her gently. "Not anymore, not really. It's mostly automated."

Desmond piped back in, "They do now! A couple guys I work with are picking up security shifts. All of them have twenty-four-hour surveillance. I heard the city had to pay a fine, lighthouses can never go down, it's against code.

"Were there any crashes?" Ivy's interest in maritime safety was growing.

"No, thank God." MyKayla said, still looking up at Desmond, who nodded in agreement.

Rocco was looking around at everyone with his eyebrows up, more lucid than I expected. He gave everyone the lobsterman's perspective. "To be honest, GPS and colored buoys are a lot more help in the fog."

As happy as I was to see Desmond brought down closer to my level, I couldn't shake the sick feeling, something felt off. Who would destroy a bunch of lighthouses? Especially so soon after they found someone in the water.

"Do the police know who did it?" Someone asked, while I had my head and beer tipped back again. When I put both down again for air, Ivy was looking at me and Desmond was answering the question.

"No, that's the thing. They've been focusing on Cadie stuff. There's only like five of them."

While the group tried to name the five cops, I tried to grab my beer for another sip, but Ivy put her hand on my arm. She leaned into me, "Let's take a walk." I started to stand up, realizing about three quarters from vertical how drunk I was. Ivy helped steady me, but once I got to my feet, I stepped away from the circle quickly, to show her I could still stand and move on my own. I hated being drunk in front of her.

Only a few steps away from the fire, it surprised me how dark it was. I looked back at Ivy and she looked like she was walking towards me from a sunset: a black outline against the orange burst. As she got closer I expected angry features to come into focus, but her expression was calm. She put her arm on my side, her way of showing affection in public. If anyone were looking at us from the fire, they wouldn't have been able to even see our outlines.

"How are you doing?" She moved her arm up and down along my ribs. "You suddenly got white as a ghost and started slamming beers."

I wasn't expecting her to notice my unease, but I was expecting a comment on the beer, so I went with the response I crafted and rehearsed in my head on the walk from the fire. "My friend is dead, Ivy, it's a really shitty day." It probably needed more time in workshop.

Ivy blinked in what I recognized as annoyance, but with her tone she opted for steady and gentle. "So it wasn't anything anyone was saying about the lighthouses? Or cops?" Her gentle look morphed into a more conspiratorial one. "That's crazy, by the way. Has it happened before?"

I wasn't too drunk to realize how smooth she was, how she shifted from accusing me to making me feel helpful in the middle of a sentence. But I was drunk enough to find it a little manipulative.

"Not that I remember." I said quickly and tried not to avoid eye contact.

"Well it doesn't make any sense if it's vandalism." As usual, she had thought about this. "Vandals destroy and move on. Spray paint - tag - and move on." She looked up at me and smiled slyly before getting back to her point. "Vandalism is breaking a window. This is like breaking every single window in a house. It's either like OCD obsession, or it was for a purpose."

She made a good point. The lighthouses were all on opposite sides of East Hook, two on islands you couldn't even drive to. Whatever they were doing, it wasn't a crime of passion. "What purpose could it be?"

"Well if ships don't actually use them, maybe it's just symbolic. But if whoever did it doesn't know that, then maybe they want a bunch more shipwrecks."

There's a huge difference between having a morbid fascination with shipwrecks and trying to cause them. I figured Ivy was being dramatic, but I couldn't shake the thought from my head, and imagined I wouldn't be able to for a while. Who had destroyed the lighthouse lights and why?

The door back into the house swung open behind us, like a portal to another dimension. A rent in space-time, giving us a madness-inducing glimpse of unimaginable horrors. Or in this case unimaginably horrible music. It's how we could tell it opened: a quick burst, less than two seconds of aural assault, then back to quiet when it shut again.

Like the portals to other dimensions I'd read about, something came through to our side, as alien to our backyard funeral party as some toothy, clawed blight. A woman stood on the patio in front of the closed door, with midnight black hair cascading around her tanned and noticeably muscled shoulders. Her body was so still and balanced, that despite only having been there a few seconds, she looked like she was built into the patio, attached at the feet, which were bare.

While her body didn't so much as twitch, above the neck she was scanning the backyard, taking all of us at the other party in, seeing if the fresh air and relative quiet was worth dealing with a different kind of weirdo. I wasn't the only one, most of us were looking back at her from the darkness of the lawn, our bug-eyed stares reminiscent of lemurs staring out from the trees of the jungle at night. Whatever animal vibe we were giving off didn't repel her, as she made her way off the patio and down onto the grass. Walking with confidence, grace and purpose, directly towards me.

And Ivy, who had been alternating her stare between the approaching mystery woman and me, and judging by the squeeze on my hand, too sharp to be affectionate, wasn't excited about what she was seeing from either party. I got the message, turned my head to see Ivy looking up at me with her eyebrows raised. Before I could shrug, which wouldn't have been the right gesture to diffuse the situation, the woman was upon us. She had closed the distance in a few strides.

Bathed in light on the patio, I had been able to only take in her generalities, like seeing a singer onstage from the front row. Her hair, her dark pants stretched tight over her thighs and yellow tank top not covering those shoulders and arms. She didn't look like a body builder, she was way too slender, she just looked powerful. Like an athlete, in a way, but that wasn't quite it. Now that she was up close, I was able to see the details, even just through furtive glances that tried to balance in the sweet spot between being rude and pissing Ivy off even more. Up close, she was beautiful.

Her eyes were a pale green that flashed seafoam in the light and almost a glowing peridot in the dark. Her face showed the same leanness as the rest of her body. Her angular jaw took some of the warmth out of her smile, replacing it with something more leonine. I had never seen anyone like her before, not in East Hook, not at school, not even in any paintings.

"I did not realize there was another party out here" She spoke slowly, with an accent that could have been from anywhere, adding to her otherworldliness. "A better one!" She was looking at Ivy while she talked. Lucky for me, because I was still thawing out, and not prepared in the least for a charming response.

Ivy seemed a little rattled too, which made me widen my eyes. She got rattled, all the time like everyone, she just never seemed rattled. She laughed, at a much higher pitch than her real one, and sputtered out, "I know. We were inside for like, a minute, and it felt like we were underwater."

The girl matched Ivy's laugh, it was hearty and genuine, and I wanted a chance to cause it. "Did you see the shrimp guy?" This line had been killing at the outside party, but she just furrowed her brow at me. Her intensity knocked me off balance, I started flailing, moving my arms up to my face and making the pincers with my fingers, with a desperation to my movement I knew was obvious. Thankfully, her face opened with recognition.

"Aahh, yes I did see." She leaned in closer, she smelled like cinnamon. "What did you call him? Shrimp guy?" I nodded, smiling, but no recognition came this time. Either she didn't understand, or understood perfectly, and didn't think it was particularly clever. We stood there, smiling in awkward silence, until Ivy saved us with small talk.

"I love your tattoo." I hadn't noticed one, but after Ivy's compliment she turned in her left shoulder to look down at her back. Ivy had only seen it because she was on her left side.

The girl smiled as she took it in. "Thank you." I moved toward Ivy to get a better look. It was crude and simple, a thin outline of a hammerhead shark, but from the side, where the telltale head protrusions barely stuck out. Yet, there was no mistaking it was a hammerhead. It fascinated me.

Ivy was introducing herself as I was examining it, and I blurted out as the girl was saying her name. "Is it traced from a photograph?" I talked slow and with my hands, mimicking taking a picture with my index fingers and thumbs in a square around my eye. I didn't want to be misunderstood again by her, it hurt too much last time.

"And this is my boyfriend Ellis, he's an artist, and a little obsessed with technique." The girl looked up at me with a different intensity, turning her head and widening those glowing green eyes like she was impressed. I felt butterflies in my stomach, followed almost immediately by guilt.

"An artist?! What do you do? Paint? Sculpt?" She kept the same expression, powerful enough to paralyze me. "I'm Marika." She didn't reach out a hand to shake, but moved closer, awaiting my answer. Ivy again picked up the slack, speaking for me. "Yeah he paints. Sea Monsters." I tasted a morsel of dismissiveness in the way she said it, but it washed away when I saw it had to opposite effect on Marika. She looked even more impressed.

"Sea Monsters! Of course! They told me this is a town of monsters."

Her look still had me a bit below full capacity to move, but

I was able to somewhat coolly force out "Yeah. East Hook is scary place." She didn't respond, just kept looking at me, like I was full of things I could teach her. It felt so good I almost flinched when Ivy spoke up again, this time to keep herself in the conversation rather than rescue it. "You're not from here, right?"

Marika looked away, and I thought I saw fog fill in the air between where our eyes were. "No, I am here for only a short time." No mention of where's she was from. "What should I see?" She looked back at me. "Where are the monsters?"

Again Ivy responded for me. "We live in the city, but they…" she pointed to the crowd around the fire "they're the locals. They know about all the monsters."

Marika's face fell slightly. She looked disappointed, I hoped I didn't too. She kept her smile, nodding at Ivy and starting to break away from the group. "Nice meeting you Ivy." She took a step away, turning towards me and giving me one last look I knew I would remember. "And you Ellis, the artist." She walked away with the same confident athletic stride she walked out with, heading towards the bonfire.

"This fucking party." I looked back at Ivy as she shook her head, in a combination of disbelief and annoyance. "I've seen more bizarre people here than in three years of art school." She looked up at me, catching me glancing back towards the fire. "What is this place, Ellis? You seem to fit right in."

It was only at this point Ivy started feeling like the anchor I worried she'd be when we decided she'd join me on the trip home. I was having a good time, slipping easily back into the shoes of the Ellis I'd been for the first seventeen years of my life. Ivy didn't want that Ellis, she wanted the one who would leave the party now, go home, and start working on his final painting. I wasn't ready to be him again. Or I wanted to talk more with Marika.

Feeling like the bad boyfriend I knew I was, I put my arm around her and squeezed her shoulder. She leaned into me, and I nodded toward the other side of the yard, away from the fire and house. "Want to go over there?"

She looked up at me, making her eyes big like she'd been crying and said in soft, almost baby-like voice. "Away from the country music?" I laughed and she broke and laughed too, both of us feeling like we'd be alright once we got a little alone time.

Before we started moving, I saw a huge, stumbling shadow against the fire. Rocco was making his way toward us, and bringing whatever nonsense he had with him.

"I—VEEE, I'm drunk!" Rocco staggered up to us, trying to stop short, but his freight train momentum carried him forward, pitching him into us and almost falling before putting one hand on each of our shoulders to steady himself. "You having fun?"

Ivy winced from his breath but willed out a smile. "Yeah! Crazy stuff happens up here."

"Try dealing with it every day." His tone went sober quickly, but he was still swaying. Ivy dialed back her pretend enthusiasm.

"We were just talking about the lighthouses…" She trailed off as it was obvious Rocco wasn't paying attention to her. He had lifted his finger and was jabbing it into my chest.

"What are we gonna do?"

I pushed his finger away. "Rocco, what?"

"You heard Desmond; people are celebrating this sea monster thing way too seriously." I nodded, not following his point. "You don't think they would do something to Cadie right? Like her casket."

I hadn't until then, but it quickly became a very real possibility.

"Has anyone done that here?" I had heard of grave robbers, but not in East Hook.

"Not yet."

We had been together all day, mourning and drinking at the same speed, and our thinking was starting to become parallel. "But until now no one knew exactly where someone is buried."

"What do you think is gonna happen?" Ivy made her presence, and her annoyance known. My passion got deflated a bit, but Rocco was either immune to her sharpness or too far gone to pick up on it.

"People are messing with everything… our lighthouses… nothing is sacred anymore. I wouldn't put it past them to mess with her."

Ivy tugged at my arm and tried to take my hand. She put her head up to try and whisper in my ear. "Can we just go home. This day needs to be over."

Still not ready to be the new me again, I made a big display of checking my phone. "It can't be over, it's barely nine." I spoke in her ear, but I definitely didn't whisper. Rocco, whose focus was sharpened by whatever he was on, heard every word. He didn't whisper either.

"You want to leave?! No!" He looked genuinely sad at the prospect. The same sad we'd seen all day.

Ivy looked up at me and held my gaze long enough to sting. She turned back to Rocco, then looked toward the house, but through it, like she was considering. "One more drink." Right after she started a slow smile that started to get wide as Rocco

74

hooted and hollered and gave her a one-armed hug. By the time he hopped off to get drinks, the smile was gone. She pointed at Rocco tilting towards the deck, struggling to stay upright but unbothered by it.

"That's what you look like."

"It's not what I am." It felt right at the time, but only after I heard myself did I realize that it was what Guardado told me about my painting while he was tearing into it in front of the class. I was perpetuating the cycle of bullshit.

"You're gonna be a lot of fun tomorrow." She shook her head, basically talking to herself. "We have so much to do."

I started walking back towards the fire and she caught my arm. I knew she was going to be watching me closely for this last lap, but I didn't know she'd be controlling my movements. I dipped my shoulder to pull out of her grip and took a couple of big steps away from her.

She caught up to before the fire. "This party turned. You're too used to them to notice." She pointed at the fire. "Everyone's starting to get angry." I looked at the group, their motions were more exaggerated and more violent. Their voices were louder and sharper. They weren't being warmed by the fire; they were becoming consumed by it. Against the bright flame they all looked alike, anonymous angry shadows with plans to solve things that were more likely to hurt people. I felt the closest thing to inspiration I'd felt in weeks, I could paint this as my final project, or at least paint something nasty in front of a fire.

I reached into my pocket to grab my phone so I could take a reference picture, but Ivy caught my arm. "Ellis!" I turned to her. "You're a space cadet." I noticed her turning inwards, seeing me as useless as a conversation partner. "I didn't come up here to babysit you."

Ivy had miscalculated what kind of drunk I was. I wasn't a space cadet, I was a berserker, just like everyone in front of the fire. I didn't lash out with an aggressive point but made my voice as disdainful as I could. "You are stopping me from getting my phone out to take a reference picture of the fire for my final project. You're like the babysitter that makes the kid drink bleach." I scored a hit, I could tell, maybe drew blood. No need to go in for the kill. "I'm better off without whatever help you think you're providing."

She didn't flinch or visibly react, except for narrowing her eyes slightly. She looked away and grabbed her phone from her pocket and started tapping. "What's your mom's address?" She asked, without looking up or stopping her tapping.

"What? Why?" She didn't answer, just kept tapping. Finally she looked up, her face a bad mask of curiosity. I thought I would play along with whatever she was doing and told her. As soon as she heard the number she put the phone to her ear and walked towards the fire. I stood there confused for a few seconds before I started jogging after her. I stumbled on a root but caught myself before I fell, thankful Ivy wasn't looking back. I saw her tap Desmond on the shoulder. He was in the middle of some speech but smiled when he saw it was Ivy. She kept the phone to her ear and seemed to be talking to both Desmond and whoever was on the other line. By the time I got close enough to hear she was putting the phone away.

"What was that?" I said when I got close enough to talk to her without Desmond hearing. Not that he was paying attention, he was back on whatever lecture he'd been on. Ivy looked me up and down.

Her answer never came, and Rocco barged in between us holding three filled shot glasses. Whatever was in them didn't look clear, but I couldn't tell in the orange light.

"I know you said one drink, but let's do two!" He handed us the shots. Ivy put her phone in her pocket and took hers. Once we had them he grabbed one beer from each front pocket, and handed them to us.

"What's in this?" I started to ask Rocco but started trailing off when I saw Ivy shoot hers down.

"Cab's here." She said as soon as she finished, then threw the beer on the ground and started walking away. "Enjoy the fucking party." She walked towards the side of the house, avoiding the shortest route back through the house party no matter how pissed off she was. I gave Rocco the shot so I could follow her. I held onto my beer though.

I stumbled again, and couldn't find a root this time to blame it on. In close to the back of the house I could hear the music again, the scratchy, industrial, slaughterhouse rock. I looked up through the kitchen window. From my angle I couldn't see any people, just the light show reflected on the ceiling. The movement of it reflected the way water reflected on ceilings, like the whole party was an indoor pool.

I walked fast around to the front, but only made it in time to see the taxi door shut. It drove away right after and I stood there, wondering what to do next. I thought about calling Ivy, or calling the taxi driver, but settled on cracking open the beer and walking around to the back of the house, keeping a safe distance from the walls.

I found Rocco standing by Desmond at the fire, still holding my shot, and his. It seemed like he was expecting me back.

"Ivy leave?"

I reached out for the shot and he handed it over. "Yeah I couldn't catch her." We clinked and knocked them back. It was minty and horrible, but I didn't cough. "It's been a shitty day, Rock." He just nodded. "It's good to see you." We were standing behind Desmond, so I clapped him on the shoulder. He didn't turn his head around, but lifted his drink behind him so I could clink it. At this distance, the fire's warmth was soft, and at this distance from the house, I could only hear the bass from the psycho trap metal, and it blended well with the twanging ditty playing outside. The song was about cold beer, good friends and woman trouble. I was starting to see the appeal of country.

I took a big gulp of my beer and leaned into toward Rocco, who was swaying, but still pretty solid. "So you really think someone might rob Cadie's grave tonight?"

# Symbolism

R occo and I stumbled out of the trees into the back of the cemetery. In high school, I did a charcoal drawing of a cemetery at night, smudging and erasing in places for the mist. The headstones, flowers, gates and branches blended to make ominous shadows. I tried to arrange it so every spooky unnatural shape had a theoretical natural explanation. Tentacles could just be twisting vines, devils could be angel shaped headstones with their wings broken off, that kind of thing. I wasn't as good with perspective then, but at first glance it was creepy. Mr. Sinclair hung it on his classroom door for all of October every year I was there. I wondered if it ever got back to my mother's. I decided I would look around for it and polish it up. I could convince Guardado that it represented how we all see monsters that aren't there.

Our flashlights weren't casting ominous shadows, still it was a cemetery at night, in the mist. Looking out over what the beam caught, it was much bigger than it looked from the road.

"You know where it is? What section?" Rocco was thinking the same thing.

I'm sure it was the drinks, but I was still optimistic. "No

idea, but it'll have a lump still. Shouldn't be hard to spot if we split up."

I took South, deciding to walk the perimeter and spiral in until I found it, and because I wanted to make a quick stop. A couple of times I saw headlights coming and turned my flashlight off. Rocco did the same. Every East Hook kid knew how to evade notice in the woods, except this time we weren't holding any beers, just trespassing.

Most of the names on the headstones were familiar, it's a small town and all the new people moving in will probably be buried in their winter cities, in garish mausoleums. None of them were familiar enough, but knew I was still a few hundred feet from the general area. I noticed I was breathing hard from the hike. I always noticed my own breath while alone in a cemetery, maybe just because how much it made me stick out amongst the locals.

After three minutes of walking, my mind was going, and I started seeing the demons and ghosts in the mist. The drunken invulnerability was wearing off, or morphing into a drunken something else. I turned down a familiar row and felt my stomach drop down into my legs as I passed his eternal neighbors, and almost retched when I saw his tombstone.

It was a little wider than the others around it, and the only one I could see with a police badge carved on it. Underneath was his name, birth year and death year, then below that an inscription: Beloved Son, Husband and Father, who gave his life saving a child from drowning. The whole thing had a concave bevel from the border, leaving a little less than an inch on the outside. Half-buried in the ground before it was a small iron cylinder, empty of flowers for at least eight months, since his birthday. And that was it. My father, the hero of

East Hook, now just a decorated stone. Among many others.

I looked straight up, mimicking what his view would be, if he could still see and if there weren't six feet of packed silt loam blocking his view. At least he could have looked into the mist. Whatever it was hiding from him, he didn't have to fear it anymore, he'd never see it again. Maybe, like most mist around there often does, it was hiding the water from him, the real place he was laid to rest. I looked back down and put my hand on the stone, it's cool slick surface offering neither support nor warmth. I guessed it fit him better than I thought.

I could have used him now though, the whole town could. He would have figured out what happened at the lighthouses before he got out of his car at the scene. He wouldn't have a problem recreating Cadie's desperate last hours. He'd know why so many people kept ending up in the bay, a fate I wouldn't wish on anyone's family.

"What's happening here Dad?" I kept my voice low, not because I didn't want Rocco knowing I was talking to my father, I was embarrassed by the sincere curiosity with which I was asking it. I even waited for an answer. The silence didn't mean he wasn't listening, and didn't mean he wasn't helping. Maybe he was just watching me and waiting to see if I could see all the differences, see what was wrong, see what he saw. See if I was like him after all or if he was alone as he feared.

I knew if I were more like him I could bring closure to Cadie's family. I could pull Rocco out of whatever he was in. I considered the possibility my dad been training me for it, after seeing obscured, warped pieces of the future in the mist. I wondered if he knew that someday, I would need to see all the details, at least for a weekend. That maybe I could be like him and do some good for the town. Do something for Cadie's father other than stealing his favorite book.

I knew what he would do now, keep walking and find Cadie's grave, but at least for now, I wasn't enough like him, good and bad, to move on so quickly. I went down to one knee and ran my fingers across his engraved name and down the inscription, putting my full palm over the word Father. I stayed that way only long enough for the patch of stone touching my palm to warm a few degrees. When I stood up to leave I wondered how long the mist would take to wash any trace of me off, but I didn't look back to check.

I moved back to the outside of the lot, returning to my spiral approach and trying to focus my mind on Cadie and finding her grave. With fathers on my mind, I thought more about her father, how he tried to nurture her imagination and just couldn't. She didn't miss out on much, I thought, imagination only makes the real world that much more disappointing, and in a graveyard at night, it can scare the shit out of you. To keep my mind off what I would do if my flashlight caught something moving, I thought about if I saw Cadie. I thought about what she would say to me if she saw me prowling around. And what I would say to her. As I heard dirt moving on the other side of the cemetery where Rocco was walking, I started having a conversation with her. The real panicked me was replaced by the imaginary, bloodless, version.

"Drowning's a hell of a way to go." I said under my breath. She didn't seem too troubled by it.

"How'd you end up in the middle of the bay in party clothes?" She would shrug I bet, not making things easy this time.

"I'm gonna find who was with you, and I'm gonna get answers." She'd laugh at this, maybe shrug again. She wouldn't want me to dwell on this, she'd want me to just keep painting. Maybe she'd get revenge, but what good would it do her? Maybe the dead only care about the living because they can stop caring about themselves.

I heard her then, not rasping, not whispering, her normal voice, which I had already started to forget. Saying, almost singing words her father and I knew, but that she'd never learned.

*She bid me take life easy, like the leaves grow on the tree.*
*But I, being young and foolish, with her would not agree.*

"Ellis!" "What the fuck!"

Oh no, I thought, Rocco found her. Grave robbers got to her. I didn't know if I was ready to see what Rocco had. I didn't want to see her body in an open, dug-up casket. I steeled my nerve, and jogged towards his light, sticking to right turns so I didn't trip over a grave. When I got close and shined the light on him, he was touching the headstone, Cadie's headstone, with his finger, maybe tracing the name? There was no bump in front of it, it looked like the ground hadn't been disturbed all season.

When he heard me he turned around slowly, then jumped up and stomped toward me. Before I could react he shoved me so hard I fell and dropped my flashlight.

"What the fuck Ellis!"

I got up carefully, keeping my weight on my toes in case Rocco was having a freak out and was going to attack again. Instead he slumped his shoulders and looked me in the eye.

"What's wrong with you?" He still sounded pissed, but also like he was about to cry.

I felt around for my flashlight and found it. "What are you

talking about?"

He put his hands up and mocked me, "What are you talking about? He pointed his flashlight at Cadie's headstone. "That!"

The light showed there was nothing carved on the headstone at all, we were looking at the back of it, which was defaced with fresh-looking spray paint.

A stenciled pointy blue E over a yellow H.

Ellis Hook.

My tag.

# IV

# Sunday

# Post Modernism

I got back to my mother's house after a frenzied three-mile hike I don't remember taking one step of. I must have crossed some streets and taken some turns, but the single-minded intensity that got me home so fast wasn't focused on the route, it was focused on survival. I went through every excuse and action that could shift the blame for tagging Cadie's grave away from me.

Rocco came around, or at least stopped trying to punch me, when I convinced him he'd been with me since we left the funeral. That method would only work with one person, Rocco, and even then, we hadn't parted on great terms.

I knew that to shift the blame I would have to provide a plausible alternative, and I tried to answer the question: Who would do this?

I had no alibi and the lines were clean, no dripping. Someone with technique had held the cans and the stencil. Anyone who had experience with spray paint could likely tell the difference between someone using it for the first time, and a seasoned professional. If they brought in someone like that to look at it, the suspect list in East Hook would be short.

I knew that I'd been in art school too long, and no detective would analyze the marks for skill. I tried to think like my father, how he would solve the mystery. Not for an investigation of my own, but to know what the people investigating me would do.

Opportunity before motive, I remember him saying while watching some cop show, so I drilled in on that as my legs carried me along road shoulders. Whoever tagged the grave had experience with a spray can and the stencil, but more importantly, access to the stencil.

I was going to see HK first thing in the morning.

When I arrived home the door was unlocked and the porch light on. My shirt was soaked through with mist and sweat. I took off my shoes, wincing as I caught the smell wafting up out of them, and silently let myself into the guest room where Ivy was staying. I had seen a blue glow under the door from the hall and sure enough Ivy was up with her laptop open in front of her. Her headphones were in and she was hunched over, less than a foot away from the screen. She was editing. I got a couple steps in before she noticed me, jumping a little but regaining her calm quickly. Normally she laughs after getting scared, but not this time. She looked at me and held my gaze for a beat, then looked back at her computer. She didn't take her headphones off.

The part of my brain that was so familiar with her was flashing warning lights, telling me the best thing for both of us was to use my putrid feet and just back out of the room and shut the door. Any alerts in my head were washed out by all the other, more urgent warning lights going off at the same time. I sat on the foot of the bed next to Ivy. She tried to keep ignoring me but took her headphones off.

"I really want to finish this." She played at cold and disinterested. She was a much better director than actor.

I'd hoped she'd see the look on my face and know I needed her, but I had to spell it out. "Ivy, I think I'm getting framed for murder."

She thought it was a joke to get her to smile, and moved to put her headphones back on. I grabbed them off her head. She jumped more this time, then glared. I pushed through her ice wall without feeling my temperature drop a degree.

"Someone sprayed my tag on Cadie's grave."

She slightly raised her palms off her keyboard in a half shrug.

"The Ellis Hook symbol we were talking about! The one I sprayed all over town.

She nodded.

I tried to keep my voice low while conveying the apocalyptic nature of the news. My voice came out as a razor-sharp whisper. "Someone sprayed it, exactly it, on the back of Cadie's new tombstone."

Recognition bloomed on Ivy's face, then shifted to anger all in less than a second. "What? When did you see her tombstone? Did you guys actually go to the cemetery tonight? That's sick!"

I would have blushed in shame, but my heart was working too hard to pump any extra blood to my face. "Rocco was convinced grave robbers would come and mess with her, and I was looking after him."

She scoffed. "You're drunk. And you're wet." Her nose crumpled; she didn't have to say that I reeked too.

She had two out of three. I was sober as I'd ever been.

"I'm not drunk anymore; I ran like three miles in the rain."

She feigned great patience, set her mouth and looked at me. "Why did you do that?"

"Because I am flipping the fuck out!"

She winced at the aggression in my tone, proving, to me at least, that she wasn't buying my situation, or didn't care. I stood up, then leaned over her with my arms on the bed, trying to get close to her face slowly, and taking it as easy on the aggression as I could.

"Ivy, I'm not messing around. Someone painted my tag, the one I'm known around town for doing, on the back of Cadie's grave."

"Ellis, I don't know…"

"Rocco almost took my head off, thinking it was me!"

Ivy slowly closed her laptop and put it next to her on the bed. She found the corner of the sheets and folded them off her legs. She stood up and got her face right up in mine. Her voice the same sharp whisper.

"You drag me here to mourn some ex-girlfriend you're still really weird about. You're a different person here with a different history you never told me about. We drink with your friends all day with no breaks. You make moon eyes at some strange foreign girl right in front of me. You let me leave a party with the weirdest people on earth alone. Then you go stumbling into a cemetery and come out talking about spray paint and murder!" She sits back down on the bed and puts her head into her hands. "I was expecting you to come back and apologize."

My brain was still bucking, but it was calm enough to know not to say anything or move closer. I sat on the bed, but a few feet away, then fell back and looked at the ceiling. After a few minutes, I felt her shift, taking her hands off her face. I knew she was about to speak, and I knew I didn't want to be looking at her when she did, so I stayed looking at the ceiling, wishing there were stars.

When she did speak, her voice was robotic, no urgency or emotion. "Did you spray paint that girl's headstone?"

I sat up. "No! I was…" The question came out of nowhere, and I found all the defenses I had rehearsed on my walk home weren't as compelling or even fully prepared.

I fumbled until Ivy jumped back in. "But you were really there?"

"Yeah"

"At like one in the morning, with Rocco, both of you very drunk?"

"Yeah"

"So you have no problem trespassing in a cemetery, but defacing it is out of the question?"

I shook my head. "That's not the p…"

It was that moment my brain finally caught up with my mouth. I realized I had blurted it out to Ivy when I first walked in, even before I really admitted it myself. I didn't care about a tombstone getting defaced. Rocco and I weren't in the cemetery because we were afraid of grave robbers. We told ourselves that because it was much easier to swallow. We were there chasing answers.

Someone in East Hook murdered Cadie, and we needed to figure out who.

It's why Rocco was so scared when he saw my tag. We went looking for clues about who killed her, and the first one we found was a giant spray-painted blue and yellow arrow, pointing directly at me.

I had a cab come pick me up at 8AM, when I knew Ivy would be sleeping. I told my mother I had left my wallet at Desmond's, that I'd be back before Ivy woke up. She had wanted to lecture me since she noticed my state before the funeral the day before, and this gave her a great opportunity. I listened to her points about respect, responsibility and relationships, trying to look contrite. I had decided earlier it was the best lie to get me out the door with the least amount of questions. I was right, I slipped out the front door after less than ten minutes upstairs with a twenty dollar bill my mother gave me for cab fare.

Andy, the younger of the two cab drivers, pulled in at 8:08. His car smelled like smoke and half the leather upholstery was ripped in the back seat.

He turned around when I got in. "How's it going, Ellis? Haven't seen you in a while."

I was a little tired for small talk, but Andy was always good to me. "Yeah, I'm at school in the city, just back here for the Cadie O'Reilly stuff."

He put the car in gear. "It's so awful. I knew her pretty well. I tried to get to the funeral yesterday, but I had a few fares that took me out of town."

"It was a good service, lot of people."

"Yeah well you know, she was the type that makes friends." He looked back at me through the rearview mirror. I held his look, trying not to move a muscle. He looked back at the road. "You going to Standish St.?"

"Yeah."

He stayed quiet for a few blocks, which was okay by me. Even his wipers, wicking the mist off the windshield on the slowest setting were making my headache worse. I saw him open his mouth a few times, but no sound came out, and his eyes kept darting up to the rearview mirror. I tried to discourage him telepathically from whatever conversation he wanted to have. He took a breath and looked up again.

"It's crazy, how she went, you know."

Great. "What?"

"How she ended up in the water. That's like three people this year."

My headache got worse. I leaned forward, ready to strike with some of Desmond's righteous fury, but sat down. I knew if I was going to confront HK, I couldn't waste my strength disproving the great East Hook conspiracy. "Two I thought. Cadie and Jim Minnone."

"There was another back in January, Ed Levesque, fell through the ice by the bridge."

I downshifted into agreeable autopilot; my head ached a little less. "I guess the deep is hungry this year."

"Yeah, like that's exactly what Cadie was sounding like last time I gave her a ride."

I thought I heard wrong, I hadn't slept well the night before, and it sounded more like a nightmare. "What's that?"

"Cadie, like two weeks ago. I was giving her a ride and she kept going on about the water. How stuff was going on under the waves without us seeing. I thought she was maybe on something, you know, sometimes she was…"

I could almost see his foot go in his mouth. But I suddenly needed to hear where this was going, so I let him off the hook.

"Sure."

"I mean, like no judgment, we've all done it, but I thought she was just spacing. But she kept going, talking about 'the darkness coming in on the tide' and how 'the town is being choked by tentacles', and 'we'd all go under, one by one.' I give a lot of rides, and it stuck out to me you know. Not just the sea monster stuff, but how scared she seemed about it."

I was waking up. "Andy, are you joking?"

He looked hurt. "No, Ellis, I swear. It's messed up, I know, but it's been gnawing at me. Like I wish I'd imagined it."

We were a block away from HK's.

"You're actually only like the second person I told" he sheepishly admitted.

We pulled onto HK's street. He lived on the second floor of a small two-story house a few blocks from the harbor. The entrance was in the back, up a wooden set of stairs. "Want me to turn in the driveway?"

"Actually, I'm a little early, let's go around the block. Leave the meter on." Thanks Mom. "You said this was two weeks ago?"

I saw him nod in the mirror. "Yeah, the Thursday before last, or I guess two Thursdays ago."

It wouldn't have been last Thursday "She died Monday, was it the Thursday before that?"

He turned left down a side street. "Yeah, shit, it must have been. It was Thursday because I picked her up at trivia night at the Porpoise."

"Was she alone?"

I could tell Andy was happy to be telling someone, so I kept pressing, wondering if it would somehow lead to a spray can. "Yeah. I think she was heading to meet someone though. In Drydon."

I realized I didn't know where Cadie lived, but I doubted it was Drydon. It was half farmland half junkyard. "What street?"

Andy slowed down, pulled over and turned off the meter. He turned to look at me, not sheepish anymore.

"So you and me are thinking the same thing. You know how they found her, right?"

We were. "Yeah, in the harbor in a dress and shoes."

He shook his head, disappointed with himself. "I don't know the address, and I went back there a few days ago, driving around, trying to remember where I brought her, but I didn't recognize anything. Last Thursday was the thickest fog I've driven through. I should've pulled over, but we followed her GPS and I remember we turned down one of the hidden private driveways off Rivercrest. She got out down when the road opened up, but I never saw a house, it was just pea soup. I couldn't see ten feet in front of me, she was creeping me out with all the talk about the deep and the monsters coming for us, I didn't know what I was doing."

Andy was freaking me out, but I felt validated at the same time. Rocco and I weren't the only ones looking for clues. "How many of those driveways are off Rivercrest?"

"More than you'd think. And listen, man, we were going like five miles an hour, we had the radio off so I could concentrate on not going off the road. Even if I could have seen street signs I wouldn't have noticed them."

He pulled back onto the road, then turned left again. The neighborhood was quiet.

"I might head back out there again later today, see if something jogs my memory, you can come if you want."

I didn't respond.

"Ellis, you want to come out to Drydon later today with me? See if I recognize something?"

I stayed quiet. We were driving behind HK's house and I could see his backyard through the mostly leafless trees. Up a wooden staircase, the second-floor door looked smashed in.

Andy saw what I did and sped up to get around the block and drop me off in front of HK's as quick as possible. He offered to call the police while I was getting out, but I just shook my head, showed him my phone and gave him the whole twenty.

I tried calling HK one more time as I walked around back, but he still wasn't answering. The mist had thinned into a light rain. With the door open I knew I could just look for the stencil and paint and leave a note. Or wait for him inside. What else was I going to do today? Fight with Ivy?

As I started walking up the stairs, I could hear that HK was home. Music was playing and I could hear banging. My heart started banging too and I felt the same dread I had the night before. I tried stomping a little on each step because I wouldn't have a door to knock on. Still I paused before I went in.

"HK?"

The banging stopped. My stomping hadn't worked.

"HK, it's Ellis."

He came to the door holding a baseball bat. He was thinner than he had been, and had a droopy mustache and pointy goatee, with what looked like a week's growth on his cheeks and two weeks on his neck. A tattered coat hanging on a stick. His eyes looked unfocused, but he recognized me right away and rested the bat on his shoulder.

"Ellis, what are you doing here?" He pointed to the busted door. "You believe this shit?"

I shook my head. "What happened?"

"The fucking Quebecois." He saw my expression, started to say something then shook his head. "Come on" he beckoned me in.

His place was a mess. The entrance opened into a window-less living room. The floor was strewn with torn posters, clothes, furniture stuffing and trash. In addition to the open doorway, natural light was coming through what looked like the entry to the kitchen off to the left, which looked covered in trash too. You could tell someone had gone through the place, but also that it probably hadn't looked too put together before.

"Look at this shit." He gestured expansively, "And the fucking door is busted." He walked further back into the house, into what had to be the bedroom. There was a full-size mattress on the floor, slashed open with stuffing coming out. The mess in this room was an order of magnitude worse than in the living room. In addition to the trash and clothes there were wood splinters all over the floor, the source of which became apparent when I turned back to HK. He was standing over what looked like a destroyed bookcase, with two random looking unpainted 2X4s nailed across the gaping hole in the middle. A hammer lay on the floor amidst the trash, and one of the nails was only half in. I had solved the mystery of the banging in the apartment, while about a hundred new mysteries popped up.

HK set the bat down against the wall. "They're fucking dead."

"You know who did this?"

HK looked at me like I was stupid.

"Yeah, the Quebecois. Those fucking pussies took every-thing."

I risked another nasty look. "What'd they take from there?" I asked, pointing at the broken bookcase.

I got the look again. This time I was just acting stupid though. I had a good idea what was gone. "Money, right?"

He glared at me. "You become a cop? It's been awhile. You have to tell me if you are." I was sure that wasn't true. He stepped toward me. "Why are you here?"

While I wasn't there in an official capacity, I was following the clues. "It's about Cadie."

At the mention of her name he shifted his body away from me. His eyes got wide, but he seemed to catch himself and made a show of sighing and looked out his little window at the harbor, just like Rocco did. "I can't believe it." He paused. "How was the funeral? I wanted to come but had to take care of some stuff."

"It was good, a ton of people came, her Dad gave a good speech."

"She's like the fourth one in three years from our high school to die, it's crazy." He had been avoiding my eyes, looking at the floor. He spotted his hammer and went to pick it up. Once he had it he used it to point to the bookcase. "Yeah they took a couple grand and about that much in weed." Now he looked at me, faking wounded pride. "No surprise I'm still dealing?"

I waved his fake concern off. "Yeah I figured. Are they like rival dealers?"

"Yeah they've been here since the summer. Thought they were just like a big family on vacation, but they stayed around. They mostly do harder stuff though, pills and powders, but lately they've had some good weed, so I started buying more and more from them. Last month, they ripped me off, stuffed a lot of low-grade shit in with the good stuff, so I went back to buying from down the coast, and steered everyone who asked away from them."

He might have seen my eyes glaze over, so he skipped ahead. "Last night one of them was at the Gannett and came up to me. I'm alone but figure everyone else in there hates them if we're gonna fight, but he was all smiles. He bought me a few drinks, to make up for it, he said, and we talked about a lot of things, actually a lot about Cadie." He looked up at me and grinned. "I even showed him your painting of the sailors, it's still hanging there."

I realized he'd given me a non-confrontational in. "Yeah some of our work is still up around town too, not as proudly displayed though."

He laughed, a little too loud. "I still smile when I see those EH's."

"That's why I'm here, H. Do you still have the stencil?"

He looked at me for a bit and stopped smiling. "No man." He looked around the place. "I don't know where that went, I haven't seen it in years. You still have yours right?"

"No I burned it back in high school, remember, when I thought the heat was on. You gave me a lot of shit."

He laughed again. "Yeah you probably panicked."

I laughed too, just a couple of old friends pretending to be enjoying each other's company.

"Why are you looking for it?" He looked at me then looked down.

I came clean, still not ready with an alternate story. "Some-one tagged Cadie's tombstone with the EH. I know it wasn't me."

"Well shit, it wasn't me! I haven't seen that thing in years. Haven't touched spray paint since high school either. Who the fuck would do that?" HK's story was better, but I wondered if it's just because he practiced it under calmer circumstances.

I played nice. "I'm trying to figure it out. Everyone's gonna think it's me!"

HK had a gleam in his eye, the same gleam when I suggested tagging. He did it when he saw my inner troublemaker. "Someone come ask you about it?"

"No, Rocco and I went to the grave last night. He was convinced there were grave robbers. We saw it and he almost killed me."

I could see HK's wheel turning. "Shit man, this isn't good!" He sat on the bed. "What time did you see it?"

"Like one AM."

HK didn't follow up with asking why we were there at one AM. "I don't know. When I had it I showed it off to a lot of people. I don't think I gave it to anyone, but a lot of people probably know how it works." His eyebrows went up. "You showed it to Rocco and them, right?"

The list of suspects grew. "Yeah, in high school I showed Rocco and Desmond. But they were both with me all day before."

HK looked deflated, he started turning the hammer around in his hands. "Well Ellis, we gotta get our stories straight. I don't need someone asking you and you giving them my name. This place isn't exactly cop friendly right now." He looked at me, half pleading, half threatening.

I put my hands up, trying to calm him down and to have them ready depending on what that hammer did next. "It's why I came here first. You had it, but you also know a lot more people in this town, I figured we have to figure this out."

He put the hammer down and looked at his bookcase. "So I swear I haven't had it for a long time, but we might be able to buy some time saying someone broke in here and took it."

I was skeptical HK had my best intentions in mind. "Now you want cops coming here?"

"God no. But if you have to say something, maybe we say that's what was stolen. Send them looking somewhere else." He nodded at the bookcase.

There it was. "And the Quebecois' house probably isn't cop friendly?"

"I hope not. But they've been there a few times, never found anything. They must have a stash house somewhere else. Hell, they can't be lucky forever though."

I was losing patience, even now, HK was only looking out for himself. "We gotta find who really did it!"

"I know! This will give us some room though. I swear, I will help you figure this out. People can't just fuck with Cadie like that and try to blame us. But you gotta understand, people can't just fuck with me, either. It's either this or something worse."

I shook my head, disgusted with his greasy looks, his filthy house, and how stupid he thought I was. He didn't notice, was too busy marveling at his own cleverness. He gave me a cocky smile, and continued. "An unrelated police visit to Drydon might be the perfect thing."

My hands started sweating and it felt like someone punched me in the heart.

"Drydon! Are you fucking kidding me!" His eyes got wide again, as I leaned into him. "Where in Drydon, exactly?" I couldn't believe it; my first lead had paid off. I really was getting more and more like my father every day.

He told me and started trying to confirm what we'd say if people talked to us. I agreed to everything he suggested, my headache was gone. I wrote the address on my phone, and charged out of there like it was on fire. As I descended the wooden stairs, I called Desmond.

# Outsider Art

D esmond didn't pick up on the first few rings, but right before I hung up I heard a click and a gravelly, annoyed "What?" I chose to join him in avoiding niceties and told him I needed a ride to Drydon.

"You don't have a car?"

I reminded him about Ivy, and I thought I heard him laugh when he remembered her leaving, he may have been just clearing his throat.

"When do you need to go?"

I answered "Now" figuring I wanted to get this whole thing figured out before Ivy left. What I hadn't figured out though, was what I could find in Drydon that would neatly answer all the questions I had. It's one of the reasons I wanted help and knew Rocco might still be thinking of tackling me.

In high school Desmond would have already been in his car, started getting his stuff together right after I said I needed a ride. "Can't do now." Relationships change, especially high school ones. "What's in Drydon?" I wasn't stung by his reticence to help, but I did want to see how little I could tell him before he agreed to help.

"It's about the cemetery, and Cadie."

"What?!" His voice was getting less gravelly, and I heard

fabric move in the background, suggesting he moved into a sitting position. "What did you find?"

"Can I explain in person?"

"No."

That one stung a little. By the tone more than the refusal. I debated telling him to fuck off but looked back at HK's house and the urge to get far away outweighed my pride. I looked around to see if anyone was listening, but it was just me and the crows. I told him about the graffiti, the cab ride and H.K.

"Shit man. So what do you want to do there? I mean, I know them but…"

I cut him off. "I don't want to talk to them or anything, just see the place. They're not supposed to be home."

"Alright fine." I heard more movement in the background, he was probably getting out of bed. "I've got brunch at…" I heard a muffled voice. "Eleven thirty. At eleven, I'm kicking you out of the car no matter where we are. I have to change."

"Fair enough." I told him, happy I got what I wanted but wondering what had sharpened him these past three and a half years. He was working full time, which I'd always been told doesn't improve people's moods, and so was Rocco. Both weren't exactly pumping me up for the post-graduation life.

Desmond confirmed H.K.'s address and said he was ten minutes out. There was no dry place to stand, so I paced under the branches of some trees in the road. I thought about calling Ivy, she hadn't sent me anything since late last night, and we hadn't talked in the morning. I wasn't looking forward to the conversation we were going to have when she woke up, but I thought she'd eventually understand why I needed to be where I was. As good an excuse as I had, I didn't call her. I let her sleep.

The light rain had pushed out all the fog. You could see a patch of the harbor from the sidewalk. I wondered if the weather had turned a corner but knew in my East Hook bones it was a reprieve, and the fog might be back in an hour.

I had never done any paintings with the mist coming in. Impending always interested me a lot less than occurring. Why commit the moment before something big happens to canvas, when you can just as easily paint something big?

A crow flew low overhead, his caw almost deafening as he passed over me. He joined a group of his friends twenty feet away on the lawn next door, all their feathers getting wet, hopping around something. I guessed it was dropped bread, maybe a pretzel and took a few steps towards it. The birds didn't scatter until I was almost on top of them, refusing to leave what I then saw to be the carcass of a woodchuck, it's head almost picked to a bare skull. Its tail spilled onto the sidewalk, but it was a good ten feet from the road. I shook off the peculiarity, considering it could have easily been flung from the impact with a car and landed on the lawn, or one of the crows tried to move it and it dropped. I knew woodchucks died for all sorts of reasons, being roadkill was probably the least common. But the details didn't add up, I spotted another difference with the reality I knew..

Desmond pulled in front a few minutes later and I hopped in his car, soaking the passenger seat when I sat down. He handed me a cup of coffee and a folded East Hook Express, the semi-weekly local town paper. Desmond never struck me as a news junkie or a big reader, but I was realizing how little I knew everyone. "No fog." I stuck with small talk as I grabbed the paper from him.

"Not yet. How's H.K.?"

"Still sketchy."

"I keep forgetting you were boys."

We weren't even friends, but I was a little embarrassed to have any history with him at all, reinforced by what I had just walked out of. "You see him around town a lot?"

Desmond laughed. "Oh yeah." But he didn't elaborate, and changed to topic, keeping a thin smile. "So what's the address?"

I told him and he pulled a U-turn to start us on our way. I looked at the paper.

Lighthouses Vandalized stretched across the entire front page, with a picture of the Buck Island lighthouse below. The door was hanging open its window smashed. Police tape surrounded the base of the tower, I thought the yellow caution tape and broken door would make for an interesting juxtaposition in the idyllic setting, but the picture was black and white, so any color clashes were only in my imagination. I filed it away, wondering if Guardado would like something like that: the suggestion of monsters instead of actual tentacles.

I started to read about how the police were baffled at the audacity of the crime, and while they've opened an investigation, stuff like this just doesn't happen in East Hook. A thin vertical opinion column ran next to the story, bemoaning the wanton destruction and how far East Hook had strayed from its mid-century values. "Something insidious has slithered its way through the fog into our - until now - protected hamlet, squirming wetly up our rocky coast and into our homes like an unwelcome return of Foamfang, the legendary serpent of Hock's Sound." I read the opening line to Desmond out loud. Was everyone in this town like that now, comparing every fucking thing that happens to a sea monster?

"What is that?" he laughed and looked in the direction of the paper.

"An Ominous Sign. Some guy writing about the lights being smashed."

He shook his head. "That's all they care about now. It's like they forgot about Cadie. They pushed her back to page three. For some kids breaking stuff."

I understood that's why he gave me the paper. I flipped past page two, reading half a headline about the mayor's cuts to social services to expand tax incentives for restaurants, but flipped to the third page before forming an opinion. Memories and Tears at the Funeral for Cadie O'Reilly. "Is this just about the funeral? They're still not saying how she died?" I can appreciate societal collapse leading the news, but wasn't murder a clearer sign of that than vandalism?

"Nothing." Desmond looked just as mad as me. "I bought it at the gas station after I flipped through and saw the article, but the whole thing is about like what her Dad said and what the priest said. There's a small part at the end mentioning that she was found unresponsive in the water, and ..."

"Let me guess, how she's the third body they've pulled out this year." I snorted an interruption.

Desmond thought about it, I almost saw his lips moving trying to read the article in his head. "No, I don't think they mentioned it this time." He nodded toward the paper, "Not sure though, check."

It was mostly about the funeral, how many people came, with selections from Mr. O'Reilly's speech "It's so terrible she was taken from us while she had so much more love to give" and oddly "her ability to find mystery in everyday occurrences." I got to the part at the end Desmond was talking about. Cadie was found deceased in the water early Tuesday morning by the Deputy Harbormaster. "This is bullshit!" I yelled when I read it, throwing the paper into the windshield. Desmond startled a little at my outburst, even I didn't realize how angry this all made me. "Why don't they say?"

I hated not knowing. What happened to her and what was happening to me.

"When do they publish this? The funeral was yesterday." A lot had happened yesterday that I hoped never made the papers.

Desmond knew everything about East Hook, he went into basically half the stores with deliveries every week. "They publish early Sunday and mid-day Thursday I think." We were only a few minutes from Drydon, Desmond took some back roads I didn't know about. "They are thinking they'll turn into a weekly soon, though. Most of their subscribers are out of town until June. They're gonna start an online version. Some summer guy bought it, said he'd keep it all exactly the same, you know, save it. A few months in the red seemed to change his mind though." Like I said, everything. I was about to ask him what "in the red" meant when I felt my phone buzz in my pocket. I didn't take it out, assuming it was a message from Ivy, and not being sure I could control my expression as I read whatever it said. To take my mind off it, I started thinking of other things to ask him, but Desmond beat me to the draw, asking me something first.

"So what are we doing there?" He didn't seem nervous, but the Desmond I was used to wouldn't have asked that until we were already out of the car and on the property.

"First we see if anyone's home. Then we park nearby and

check out the garage. The stencil should be in it and maybe other stuff we can tell the cops about." Desmond was trying to protest but I powered through his raised hand. "Anonymously, once we're a good distance from the house." What came out of my mouth more closely matched HK's plan than my own, which was to find someone on the property and ask them why Cadie was there the night before she died. I wondered why I was hiding my true intentions, or if my intentions were tilting more toward self-preservation.

He still looked like he wanted to protest, but instead asked another question. "What kind of stuff are we going to find we can tell the cops about?"

"Drugs, I think it's a grow house in there. Apparently they keep all the bad shit in there, just police have never had probable cause to actually open the doors."

"So how are we getting in?"

Now I felt like the East Hook expert, and relished it, trying to be as condescending as possible with my answer. "No one locks their doors here."

Desmond slowed down as we got near the address. We crawled by the driveway, looking down the hill at the house and seeing if we saw any cars parked or other signs of life. The property consisted mostly of thick woods that separated it from the neighbors, and backed up to the Canoe River. There was a big separated garage that looked like a converted barn, it was two stories and had a boarded-up window above the garage doors, towards the point of the roof. The main house was small, it looked like a prefab, but new. The paint looked fresh and there were shutters, it wasn't what I was expecting. The woods came almost right up to the house, so there wasn't much in the way of yard. There was a patchy square of lawn between the house and the driveway, but it was strewn with what looked like car repair equipment and other mechanical refuse.

We were perched high above the house, which sloped down to the river from the road. I was surprised to see a dock behind the house, with a boat tied up to it. These Quebecois were living large. No wonder they were able to keep the parties supplied.

Desmond parked a hundred feet past the driveway on the opposite side of Rivercrest. There was a large dirt shoulder and it was hidden from the road for northbound traffic, the direction we expected them to come. When we got out of the car I checked my phone. The missed text was from Ivy, she was on her way back to the city.

As we started walking down the hill, I asked Desmond what else he knew about the Quebecois.

"I don't know much. They're better friends with my roommate, but they're just weird guys who sell weed and dress like monsters."

"How long have they been in town?" I was last in East Hook over winter break, and thought I got around town then. I would have remembered seeing them.

Desmond let out a long 'hmmmm' as we walked, so he could think about it. "There were here last summer, but I thought then they were just summer folk, but they obviously stayed. I'm trying to remember if they were there the summer before. I think so, but maybe they looked different."

"No pincers?"

Desmond laughed. "Honestly, the first time I saw those was at last night's party."

So maybe I had seen them before too. I wondered why the

monsters were finally revealing themselves.

Before we reached the driveway, Desmond hopped down from the road into the woods of the property. "Let's stay in the trees, in case they're home." It was a good idea. I jumped down with him and we started descending, trying to move from tree to tree, blocking us from the big house. The ground was wet but not too slippery. We still needed to watch our steps. Desmond's big, sure steps took him down a lot faster, by the time I had my feet under me, he was already twenty feet away.

It surprised me how much less scary everything was in the daylight. Not just how I wasn't expecting something to jump out at me behind every tree, but mundane, realistic problems seemed more manageable. I figured if someone saw us we could just say we wanted to get down to the river. If pressed could say I wanted to paint it, it was an excuse I'd used before. Typically no one believed me until I grabbed a stick off the ground and started sketching the property or house or even the interrogator in the dirt right in front of them. Art school had developed a few skills suited for trespassing. Maybe it wasn't such a waste.

"Dammit!"

Instincts had me looking toward the house first, to see if someone was coming out, and I looked for a tree to duck behind. It was still all clear. So was the driveway, and I couldn't hear any cars on the road above. I looked at Desmond and he was jumping back with one foot in the air. He kept it in the air and steadied himself on a tree.

"You ok?!" I ran over to him, noticing a strong acrid smell.

"Yeah." He sounded annoyed and not in pain. I looked at the ground for whatever he stepped on and saw it. Lying next to the tree was a dead skunk, fur covered in maggots, with a big footprint near its back legs.

Desmond started wiping his shoe off on the leaves and pine straw. When it looked like he at least brushed all the maggots off we kept going down. The ground started to flatten out when we neared the garage. We moved sideways a little, making sure to put the structure between us and the house. It did leave us exposed to anyone coming down the driveway, but the back of the garage was only a few yards from the deeper cover and the easy escape the woods provided.

Desmond got to the edge of the clearing first and waited for me next to a tree. He looked down at his shoe and scraped it against the bark. When I caught up to him he was shaking his head. "These were my brunch shoes." We both started to laugh but caught ourselves and shut up.

Up close the garage looked normal, it didn't have a generator next to it or any extra ventilation. If it did used to be a barn then it wasn't a big one. It was probably just a normal two car garage with a fake rustic design. The vinyl siding looked new, just like the main house. From here we couldn't see into the back windows, they were just reflecting the gray forest back at us. I had expected that if there was a grow house in there, something would be obstructing the view, maybe blackout curtains or cardboard. So far, everything looked normal, and away from the skunk, smelled normal, like pine and salt. It didn't quite feel normal though.

I whispered to Desmond before we left the trees. "Have you seen a lot of dead animals lately?" He thought about what I said and just shrugged, then stepped into the clearing and walked to the back of the garage. I followed quickly behind.

He checked the left window and I walked to the right. They

were high off the ground. I had to get on my toes to see over the frame. When I did I couldn't see anything, it was too dark. They didn't look blocked by any material; I just couldn't get high enough to block the reflection and see through the window. I tried moving a hand over my head but couldn't keep my balance.

Desmond was about three inches taller than me in high school, but must have gone through a growth spurt since, as his entire head was above the frame, with him standing flat footed. Maybe I spent so much time hunched over drawings, it had warped my back. He was leaning close to the window, cupping his hands around his eyes, darkening the glass so he could see into it. "Holy shit!" He said and looked back at me.

"What?" I responded, and he nodded to the window behind me. I didn't want to, but I admitted it. "It's too tall." He waved me toward him. I felt like a child. Was he going to lift me up to look in? As I got closer I realized that Desmond wasn't the giant I thought he was. He was just standing on the higher side of sloping ground. I leaned in and cupped my hands around my eyes to see.

It took my eyes a few seconds to adjust. All the lights were off in the garage, which eliminated the grow house theory. The light, weak and gray as it was, shined through the windows in illuminating shafts. It was interrupted in places, blocked by jagged, odd shadows. As my eyes adjusted the shapes came into focus but remained odd. Near the window towards the house, I could make out the silhouette of a six-foot fearsome kraken statue. Its head bulged with eyes and teeth and each tentacle I could see was lined with suckers and spikes. It was black in the darkness, the light was hitting the side we couldn't see, but I thought I could make out a brown halo, like it was made of wood. Not the kind of thing that stays in a garage.

My eyes were seeing more the longer I looked into the darkness, near a window on the opposite side I noticed a table with blocks stacked in an irregular way. When I looked closer details started to emerge, the blocks were buildings in a miniature town. Something on the table was shimmering, like the base was made of aluminum foil, but the shining spots kept changing. I knew the light wasn't a strobe or laser, and it wasn't flickering anywhere else, so whatever was shiny had to be moving. I stepped away from the glass, planning to take it in from the other window, get a look at the tiny town from a brighter angle. I just hoped I was tall enough.

Desmond saw the purpose in my step and didn't say anything, just took my place by the window. I was more than tall enough. After I'd cupped my hands against the glass so I could see, my shadow loomed over the tiny town like an ancient giant. In the light I noticed two details I couldn't make out from the back view, each more unsettling. One, the tiny town model I was looking at was downtown East Hook, cast in plastic and stylized, not quite to exact scale. Two, the shimmering base I was seeing was water. The edges of the table were raised, to keep water on top, and the water level in the model was high enough to flood the whole town, entirely submerging the shops on the harbor.

I felt a cold sweat break out at the base of my neck and start trickling down my back. I backed off the window and bumped into something moving fast on my first step. It spooked the hell out of me, I jumped and gasped, turning around to see Desmond, trying to get me under control. His finger was up to his lips telling me to be quiet. I nodded, trying to hold my breath to hear what he heard, and when I was still he took the same finger and pointed to the woods behind the garage.

I heard it then, a car motor and tires crunching gravel, getting louder. I started running for the woods, and Desmond was right behind me. He beat me to them and kept running deeper towards the neighbor's house. I followed him, seeing him turn around and slow down once we were seventy feet in or so. He put his arm up for me to slow down. I stopped running and turned around. The car was in the driveway, coming to a slow stop between the garage and the house.

I expected everyone to be moving fast if they saw us, but once the car stopped, no one came out for a tense half a minute in which neither Desmond nor I breathed. Finally, the driver door opened, and someone stepped out and moved around to the trunk quickly enough that I couldn't tell if he was wearing the prosthetic pincers. Desmond and I exchanged a quick look confirming our luck, but we both remained content not to press it and stayed put.

The trunk slammed down, and the driver emerged struggling into a raincoat and carrying what looked like pieces of cloth, or empty bags. He walked around the front of the car and towards the house, only he didn't go to the house, he walked right past it, and the garage, through the gap between the two buildings and down the backyard forest path.

We both flinched, thinking he was headed our way, but he never turned in our direction. He walked away from us, toward the river, with a sense of purpose.

"What is he doing?" I whispered, for no reason. I knew Desmond couldn't answer. He just shook his head, as we watched the lone Quebecois march down the dock, and start preparing the boat for launch. Paralyzed by confusion of what

I saw in the garage, and the fear of almost being discovered, I just stood there, leaning against a tree, as the engine caught, ropes were tossed, and the boat took off southwards, towards the river mouth and open ocean. As the engine sound started to fade, I heard a thump next to me. I looked down, and saw a robin, legs in the air, one wing half spread, dead as a stone.

# Fauvism

P equod Point was the first vacation settlement in East Hook and its small, close-clustered houses better reflected the town's much more modest history. A few were right down on the rocks, most were across a small road from the water, none of them had a yard more than fifteen feet in any direction. During the winter, they were largely boarded up, I don't remember ever knowing anyone who lived in one year-round. Starting in May, they were rented one week at a time to summer folk, turned over every Friday, and boarded up again in September or lately October. A small blessing for the unlucky people who rented in May was that the fog was the only way they'd have any privacy, the only way your neighbors couldn't see in your windows.

It was beautiful though, especially on a clear day. You could see the coastline winding North, dotted with smaller, paler blue lighthouses the further you looked. Straight ahead East was Indian Island, and behind it towards the horizon the outer islands. If you looked South you saw Little Hook, Big Hook, the Stains, and in the small gap between them, Lincoln Head across the bay. I used to go on walks there when I was little, in the winter, when the wind's so strong you can actually lean with all your weight over the water on the rocks and it'll blow you back. I remember I painted a sunset over the harbor on some perfect October day, starting as the sky flashed orange, and finishing while the high clouds still had a pink tint. I gave it to my aunt for Christmas after she had done a walk with us there the previous summer and kept talking about how lovely it was.

Desmond and I were parked at the North end of the point, and while the day was far from beautiful, the visibility was a lot better than normal for this time of year. We could see a long way Northeast. The rain held steady and it was windy. The water had some whitecaps out past Indian Island, but the Pequod inlet looked calm enough and a little research on my phone confirmed there was no small craft advisory. Still there weren't many boats on the water.

I doubted any charter was even booking in May anymore. The Salt Cod, the daily ferry to Haven Island puttered past us, and I watched it with morbid fascination, praying to myself that no one would jump off the stern. A large sailboat was listing near the Stains, a bad place to be ceding control. Everything on the water felt so fragile and fraught.

We kept our eyes North, until we saw a little blue boat motor up from the river into the inlet. I looked through Desmond's small set of waterproof binoculars and confirmed it was the same boat that left Drydon.

I had the idea to park out at the point and just wait for them. If they were going somewhere, this was the mouth, and we could see every move they made. Even the small chop caused by the wind would keep their boat under twenty miles per hour, and unless they went behind Sands Island, there is no place to hide on the ocean. That was also the reason we didn't want call Rocco to jump in his boat and follow them from there. We could stay closer, but they would be sure to notice us. Also, with all the bridges and coastal roads, it was much faster to drive between any two points in East Hook, other than Lincoln Head, than to go by boat. And without the fog, you could follow a boat wherever it was going without losing sight of it.

As picturesque as the North coast was, I doubted the boat was out for a pleasure cruise. It would most likely be headed somewhere in East Hook. So I wasn't surprised when it turned to starboard and came up the inlet towards us, but my heart started beating faster anyway. Something about the Quebecois freaked me out. Desmond sat up straighter and turned the radio down when he saw it turn, so it wasn't just me.

We hadn't said anything to each other since we parked about ten minutes before, but seeing the boat made me break the silence. "Think he's going downtown?"

Desmond shook his head, "Nah, he'd just drive there." He was right, I couldn't think of where they could be headed then. We kept watching as the boat crept toward us. We watched it come and go, swapping turns looking through the binoculars at the ship and captain.

Once he passed us Desmond put the car in gear and we did a U-turn, heading for the bridge to Big Hook. We took our time, there was still a chance he'd head into Athena Bay so we didn't want to get too far ahead of him, but most likely he would stay the course and loop around Little Hook and the Stains. We wanted to beat him there and watch from a stationary position. We definitely didn't want to be on the bridge if he came under it. He would recognize Desmond's car from his house. He also could have seen it parked on the road in Drydon. A parked car is a lot less noticeable than a moving one.

Big Hook is bigger than Little Hook but is still a small island. There are only two roads and one is a dead end. The main road snakes through the properties and ends with another bridge connecting it to the middle peninsula in East Hook, East Center. Unlike Pequod Point that road did not offer unobstructed views of the water. You can see it from some certain angles, but mostly you saw tall bush fences and iron gates, with the occasional shingle roof and dormer window among the trees.

We were headed to the one publicly accessible part of Big Hook, a small strip from the road to a landing that families on Little Hook used to access the mainland. The two islands are close enough at that point that people usually row across on kayaks or row boats, if they have a lot to carry. The sewer, water and power lines to the island ran under the crossing at that point too, so no one wanted it on their property. We parked in one of the two dirt spots, grabbed the binoculars, and jogged down a dirt path between two immaculately trimmed hedges guarding expensive empty summer properties on either side to the landing.

The landing was in better shape than the path, with a newly built rack for kayaks next to a few upturned rowboats. The new wood repelled the rain, and the rock walls, which replaced the hedges close to the shoreline, were protecting us from the wind. There was even a new decoration on the rack, the same sign with the bright red warning saying the same thing: DO NOT GO IN THE WATER. It was only three hundred feet or so across the inlet to Little Hook, where it looked like the landing there had gone through similar renovations.

We could see the almost all the Stains south of little hook, but with the rock wall, couldn't see the outer harbor. As pleasant a place as this was to pass some time, we'd probably have to find another vantage point soon.

The little blue boat kept on the expected path while we were moving, and we only had to wait a few minutes until we saw it appear Southwest of Little Hook. I focused the binoculars on the tentacle logo to confirm. From so far away, the progress looked plodding, but it was about to go out of sight. I asked Desmond where we should go.

He tilted his head like he didn't have an easy answer. "Uh, it depends on which way they're going. Can I see those?" He gestured toward the binoculars and I handed them to him. He looked out at the boat then tilted them down and readjusted the focus, looking at something closer. "They should turn towards the harbor soon, otherwise, we can go to Lincoln Head. We would just be blind for so much of that it'd really be a guess." I was feeling like less of a genius tracker and looked around for something to do while Desmond was on the binoculars.

"Shit." I turned toward Desmond and saw he was trying to lean around the rock wall, with a hand on it to steady himself while he tried to keep his feet dry. "Do they really it to go all the way to the water?" He stepped hesitantly into the water, testing its depth. It sank about halfway up the shoe and he pulled it out.

"Did it turn yet?" I looked behind me to see if there was a better angle or higher ground we could use.

"Yeah, it's actually doing circles, looked like he was slowing down, and I thought I saw movement on the deck, like he was getting ready to do something. It's just..." He looked down at the water for some place he could step. "It's just out of sight. We just need three more feet."

"You don't want to get your shoes wet?" I didn't understand.

He was still looking down at the water, not offended. "It's not that, we just don't have a foothold, it's smooth rocks like four feet down. There's no guarantee we could even hold footing in there, it's like a cliff."

I thought about running right in, swimming out far enough past the wall and treading water while I watched them. It wasn't the sign by the rowboat that kept me from it, but its words were going through my head, in my father's voice. I may have known what was in the water, the Quebecois, but I didn't know what else. I looked to the flipped rowboats, wondering if the oars were stored underneath like they were on most docks. I even started walking toward them when I heard a splash.

Desmond was chest deep in the water, struggling to pull himself up or get a foothold on whatever jagged and slippery rocks he had jumped on. After a minute of flailing, he seemed to press his chest down below the surface and slide up like a climbing seal. Succeeding at clearing the barrier, he rolled forward and fully submerged face first. He stayed under for a few of my quickening gasps of breath, and I noticed myself exhale when his head finally popped up.

His arms were moving, but not quickly like he was treading water, instead methodically, feeling for something to grab. They must have found it, because his head became still, with his jaw clenched tight. He was balanced on something but needed tension to stay there. He finally looked back at me.

I burst out laughing, convulsing in relief and entertainment.

Desmond laughed too, almost an animal howl, more relieved than I was. He was shaking too, but from the cold.

"Can you…," I couldn't get it out without another laughing fit overtaking me. I tried to compose myself, shaking my head "Can you see it?"

Desmond looked confused for a second. The shock of getting in made him forget the purpose. He looked to the West, squinted and nodded. "Yeah I see the back of it. It's not moving, just bobbing." He was breathing hard from the cold and the effort. He brought his left arm up slowly from below, careful to keep his balance and his hold, and pulled out the binoculars. He shook them a little, and put them to his eyes, adjusting the focus with his middle finger.

"He's off the side playing with a huge shiny metal box, like balancing it on the edge… He just took something out and threw it on the deck… Ok, now he's closing it and… Holy Shit! He just pushed it into the water. Must have been heavy it made a giant splash!"

I knew lobster traps weren't metal. In fact, I couldn't think of anything metal that just gets thrown into the water. I looked at the sign on the rock wall and said the unwritten part to myself. You never know what's in there.

"Ok now he's got a hook around a line and this dark lump, it's getting tighter, must be attached to the sinking box… The black lump is floating. I saw him spin the focus again, sharpening his view. "It's a buoy, a black buoy."

"A black buoy?" I yelled back. "Like solid black?" I thought I heard a motor change pitch.

"Yeah, but like a dull black, no shine." Matte. "They're headed back, I think." Desmond confirmed what I heard and turned to me and tossed the binoculars into a patch of seagrass by my feet. He started making the climb back onto land. "Let me know when you can see it."

I kept the binoculars focused on the edge of Little Hook, so I didn't see Desmond's exit, but from the sound of it, it was no more graceful than his entrance. The blue boat came into view, turning back around Little Hook. When it was out of sight behind the island, I looked down at Desmond lying on his back at my feet, breathing heavily and still shaking. "You earned your omelet."

I helped him up and we started immediately moving to his car, where we could crank the heat, because he didn't have any towels or dry clothes. He stopped me before we got to the trail, and walked back to pick up his phone, keys and wallet from the ground by the sea wall. I was glad I hadn't stepped on them.

Desmond made it to the car under his own power, but he didn't have the same long stride he had at the Drydon house. He was still shaking, and his clothes were sticking to him. He said they felt like they tripled in weight. A familiar, high school feeling stirred within me as we walked together, his arm around my shoulder as I helped him to his car. Envy. I wished I had been the one to jump in the water. I wished I could say monsters be damned sometime. Maybe Guardado was right, maybe I was too afraid of monsters to ever paint them right.

I deposited him in the passenger seat, he didn't protest me driving. We had the heat on to full blast while Desmond rubbed his hands together and started to regain feeling.

I asked him about the buoy. I couldn't picture what a black one would even look like. He repeated that it was a dull black, that there didn't look to be too many others around it and that from the angle, it was probably between the second and third Stain, fifty feet towards the harbor. I let him get warm in silence.

He broke it. "Maybe it's a city trap, or county, something public."

"What are you talking about."

"Out behind MyKayla's parents' house, you know the animal kingdom, Sherman's Pond, there's a solid black buoy there that looks just like it."

Sherman's Pond was the largest freshwater source in the East Hook region. The properties around it were nice, probably the best off the coast, the best for locals. I had forgotten the twins grew up in that neighborhood. Good for Desmond. I looked at him in his soaked clothes and was no longer jealous. I just wanted to tell him how happy he looked with MyKenzy.

Instead I opened my phone and dialed Rocco's number. He picked up on the first ring, with no noticeable grudge from the night before. If anything he was anxious to help me find out more. The curiosity only grew when I told him what Desmond and I found. He even said, "What are we gonna do next?"

"Let's go out tomorrow morning, early, and pull up that black buoy." His excitement must have grown enough that he was beyond speech because it was total silence on his end. "Can you do that?"

Rocco laughed. "No, it's illegal and if anyone sees us do it I couldn't fish in the state again."

Sounded like a plan. I would stay another day.

# V

# Monday

# Luminism

hrough the fog we took the inlet to the harbor from the marina where Rocco kept his boat. It was dead calm, even around the point, but visibility was less than thirty feet. Rocco could have navigated with no visibility; he had been on East Hook bay every day. Good thing too because he rarely took his eyes off the water right beside the boat. Still looking for bodies.

Locals joke that the fog is the town's way of punishing the summer folk. They set out following real estate listings, looking for a coastal spot to escape their lives and their cities and heat for a while. Find some old family home being sold by descendants looking for their own escape and make offers over the asking price. Then they move in and immediately start using their money to make connections and use those connections to slowly morph it back into the towns they came from. Trees keep growing and more are planted around the perimeters of these waterfront properties, rendering them impossible to see from the road. From the water they are the only things you can see. Shingled, mostly empty levees standing between everyone who actually lives in East Hook and the East Hook bay. In May, when the summer folk start arriving, the town gets a small revenge. The fog renders the deep-water properties both hidden from the water and blocked from the view like the rest of town.

The blanket of fog felt like a real blanket, working with the vibration of the engine and the salt air to keep me on the verge of drifting off. I had a relatively calm night after the drama of the day before, but still didn't get much sleep. A risotto primavera dinner with my mother filled with questions about why I wasn't yet going back to city, why Ivy was, reminders that she hoped I knew what I was doing and a lot of verbal and nonverbal suggestions that she knew I didn't. The dinner was interrupted by a call from Ivy, the first I'd heard from her, and I was so thankful for what the call got me out of that I forgot what it would bring me into. I knew I had been a jerk and I knew I was acting strange, but the way Ivy talked down to me, like a concerned parent, did not sit well. I already had one of those. We didn't leave it on great terms. She hung up and blocked me. Intending to paint until my mother went to bed and I could go up and raid the liquor cabinet, I went into my supply closet downstairs for materials and saw Cadie's dad's Yeats book staring back at me.

For so long, the book had been my proudest trophy, cherished much more than any recognition I ever got for painting. Almost every day in high school I would take it out of its hiding place, right next to the spray paint, and read from it. It started as a reminder of my manhood and conquest, typical feelings associated with reading poetry alone by yourself in your room, but I kept returning to it because I loved it. A lot of Yeats' poems were like songs. Simple childlike rhymes about love and mythical creatures in a foggy seaside setting. It was the way I wanted to see East Hook. I had been using his words to describe my feelings almost every day since high school.

The book looked different in my closet. Instead of leather and paper, it was another, significantly less important, Stolen Child from Mr. O'Reilly. I thought about returning it before remembering her grave, which he surely had visited since the burial. Then I thought about throwing it in the water. Instead I took it out and opened it, reading about Irish elections and Greek heroes, knowing I had a painting to start and an early wake up in the morning. I didn't hear my mother go to bed, and I didn't put the book down or pick up a brush or pencil before I fell asleep.

On Rocco's boat I stayed awake by looking at how the buoys reflected on the empty navy water, shimmering brown blobs, no matter what color they were painted, that thin out and merge with the shimmering gray sky reflection as they stretch toward the boat. I wondered what the light was like when they found Cadie, how her reflection must have still rippled and stretched, while her body lay still.

The Stains were a straight shot from downtown. Once we passed under the Outer Harbor bridge there were no speed restrictions, but Rocco barely pushed the throttle forward. He respected the fog too much to rush anything while in the middle of it. Even at the slow speed I turned to watch the wake fan out behind us, the white foam spreading and thinning as we left it behind. Long before we turned and came back through this area, it would be glass, nothing to show we were ever there.

The spot Cadie floated in was just as glassy and calm.

"Right up around here, right?" Rocco started slowing down as we turned back toward Big Hook. In the mist I couldn't see the Stains, but I knew we were close.

"Yeah, it's a black buoy, the only one in the area."

We didn't speak as we crawled forward, looking for the dark buoy. The visibility made it tough, Rocco would pick a heading, go all the way to the first stain, almost at Little Hook, then turn and set a heading 180 degrees opposite. We couldn't eyeball the lines, with the current and fog we'd go off course too quickly.

Rocco broke the silence after four unsuccessful back and forth trips. "I haven't fished this part of the bay in months." We were going slow, so the engine wasn't so loud. Rocco's voice went lower to match it, almost like he was talking to himself.

"What do you mean?"

"A couple months ago we pulled up our traps here. All the lobsters were thin, looked sick, and one out of every four were already dead."

It looked like there were still a few buoys in the water, but we'd go past a lot of empty water between seeing them. Rare for East Hook, especially in the deep water close to town. "Do you know what it is?" I thought about the dead raccoon on my mother's porch.

"Some disease, something their eating, the pH in the water. Everyone's got an idea."

Something sinister.

We stopped talking. After going back and forth two more times, I thought I spotted it to the right.

"I might see it, off the starboard."

Rocco looked right and chuckled to himself.

"I'm from here." I knew I was trying to impress him. I act like a salty local when I'm back at school in the city, helping everyone crack their lobsters (which I try not to eat outside of East Hook, too small and expensive and dressed up), but back home, with the real thing, I was the city kid. I'd have more luck impressing him parallel parking or using a laundromat. Seemed no matter where I was I was faking it unless I had a canvas in front of me. Even then I wasn't impressing everybody.

As we got closer the black buoy came into focus. Its reflection wasn't a brown blob, even in the fog, it was jet black, like a rippling void in the water. We got close and Rocco shut the engine off, so we could hear if any other boats were near. Nothing but the lapping of the waves on the hull and the distant clang of a buoy bell.

Rocco started the engine again, to keep the boat steady, and told me to use the hook stowed next to the port bulkhead. I grabbed it and tried to hook the buoy. It took me two tries, and once I had it, I brought it in and threaded it into the pot puller. I didn't know how to turn it on so Rocco came back and did it. I was surprised how quiet it was. After only ten seconds, I saw the pot coming up through the water. It wasn't a pot though, it was a box made of dull metal, just like Desmond described.

When it was almost at the surface. Rocco turned off the puller and we started pulling it up by hand. It was heavy.

"This thing's heavy." Rocco said, to my relief. I wasn't going to say it because I had nothing to compare it too.

After struggling for a minute, we got it up the side and onto the edge. It was a dull, almost green metal. There were four clasps, two on the front, one on each side. The mechanism was simple, like clips on a briefcase but bigger and sturdier, probably to create a seal. No locks though, so the bolt cutters would go unused. I fiddled with the left one as Rocco tried on the front. You had to push down hard on the top then unhook the catch. Rocco got his two open before I finished the first one, so he took on the last one on. He struggled with it, but popped it loose as I stood watching, trying not to think about what I'd find inside. I breathed in and lifted the lid.

Inside were a bunch of papers, individually wrapped in plastic, to keep them dry. It seemed like the seal mostly held, I didn't notice any water inside, but the top plastic did look a little foggy, like there was a layer of condensation under it. It couldn't have been good for the documents and kept us from seeing through the plastic.

I reached in and pulled them out of the box. Looking closer at the one on top, I noticed the colors, deep blues and grays extending to the edges of the page. It wasn't anything typed. Unwrapping the plastic, I felt another, more solid plastic, like a laminated sheet surrounding the paper. I pulled it out.

"Ellis." Rocco paused as nausea rolled over me. "You gotta tell me what's going on."

My first thought was to duck in case he tried to tackle me again or swing at me. When I saw he wasn't going to, my second thought was that I fell asleep on the boat, and I was in a foggy nightmare caused by the insanity of the last few days.

The smell of the salt and engine fumes were too sharp though. I was awake. Just living a nightmare.

"Ellis? Talk to me."

On one side of the laminated paper was a painting of the front of an old ship, with a big rope line hooked right below the eye of a mammoth squid, who was churning in fury and already starting to drag the ship down with two of its horrible tentacles. It was eight and a half by eleven version of a bigger painting I'd done for the yacht club five years before called

"Got One." On the other side, the blue and yellow EH of my tag.

I staggered to the side of the boat and leaned against it, reeling. Rocco didn't jump at me; he must have seen how green I looked.

"It's the tag again. What do they mean?" He looked at me and after a few seconds I got out of my own head enough to raise my palms and shrug.

Rocco went back to the box and started rifling through it, looking through the other papers. He brought them to me and even though I didn't want to look, didn't want to get dragged further under, I took them.

There were three other laminated pages. Two were my paintings: "Early East Hookian," showing a caveman with a peg leg crawling onto the rocky West Town beach that I'd given to the General Store on Sherman's Neck, and "Head Down," with a little girl almost getting grabbed by a tentacle under a bridge as her lobster boat floated under, that I had done in art class, for Mr. Sinclair. He wanted me to do something with a more intricate man-made structure, and I chose the underside of a bridge with all its lattices and trestles. Both had my tag on the back.

The other one I didn't recognize, it was a different, more raw style than my own. It showed a ferry coming in during a rainstorm, with kids looking out from lit windows. On the back was an O with and S inside it, or a zero with a five inside. Freehand, not a stencil, so the O was a little warped. I didn't recognize it. While I was taking this all in, Rocco didn't take his eyes of me.

Off in the distance, we heard the motor of another boat. We couldn't tell, over the sound of our own motor, if it was getting louder or quieter, but we knew we should move.

I tried to shuffle the pages back in the order we found them in, but Rocco grabbed my arm, pulling me, briefly, back into the real world.

"Let's take a picture of them at least."

He went back front into the cabin and brought back his phone. I laid the pictures down on the deck and he took a picture. I turned the unknown one over and had him take another shot of the OS sign. After he got the shot, he put his phone in his pocket and I grabbed the papers and put them back in the box. I closed the box and was struggling to get the first clasp locked, it was the one on the right that stuck, but my hands were shaking too badly to manage any of them. Rocco quickly did the other three and reached over to grab mine. I noticed his hands shaking too.

Once the box was shut we threw it overboard and unhooked the line from the puller. We saw the box start to sink and Rocco went back front to move the engine out of idle. I collapsed into the seat in the stern. We started moving, away from the motor we heard, planning to loop around the Stains back to the Marina. I didn't see the rocky islands though, or Little Hook or even Lincoln Head. I just saw the fog, and for the first time since I was very young, I was seeing monsters in it.

# Minimalism

occo docked the boat in silence, only saying "That's fine" when he saw my second try at tying off the stern. The same motor I thought I heard earlier sounded like it was still behind us, but I really wasn't in the mood to look back out at the water. The mist was still thick, so it's not like I would have seen anything.

With my feet back on dry land, what I saw in the buoy felt less real, and made a lot less sense. Out in the fog, I almost expected to be involved. Feeling the mist stinging my skin and only being able to see ten feet in any direction expanded my sense of fatalism, like I deserved whatever personalized torture this was. Looking from the outside, I knew I had nothing to do with it. I had only come back into town three days before. I started re-confirming my alibis, not able to fully rule out that I was going crazy. As much as I didn't want it, I thought I should call Ivy back, to confirm I was actually doing what I remembered the week before. Back on shore, the hell I expected was that someone else besides Rocco would start connecting the dots until a circle closed around me.

Despite avoiding eye contact, Rocco didn't give signs he was suspicious, which I was both eternally grateful for and had my own suspicions about. It must have been hard for him to believe I had no idea what was going on, but I was starting to believe he may have known more too. He's on the water every day and he knew Cadie better than almost anyone in town. Going to the cemetery was his idea. I looked at him stowing equipment and buttoning up the cabin and saw the same big simple guy I always did. Maybe I never gave him enough credit, life in East Hook wasn't proving as simple as I remembered it.

Rocco finished tying everything down and climbed onto the dock. At the early hour, no one else needed the slip so we could tie up and eat breakfast. After eating he'd take it back out, pull and bait his traps and return it to the mooring, and I'd catch the taxi home. I was a little jealous of how structured his job seemed, and how clearly demarcated his lives were: do the same few things every day on the water, go home on land. I knew I blurred the lines for him a bit that morning, but I didn't have room in my head to feel anything, much less guilt.

MyKenzy was working at the Porpoise and from the look of it, just setting up. Her hair was different from MyKayla's, curlier and darker, more of a redwood than an umber. I didn't like being able to tell the difference, it reinforced the feeling I had that'd I'd already been back home too long. My final project was due in about fifteen minutes, and I had absolutely nothing. I was beyond getting anything turned in on time. After breakfast, I vowed to focus all my attention on coming up with a good excuse.

We were the first ones in. She looked surprised to see us, but not unhappy. We choose stools at the bar and MyKenzy had a knowing smile as we sat down. "I heard you guys had fun at Desmond's the other night." I started reflexively thinking through every embarrassing thing we did that she would know about. It was a bad night, but I didn't know how we could have heard about the cemetery. Nothing had gotten back to me yet, but already HK, Desmond, Rocco and Ivy knew about it. Things were spinning out of control faster and faster. The smart move was to call the taxi right then and go to the bus station, but I was hungry.

"What did we do?" Rocco asked, having similar thoughts. Except about leaving East Hook immediately.

"Oh nothing, I just heard you two were riling each other up and your" she pointed to me "girlfriend left you there." Oh, that. A normal version of me would have found that embarrassing. MyKenzy's smile hadn't left her face. "Where is she? She's so nice." I wondered if she had forgotten Ivy's name or just pretended to.

"Back at school, we have finals this week." I was glad to have that excuse handy.

"Oh. Do you have them too?"

"Just one."

MyKenzy was gearing up for the obvious follow-up when I was saved by the front door opening. An older man in waders wandered in.

"Hey ya Sull. Get you a coffee?" He gave her a tight smile and looked at us.

"Morning Mick, yeah that'd be great."

MyKenzy caught his look and felt the need to introduce us. "Couple early birds beat you in today."

"Hey Sull." I heard Rocco say behind me. Sull nodded at Rocco and looked at me for a second. Instead of nodding I looked back at the bar. My eye went past the liquor stack to my painting.

The Porpoise had updated its outdoor light-up sign facing the water since I painted it. It was closer to white than yellow. I was a little offended, like I had immortalized something than it was just paved over. The painting seemed darker and emptier than I remember. The mist dotting in front of the lights was the effect I wanted, but it wasn't clear how the rest of the building and the rocks were lit in areas the sign light obviously couldn't reach. And the sailors looked tired, but tired from depression not exhaustion. At least a few sailors would puff their chest out in front of their mates after cutting free of a giant squid. These guys looked headed for a bad time at the foggy pub, and it made me want to leave the place more than stay. At least Sull was smiling company.

MyKenzy went to the coffee pot and asked us what we wanted while she was prepping it. I asked for a coffee and Rocco asked for a Diet Coke. She poured Sull's coffee and walked it over to him. While she was away Rocco leaned down toward me. "I'm not gonna tell her about the buoy, don't worry." He nodded in apparent solidarity and I was tempted to say No shit but instead I just returned his nod. Worries took root wondering if Rocco only performatively had my back. MyKenzy and Sull were laughing as she took his order. "What are you gonna do?"

Good question Rock. I shrugged and was thinking about how to answer when MyKenzy came back.

"What's it gonna be?" She stood over us and asked. It took me a second to understand it was about food.

She punched our order into the computer then came back, looking like she had some time while it cooked. "So what were you doing out this early? I saw you tie up the boat before you came in." Rocco looked down, I knew I shouldn't look at him, or wait too long to answer or we'd look suspicious.

"Looking for monsters." I blurted out, trying to make it sound like a joke, not the truth.

She rolled her eyes, but a smile broke out, not in amusement, something more wistful and internal. "You sound like Cadie."

I had successfully changed the subject, but felt sick again, like I was back on that boat. "What do you mean?"

"She started talking like that, the last few months." MyKenzy was the second person to tell me that.

"About monsters?"

"Yeah, she'd dismiss stuff, like she'd have a problem and be like 'oh well, the sea's gonna rise and swallow up the town anyways." Just like the model in the Quebecois' Drydon garage. "She'd say 'tell that to the monsters when they come back."

"Cadie?" It didn't match the Cadie I remembered, nor the Cadie her father described as having no imagination. I looked over at Rocco, to see if he was surprised by any of it. He was still looking down, shaking his head.

"Yeah things got… weird at the end."

Rocco finally looked up. His voice was soft. "I didn't know."

MyKenzy didn't believe him. "You knew things weren't going well, the people she was hanging out w…"

She trailed off as Rocco got up and walked to the bathroom, faster than he needed to.

When Rocco was gone, MyKenzy pursed her lips like she felt sorry for him. I mimicked her and regretted it immediately. I was trying to come up yet another subject we could change to, but she doubled down.

"He's taking this too hard."

Why was everyone's problem with Rocco? I tried to make her feel bad, "It's a terrible thing."

"Yeah I know, Cadie was a good friend and a good customer. It's just like Rocco's running around acting like a widower, when I don't think they've talked in months."

"You know him, he tries to protect people."

She shook her head and looked toward the bathroom, to see if Rocco was coming back. She leaned over the bar to me. "It's easier to understand why you can't let this go." MyKenzy gave me a sly smile and almost winked.

My face flushed, "What are you talking about?" I wondered if she knew about the tag or the locker box of paintings.

"Nothing, just a lot of us thought that you and her got close in the last few months."

Not what I was expecting. "What? No! I don't think I've talked to Cadie in years!" I racked my brain trying to remember the last interaction we had.

"Every time she'd come in here she'd sit right in front of your painting, pointing it out to any stranger unlucky enough to catch her eye."

"No kidding." I was surprised by this information but feeling a pang of validation. I spent the day of the funeral asking myself who was I?, thinking I didn't deserve to feel so attached to this girl who, if she loved me, only did for a few days. I was just one of the least impressive notches on her belt. It turned out she did still think of me.

I felt a buzz in my pocket, someone was calling me. Not wanting to be rude, I checked my phone below the counter. The call was from a city area code, I'd guessed it was Guardado, wondering why I didn't hand him anything by the deadline. I hit ignore.

"Oh yeah. She had this whole spiel down. Talking about how you drew it your Junior year, after you'd worked on your two-point perspective. She'd make the poor saps look at the sign edges and how the top and bottom depth lines slanted in opposite directions toward the side."

I couldn't help myself, I looked at the painting again for this detail, but it was too far away. The vantage point was from below the sailors, so I probably couldn't have pulled off three-point perspective.

"If they were still listening she'd mention you were at art school in the city, and how paintings of yours were all over town." MyKenzy laughed. "She'd start rattling them off and unless the guy was real desperate, he'd had left by then."

Something about my paintings being all over town caught in my head. I looked down away from MyKenzy to try and shake whatever it was loose. I felt something catching, the fog was maybe starting to thin, then I felt a hard slap on my back and all concentration broke. Rocco had returned from the bathroom and MyKenzy turned away from us to go get our food.

Rocco headed to the boat, reassuring me that he wasn't going to tell anyone what he found, yet. It wasn't reassured. He was another variable I had to worry about and worrying was the only thing I could think of doing at the moment. I checked the time; it was only six fifty-five in the morning. I doubted either of the taxi drivers were awake, they usually worked late. I could walk home, it was only a few miles, but too much caffeine and confusion were coursing through my body to make sleep an option. I needed it at some point though, the morning's four AM wake-up and the cemetery adventure two nights before hadn't left much room for rest, and I wondered how much of the dread I felt was due to sleep deprivation. I knew it all had a sensible explanation; the world wasn't interesting enough to put me at the center of a sea monster resurgence. I walked to a park bench in front of a new boutique fashion store, to sit and think.

I closed my eyes and went back over the last thirty-six hours. The party, packed with strangers, some wearing prosthetic palpi. Cadie's grave, defaced only hours after she was buried, with my tag. The creepy Quebecois compound, with the monsters and sinking town in the garage. The black buoy, tied to an old steel box containing three of my paintings, all featuring monsters, with my tag on the back.

When I was little, my father kept little doodles I did in a box on his dresser. A metal box.

Having no answers, I opened my eyes. I looked across the road at the town library, and the bronze statue of the lighthouse out front. I got up and walked over to take a closer look.

I had meant to take a sculpture class at school, but the longer I stuck with painting, the deeper I wore the track I was on. The statue was well done, imprecise, certainly shaped by a living artist, not just machined cylinders. It was probably a replica though, some mass produced "lighthouse" order the town put in for some celebration. It didn't match any of the lights we had in East Hook. Then I remembered what everyone else in the town was worried about, the lighthouses!

I had laughed at how seriously Desmond was taking the vandalism but now that I'd seen what the town can do to your thinking, I realized how crazy it was. Some group systematically destroyed lights for all the lighthouses across East Hook. Two were on islands, one only accessible by boat, another via walking bridge. It had to have been more than one person. Could that have something to do with Cadie? With me?

Desmond claimed the lighthouse destruction was all mixed in with Cadie and the awful glee people seemed to have when something unexplained happened by the water. I wondered if they could be linked by something more than the town's morbid imagination, what if the same people were responsible for both? What if the same people were responsible for the other deaths in the water too? What if it wasn't people?

I wasn't ready to go to the police, given how I couldn't even really convince my best friend I wasn't involved, but maybe one of the harbormasters would tell me more about how they found Cadie, how they found the others, and what crazy stuff they've seen in the fog recently. I knew they were open.

The Harbormaster HQ was across the footbridge on the West side of town. On the way to the bridge I started rehearsing how I would ask what I wanted to know. I kept coming back to what Rocco said before the funeral. "Who was I?" Why would the Harbormaster tell me things they weren't telling the newspaper? I wasn't family, I wasn't a close friend, I wasn't even really a resident. I pictured being honest if they asked me why I wanted to know, "Me? Oh in a few days or maybe hours, you're going to start hearing my name connected to all this." I decided to fall back on the only strategy that ever worked for me, I'd hope they recognized my name and say I wanted to paint something from recent news. I'd say they could keep it. Maybe I could even paint the damn thing and send it to Guardado, catch him in a good mood, get a D and graduate on time.

Figuring I had put it off long enough, I grabbed my phone and listened to my voicemail. As suspected, it was from

Guardado.

"Hey Ellis, this is Professor Guardado, wondering why you didn't turn in your final project. I understand you're attending a funeral and appreciate your head may be elsewhere, but not turning something in, or letting me know is not ok. Call me, email me, or better yet, turn in your painting! I can't make exceptions. I'll fail you if you don't send me something today."

It's still early was the only positive I could take from that message. I thought if I went back home, I could paint something, anything, and turn it in later that night. I kept walking to the harbormaster though. On the way I brainstormed scenarios in which I could still pass without turning something in, including begging, bribery, even hurting myself to get an extension. A voice that had been nagging in my head for the past month, amplified by lack of sleep, stress and the complete lack of inspiration for any painting, came to the forefront: Is there any difference between having a degree in painting and not having one? Especially now that I was at the end, I had learned everything, I just hadn't crossed the final Ts.

I knew what my mother would say. I was certainly a more complete artist having studied formally, but what kind of client would commission something based on a degree instead of the work? Is that even what I wanted, to be commissioned?

If nothing else, the previous few days had been a distraction from the constant worrying about my capital F Future, something that had been dominating my thoughts for the previous six months. It was no relief though, worrying about your long-term future is a lot better than worrying about your short-term future. Like when you really have to use the bathroom, you're bursting and sweating, your bigger problems get pushed to the side, but you aren't thankful for it. The years to come had started to seem a waste of breath, only now I couldn't be sure I'd still be breathing.

I was able to walk through the fog of my own head on my way because I could walk through the fog of East Hook without thinking at all. I became aware of my surroundings when I was already halfway across the footbridge. The fog from the morning stuck around. When I looked out at the harbor I could only see the few boats moored immediately in front of me. What I was seeing wasn't matching what I was hearing though. Some details didn't match. It sounded like a hundred boats were out there. I stopped and stood at the rail looking harder. If I squinted I could make out some beams of fog lights. The ones I saw seemed to be moving, all in the same direction, toward a dock in the West side, right around where I thought the Harbormaster HQ was. From the bridge I couldn't really tell that I was seeing anything, much less exactly where they were going, and I considered I was much more susceptible to seeing patterns than I would normally have been. Still I doubled my pace across the rest of the bridge into West town.

The streets were as quiet as East town so early time in the morning. I noticed a few patrons in the couple places that served breakfast, everyone there seemed to be looking out the windows towards the harbor, where the commotion was undeniable. Along with motors and frequent blasts of boat horns, I started hearing the din of voices, growing louder the closer I got to the Harbormaster HQ. I turned the last corner, almost at a run, and saw a crowd of people, on land, around the entrance. Looking toward the water, I could only make out the end of the Harbormaster dock and maybe ten feet more, but even with that limit, I saw at least ten lobster boats. Lobstermen were crowding the dock, gesturing angrily in their waders at a few panicked-looking uniformed personnel.

I walked closer, seeing more people like me, curious by-standers, edging toward the entrance with their heads and ears up, hoping to overhear some explanation. We were different from the mini mob that had formed, demanding an explanation, for something I couldn't understand. As I walked closer I caught the end of what one of the uniforms was announcing from the entrance, his palms facing out to the crowd, trying to calm everyone.

"..information at this time, we're out there now, looking. And we'll update you when we know something."

No one was calmed. People were lunging forward, throw-ing their fingers forward at the speaker. I caught a few angry curses, someone just shouted "Idiots!" and another "What do we have you for?" I saw a younger guy turn away from the entrance and walk toward the street and me. I ran into him just as he was fishing a cigarette out of his front jacket pocket. He had a smile, but more like a snarl. I wasn't sure I wanted this guy's attention, but the choice was made for me when we almost collided. He stopped short and stood up straight, thinking which side to pass the moron on, and I pounced.

"What happened?"

He looked me in the eyes, then back at the water and pointed to the harbor.

"Someone cut everyone's trap lines last night. No one can pull up anything."

# Surrealism

I hung around with the crowd, waiting for updates. Not from the Harbormaster lackeys, but from the lobstermen who rose from the dock and saw someone they knew. Lobbies weren't usually social types unless you got them talking about fishing conditions.

Apparently a few early risers noticed their traps cut in the bay just South of Big Hook, one of the prime pieces of pot real estate in the area, and one of the first areas a lot of them fished each morning. More came to check, and found their traps cut too. Pretty soon they were broadcasting on all frequencies, and every boat with their radio switched on made for South of Big Hook or the Harbormaster HQ.

Many went out to check all their other pots and early reports indicated that the damage was mostly limited to traps near downtown. But others were reporting they found trap lines cut as far out as Indian Island.

"What do you do?" was the common question people like me asked once someone said their lines were cut. Normally if a lobsterman finds his line cut, he chalks it up to some other reckless pilot, revenge or a misunderstanding with some rival, even potentially a sea creature, and leaves the trap down there. Sure he's out a trap, and whatever lobsters were in the trap would die there, unsold and unsteamed, but not worth the trouble to send someone to dive down and get them.

Depending on how many were cut, there could be tens of thousands of lobsters dying in traps, causing prices to skyrocket across the state. So many traps and lobster husks remaining on the sea floor could impact on the ecosystem, maybe impacting the fishing for years. The harbormaster had already put in a call to the Coast Guard and they'd start diving later that day. Reconnecting where they could, but at the very least bringing everything to the surface. I liked the idea of someone going down there to look around, it was kind of like having someone confirm there wasn't a monster under my bed.

The other question no one seemed able to answer was "How could this have happened?" Everyone who spoke to the group had different theories, some sat better than others. One lobsterman who had found three of his traps cut described the break as "frayed and ragged" and not done with a knife or clippers. Another unlucky fisherman said his were cut about fifteen feet down from the buoy, whereas when lines were cut with malice, they were cut only a few inches down, to save the effort.

Even the more pragmatic lobstermen admitted that it was nothing like they'd ever seen before. Motoring through the area was treacherous, as every buoy had five to fifteen feet of rope floating next to it that could damage the boats' propellers. One described redlining into the area, only to be met with silence when he got there. Out where the buoys were concentrated closest together, the boats had their motors off, with crews rowing through the wreckage. Going slow and quiet was the only way they'd be able to fully assess the damage, to their property and livelihood, through the East Hook fog.

Putting it all in perspective was a familiar white sign with red lettering at the end of the harbormaster pier: DO NOT GO IN THE WATER. I wondered if it would give the divers any hesitation.

Rocco and I had been close to that area and hadn't noticed any floating lines. It was foggy, but we were looking down at the water almost the whole time, concentrating on buoys. I figured we would have motored right through the worst spot if it were on the outskirts of town. Trying to remember if I saw anything like what they were describing, I instead remembered the feeling I had as we rode back through the fog, that maybe I had really seen a monster. Or just sensed one, swimming right beneath the surface.

I also remembered that we heard another boat out there with us.

The increasingly familiar feeling of walls closing in around me set in and I lost control of my thoughts. If it were a normal boat then they heard us and even though we couldn't see them they might be able to identify us. Even if they couldn't, someone could have seen Rocco and me get on or off his boat early this morning, before almost everyone was up. The list of terrible things I could be credibly accused of was growing every day. I almost retched in the street and pulled out my phone to call Rocco.

Spotting a familiar face fighting her way down through the crowd kept me from completing the call. It was more a familiar body than a face, the lean frame with those muscular shoulders coming out of a tank top. She was walking towards me, but I knew if she turned around, there'd be that same hammerhead on the back of her right shoulder. As Marika got closer, I found myself walking towards her, expecting to have the answers to whatever question she was about to ask. I cut her off about three feet before the edge of the thicker crowd, as I intended. My strides got a little longer and moved a little quicker when I doubted I'd get to her first.

She didn't look startled, or bothered when I stepped in front of her, she just smoothly adjusted her step to walk around me at an angle and had passed me without slowing.

"Marika." I tried to say loudly, but my plummeting self-esteem only allowed me a breathy stage whisper. Part of me no longer wanted to be heard. She heard it though, and turned, and I got my second look at those glowing green eyes, narrowed in intense concern, then widening when she recognized me. She smiled, which I was even happier to get a second look at.

"The artist." I spun through how a cool person would respond to that greeting but was spared any failed attempt as she didn't pause, instead nodding her pointed chin at the cluster in front of us. "What is happening?"

I explained what I knew, claiming all the knowledge I gained from lobsterman about trap layouts and what could and could not be recovered as my own.

"All of them have been cut? This is not good." She almost said to herself. I felt like I had just explained how not good it was, but it was clear she was only half listening. Those eyes weren't looking at me, they were looking out at the bay, right at the section of water where most were cut. Mine were focused on her, until she started to turn back my way, and I quickly looked right, toward town. I don't think I got away with it, because when I braved another look at her, she was staring at me, a different smile on her face. "It seems your monsters are still here."

It did seem that way. "No one's saying that."

She looked around the crowd at the wild gesturing, angst and shock and narrowed her eyes. "Maybe not with their mouths." She clucked her tongue as if disapproving of the town's collective response. "Bad luck. Monsters do not fare well once they start hurting a town's profit. I hope this one gets away."

I hoped to be less scared.

We looked at each other for a beat, me with confusion, her with amusement. Without breaking eye contact or even blinking, her head perfectly still, she said, "I have to go." Blood rushed to my face and ears as I nodded. I was so bright red you could see me through the fog from across the bay. She still hadn't moved, I guessed she was waiting on oral confirmation. I moved my lips to say something only to feel something pressed against them, something soft and firm and attached to something that smelled like cinnamon. Her lips lingered, but didn't move, and by the time I knew what was happening and started to kiss back, they were gone, moving to my left ear.

"Next time you have to paint me." She whispered and gently pulled back, her thick black hair rustling into my face as we parted. She spared me a final look before turning around and walking back up the hill into town. I watched the hammerhead the whole time, hoping she'd turn around so I could see those eyes again.

She never did. *I heard the old men say, all that's beautiful drifts away, like the waters.* When she was out of sight I called Rocco.

He didn't answer. It was the first time he didn't pick up right away. I wondered if he was checking his lines, how much he had already discovered. I'd have to ask how much money losing all his pots would cost him, and if he was insured for that kind of thing. As bad as this could be for me, it was already tangibly bad for Rocco. I don't know why, but I felt guilty, even though I had nothing to do with it, I was involved. I felt I had just run out of strikes with him, too many coincidences. He probably didn't answer on purpose, probably a smart idea, given all that had happened. I resolved that if I were going to figure out what my pictures were doing in that lock box, I could manage without Rocco for a bit. As I tried to collect myself and decide my next move, my phone rang.

It wasn't Rocco, it was HK.

"Hey."

"Hey Ellis?"

"Yeah, HK?"

"Yeah, wasn't sure this was still your number." I remembered confirming each other's numbers two days before. "Did you go to Drydon?"

So much had happened I almost forgot that he sent us there. I ran him through our trip to the house and all the freaky stuff we saw through the window. He seemed concerned.

"Those weren't there before, sounds like a recent thing. Did you go inside?"

I told him about the boat, and how we tracked it from the road then went out there in the early morning. I caught myself being too honest too late and tried to correct it saying we just got back, that we were out with everyone else. I told him about all the lines being cut. He hadn't heard yet, but he seemed to take it with a stoned calm.

"Oh shit, that's gonna piss a lot of people off."

"Yeah I'm down here. People are pissed off."

"So you didn't make it to the buoy?" I didn't remember HK being this focused, or direct. He used to love a good story, love getting sidetracked. Luckily, he was about to hear an even better story. One I'd been itching to tell somebody about, and he was one of the few people who would understand.

I moved away from the crowd for privacy, and told him about the lock box, my paintings, my tag, the weird fourth painting and sign I didn't recognize. It woke him up. He told me to slow down a few times at the beginning, then made me repeat myself after I described pulling up the metal box from the water, like he couldn't believe it. Then again when I talked about versions of my paintings being inside. After he got the whole story, he was calm, contemplative.

"I don't get it. Did they see you, at the house? Or following them?"

I had considered it, but if they maybe saw Desmond's car, they didn't see me. I told him as much. I could tell through the phone his mind was going.

"Maybe they have cameras, at the house. They could have seen your face, recognized you, now they're messing with you." The thought chilled me but was much simpler than the alternatives I had been considering for the last hour. It also removed the connection between me and the cut lines. Having recently drawn the attention of those people was much less off-putting than if they have known about me for a long time, but it was probably just as dangerous.

"I don't know." Is all I managed to say.

"Yeah it's fucked up either way." HK added, before we both went quiet. HK broke the silence, "You know what I'd do if I were you?" He didn't wait for me to answer, he barely paused. "I'd go to the store they all work at, the shipwreck novelty place on Harris, the Splintered Mast."

I knew it, they offered to sell prints of my paintings when I was still in high school. Mr. Sinclair encouraged me to turn them down, telling me I might make a hundred dollars or so, but I would give up control of where my art was and who had it. I turned them down, even though I was skeptical of the value of what Mr. Sinclair described. He didn't know how right he'd be, in the end. My art was now turning up all over town in the worst possible places, and I would have sacrificed a fortune to have prevented it.

"They all work at the Splintered Mast?" It could explain why they liked sea monsters so much.

"Yeah, they were summer workers last year, there. I partied with them at their rental house. Then a couple older guys, the ones who own the house in Drydon, moved in, bought the place and opened it year-round. They all stuck around; the winter didn't drive 'em away."

When I was off the phone, I looked West and could see the Splintered Mast from where I stood. I didn't make a move toward it. If it was the headquarters for the Quebecois, I needed to be smart before I showed up. After the morning's events, they felt much more insidious, and much more interested in me.

Even if I got a brain transfusion and got smart right away, I couldn't head there right then, I had an appointment I promised I wouldn't miss.

Somehow, the night before, during our long terrible dinner, I had promised my mother I'd let her give me a haircut since I was staying in town. I didn't think I had let it get that shaggy, but she insisted I look good for graduation and all the pictures we'd take.

While I was at breakfast, my mother had texted me that her nine AM cancelled, freeing up her chair. I couldn't believe her salon would be too busy early on a Monday morning in May to fit me in, but apparently I had a small window to make. Even though there might not be a graduation to look good for, I decided to go see her, start the thaw before I really needed it.

I went against habit and entered the salon through the front door. Normally I came through the back. Growing up, I'd spend what felt like hours in the back room, leaning over the card table, sketching while I waited for her to finish up. The fridge was always stocked with generic diet sodas, so I'd go through a couple while I sat there drawing. Some of my first reviews came from the stylists as they'd come to check on me. All raves.

Caleb picked me up in the taxi. He never talked like Andy did, and that morning he was especially silent. In between confirming the address and wishing me a good day, the only time he spoke was to ask if the air was on too cold. I didn't think the air was even on but just shook my head. I looked up at him and saw his arms were covered in goosebumps, figuring the air was only up front.

Caleb dropped me in front, and I was too tired to walk all the way around the back of the strip mall. I heard the familiar tone when I walked through the door and looked around to see what had changed. I saw my painting, in the same spot behind the register. It wasn't near the same feeling as I had in the Porpoise. Seeing a painting from high school, was like revisiting a memory from the awkward years. The Medusa was from barely more than a year before, looking at it was like looking at something I was working on now, deciding if it was really finished. I remembered the reasoning behind every brushstroke, even the extra glob of background gray I had to add just above the right collarbone, to make one of the tendrils more naturally thin at the end. The technique was good, and the effect was much better, more soulful, than I remembered.

"Ellis!" Ramona, the longest tenured stylist, had her hand over her mouth in mock surprise. I couldn't imagine I looked too different, but I smiled and waved.

"Just in for a trim, boss' orders."

My mother was crouched down behind a dark-haired woman, trying to get the angle of a cut perfect, but I could see she was beaming. "You need a lot more than a trim." I ran a hand through my hair, only running into a few snags. "Give me five minutes, then I'll get the weed whacker ready." I heard chuckles all around. There were three stylists, my mother, Ramona and a third whose name I didn't remember, but had been there for a few years. I waved at her too. Each one was working on a customer, and another lady sat below one of the two dryers. I didn't recognize the customers, but they smiled at me, either in recognition or who they understood me to be. The attention I got when I walked in faded fast though, the stylists stayed focused.

I took a seat on one of the padded plastic mod-style chairs, looking at my magazine options. But instead I found myself looking back at the Medusa. The background was a gray spectrum, designed to recall the background they use for professional headshots. I couldn't make it look bland enough until my twentieth layer, but I ultimately succeeded. It gave the whole thing a level of reality that I struggled to consistently reproduce. I couldn't shake the feeling I hadn't painted anything as good since, which set my brain down an unhealthy path until I had a breakthrough.

If it were my best work, which was debatable but also not terminal if true; I could still improve. And I would have had the good fortune that none of my professors of fellow students had seen my best work yet. The monster was right in front of me, real and trying to fit in, despite its repellent look. The painting was exactly what Guardado was talking about, and I could drive it down to him in a few hours. I'd just need to ask my mother to borrow it.

I stood up to look more closely and see what I could add to freshen it up, make it look like it was recently painted. I walked toward it, pulled by the reprieve it offered me.

"Ellis watch out!" My mother's voice, in a tone I recognized at my core. Her customer had finished, and we were walking to the register at the same time, a foot away from colliding. I mumbled an apology and started walking deeper into the salon toward the recently empty chair.

When I sat down I took in the details, trying to spot the differences. She still had the same framed family photo we had done one winter when I was six or seven. My father stood ruler-straight next to my mother and behind me, a few years from his fate, each hand on one of our shoulders. He was smiling, but I doubted he was happy getting his picture taken. He wasn't happy doing anything.

My mother was back just as I was getting settled, folding a towel for the back of my neck and throwing the cape over me with a familiar flourish. I always liked seeing her in her shop, she had a confidence and aptitude there I never got to see in private. I didn't pause to wonder if it meant she was a better stylist than mother, they presented wildly different problems, and I knew I was a better painter than son or boyfriend. I turned my head towards the Medusa before my Mom pushed my chin back toward the mirror.

I had been avoiding my reflection for the last few days and catching a glimpse of myself reminded me why. It was like gazing into another inter-dimensional portal, filled with monstrous versions of people from this world. I was sickly pale, with dark circles under my red and red-rimmed eyes. My hair shot out in a couple places, giving me horns and spikes, but I didn't look fearsome, just sick. My clothes were chaotically rumpled, looking a few sizes too big, and I was sitting in the chair like it was covered in needles.

I looked up at my mother's reflection and saw she looked the same as she always did. It was a normal mirror and a real monstrous me. Or was I seeing what my dad looked like when they pulled him out of the water?

"Anything particular you're looking to do here?"

I wasn't ready to answer that. I looked back down at the family picture, then back up at the beast straight ahead. She waited a few seconds for me to answer, then tapped my shoulder. "Ellis! Hello."

"Uh, just clean everything up." I mumbled without looking at her.

"You're gonna need more than me for that." She projected so everyone in the salon heard her, they all laughed and it both embarrassed and soothed me. At least everyone knew my current look wasn't normal.

My mother kept running her fingers through my hair, massaging my scalp and feeling through the knots and cowlicks she'd have to deal with. "You see any styles you like? What are you seeing in the city?" She had moved to get a spray bottle and started spritzing around my head. The mist, in such a controlled and insignificant form, helped pull me back out of my trance, and I cast my eyes away from the mirror, down at the lineup of tools on the mantle in front. I mumbled something about the latest style with a few long tendrils and a few shaved parts I'd seen on a billboard that I thought I could pull off, and my mother scoffed as she combed out what knots she could, not pausing to go gently.

"You could pull it off today, Ellis, and you'd literally stop traffic. But that requires fifteen minutes with a blow-dryer, ten with a straitening iron, and another fifteen with paste. If you roll out of bed with that cut, it's gonna look like a comb-over." She wasn't projecting as much, but laughter still filled the room and she noticed and played to the crowd. "You know it, these cuts, men's cuts require so much upkeep those poor boys are either ruining their productivity or their sleep." I was ruining both of those without a thought for my hair.

"Let's keep it close. I don't want hair getting in your eyes as you're finishing on your final project." She moved to grab the clippers.

Ramona kept the group conversation going. "Are you excited about graduating?"

I answered like the pre-monstrous version of me. "Yeah, really excited!"

"Do you know what you're gonna do?"

"There are a few fellowships and apprenticeships I'm talking to professors about. But I can always apply for some graphic design jobs." This wasn't pre-monstrous me; it was a third, fictional art student with none of my problems or doubts. There weren't any mirrors or portals that would make him appear.

"That's news to me." My mother jumped in, earning another round of laughter.

The stylist whose name I should have remembered spoke up. "You can always move back here and teach art at the high school." I felt my mother turn back to her, but no one said anything. "We need one of those." I wanted to turn around and ask if she remembered Mr. Sinclair, but my mother's hand was on the top of my head, keeping it still, pointed toward the mirror I still refused to look into.

Ramona didn't want to linger on the topic either. "You could move back here and be a cop. We could definitely use more of those." Everyone in the salon laughed, including my mother, but when I risked a look at her in the mirror, she was looking down at the family photo on the counter.

Everyone besides the two of us started talking about the lighthouses and the vandals. I realized they hadn't even heard about the cut traps yet, or Cadie's tombstone. I could only imagine the murmurs about the town going to hell would be even more urgent in the afternoon. My mother spoke softly, but maybe because of her position, everyone stopped to listen. "Ellis is no cop." She looked at the photo, then back at me. "He is looking more like him every day though." She looked me in the eyes, and I saw them start to grow wide as she turned back toward the group. "But what do I know, I keep seeing Logan everywhere this week! It's like his ghost is here." Me too. "I thought it's because that poor O'Reilly girl drowned just like him, but maybe you're right." She pointed in Ramona's direction with her comb. "Maybe it's because I know none of this shit would be going on if he were investigating."

# VI

# Tuesday

# Pop Art

I wasn't lucky twice in a row, Andy picked me up at my mother's house. Without him I never would have agreed with HK's plan, and there he was again assisting me in following HK's orders. I wasn't ready to involve him in everything that had happened since Sunday morning, but I knew I'd feel bad lying to him. Whether it was boredom, pity or something else, he was trying to figure out what happened to Cadie too.

I'd hoped in his search he hadn't gone to her grave, getting in his car made me his captive.

He seemed excited to see me though. I hadn't even closed the door before he started, "Hey Ellis, how's your friend's place?"

I laughed, unnaturally, and tried out not lying. "It's fine. Someone broke in, but he's ok. He's getting new locks."

Andy still hadn't put the car in gear. "No shit. He know who did it?"

Not lying didn't last too long. "Someone thought he had cash. He flashed a bunch at the Gannett last week and the wrong crew saw it."

He kept his head turned around back as he shifted into reverse and started backing out of the driveway. He started shaking his head as he spun the wheel and but didn't respond until we were moving forward. "This town, man. It's changing."

Back to the truth. "It does feel different."

My agreement allowed Andy to share what felt like a developed bit, an observation he had honed through repetition to every sympathetic fare he got. "During the day, the whole place feels more deserted than it used to. At night it's like the jungle. People skittering across the roads, ducking into alleys, gathering in groups that don't make sense together. And everyone is so secretive about everything, all the time. It's like they all want the fog."

It wasn't quite the difference I had seen, but it was close. It was more like everyone who stayed here had secret lives they would never share with me anymore.

I didn't want to go too deep with him, so I used my father's certainly well-honed words just to keep up. "You never have to see what's actually in it."

He looked surprised. "Yes! I feel like someone said that exact thing to me this week." I looked surprised. I'd never heard that from anyone else. I wondered if my father had heard it from someone else.

Passengers saying weird things to Andy got me back to our common purpose. "Was it Cadie?"

He laughed, acknowledging that everything before had been small talk. "No man. It's been more than a week with her."

I wasn't going to say anything until I had to.

Andy picked up again quickly. "I went out there, to Drydon, yesterday afternoon, see what I could remember."

"Oh yeah?" Careful.

"I think I got it down to a general area. I'll ask the next fare

I get out there about the neighbors."

Andy's investigative tactics were a lot more methodical than mine.

"But get this." He looked back at me through the mirror, making sure I was paying attention before he looked back at the road. "A deer ran out into the road and just collapsed. Dead."

The Splintered Mast was filled with the stuff you'd find in an alternative kid's dorm room, which at art school, meant all the dorm rooms. It was lit with black-lights, rooms were separated by hanging beads, and crystals were scattered in every corner. It smelled like a dorm room too, incense and books. It opened when I was a kid, getting in on the darker side of the East Hook monster market. Instead of cuddly kraken on a t-shirt, the Splintered Mast sold much scarier merchandise.

Catering to the type of person who wanted to be scared in the dark on summer vacation took the already niche store into other, somewhat related niches. The store started providing for wildly different customers while maintaining a logical spectrum. The nautical history section lead to the monster section which lead to the costume section which lead to the goth section that led to the music section which led to the comic book section that lead to the medieval fantasy section which lead to the witchcraft section that lead to the crystals and wellness section that lead to the drug paraphernalia section. You could one-stop shop for tarot cards, a "Shipwrecks of the Atlantic" coffee table book, a Lord of the Rings poster, an Archie comic book and a bong.

Walking through the front doors for the first time in years, it still had a druggy feel, but it wasn't the same drug. Black lights were replaced by LED strobe lights and lasers, and the distraction helped hide the fact everything had become so shabby. Most of the sections were still there, only they had about half the merch they did before, like new orders were no longer coming in.

I wandered through the maze of high shelves, trying to identify all the workers, and spot all the other differences since I had been there last. Something above the book section caught my eye, a painting. It practically blended into the wall compared to the garish neon yellows, purples and greens in the pop art figure paintings surrounding it. The dark green, navy, and dark brown weren't what drew me in, it was the familiarity: a returning ferry waved back into port by children in windows. It was the other painting I pulled out of the lockbox that morning. I walked closer, and even though it was above eye level, I could see the S.O. signature in the corner.

I couldn't figure out what it meant that the painting was in the Splintered Mast, but I was almost glad to see it. Things had been taking on a dream-like quality, seeing things without the fog reassured me that I'd been awake the whole time. Next to the painting was the price tag: twenty-five dollars.

The colorful paintings surrounding it were all going for four times that amount, and I imagined the store moved a lot more of them. They fit better with the new aesthetic, the one in that section at least. I thought about adding more primary colors to my work, making them simpler, blockier, and putting out a new one every day. I could find some touristy store to sell each of them for a hundred dollars and make some money. Not enough to pay rent in the city, but enough in East Hook.

I had spent the last year avoiding thinking like that. I trusted something or someone to take care of it for me, the way one of those two always had in the past. I knew at some point I had to decide what kind of artist I wanted to be; what kind of life I wanted to live once I could do anything. I was able to keep avoiding the thoughts, as I got back to the business of casing the joint to see the best way to get into the back room.

I had counted three employees since I'd come in. One behind the glass counter in the drug section, one working the front register, and one roaming. It was a big place and in the new lighting, hard to see what was going on. It would make sense for at least two more to be on the floor. But it was still the slow season and the place looked like it was cutting expenses, maybe there was just one more.

The way to the back of the store went by the public bathroom. I'd had to use it one or two times and remembered hearing staff walking by constantly. There's an unmistakable retail walk sound: the quickness of the steps combined with the padded insoles on cement or hard tile floors. Out front I couldn't rely on hearing it, half the retail floor was covered with patterned carpeting.

I doubled back to the front, swinging into the witchcraft section through an aisle of ancient Egyptian curios. I looked between two Anubis bookends and saw the fourth staff member, sitting down in the crystal section stacking smudging kits into a lower shelf. I started collecting ingredients, keeping my head up for any others.

Egyptians worshiped cats, so I was able to find a metal cat food bowl engraved with hieroglyphics only a step away. Once I had that I made my way to the comic book section. I grabbed a thick, multi-volume paperback with atrocious bulging drawn figures covering about a year in some dystopian, non-superpowered comic run and then on my way out of the section, one of those sudoku books. I had to curl the comic to fit in the cat bowl and rested the sudoku book on top of it. I moved into the wellness section and picked out two mini-bottles of tea tree oil, easy to find alphabetically beneath an unimpressive selection of diffusers.

I hadn't seen any other staff on my provision run, but I was still sure someone else was there, probably in the back. I had to walk dangerously close to the girl in the crystal section for my last supplies: three lit incense sticks. I needed to cross the aisle she was sitting with her back to, so I tried to keep my footsteps both quiet and moving so she wouldn't turn around, wondering if I needed any help. I got by her and she kept her eyes on the smudging kits.

Ideally I would have gone upstairs to the costume and clothes section, there was a good clear space for what I wanted to do, and it was the furthest point from the bathroom and private office area. I was worried I would be too visible on the stairway though; it was fully exposed near the entrance of the store. Instead I walked back into the fantasy section, looking left and right through dragon figurines and shiny, dull edged swords for any staff or customers. As I walked I tipped the tea tree oil bottles onto the comic book in the cat bowl. I had to shake them a little to get more than a drop to come out at a time, but by the time I reached the tapestries the bottles were almost empty. I placed them beneath the wet books, put the cat food bowl on the floor, and tossed the incense sticks in, walking away as soon as I saw them land safely, but before I saw smoke.

Tea tree oil is one of the many, many essential oils that is dangerously flammable, and I could smell the burning coated stock comic book paper before I made it to into the Lord of the Rings subsection. I didn't risk a turn back to see what it looked like as I passed a Balrog woodcutting, and didn't think anyone else saw anything until I heard raised voices while walking, at a labored easy pace, past a collection of old concert posters, in swinging metal frames.

I kept up my pace through the drug section, consciously avoiding eye contact with the guy behind the water pipe counter, only catching it out of the corner or my eye when he jumped that same counter and started jogging toward the noise. The voices were getting louder and more frantic as I parted the black curtains separating the store from the back hall with the bathrooms. Once on the other side I darted into the men's room and put my ear to the door.

Almost immediately I heard steps running past me and fade out into the store. There was someone else in the back. Satisfied I was alone, I walked out of the bathroom down the back hallway. I figured I had at least five minutes until anyone came back there, with everything they had to take care of out front, but the first thing I aimed to find was the back door, ensuring I could make a quick exit. There were two doors in the hallway besides the bathroom. The first was a utility or custodial closet. The door was locked and had a clipboard nailed to it, showing how often and the last time someone had come to service whatever was behind it. Morgan R. was the last one to sign off that everything looked good a little more than a month ago.

The other door wasn't locked it opened to an average-looking retail back room. It was dark and mostly filled with boxes, stacked in numbered rows. There was a rolling ladder staff could use to reach the higher shelves. My eyes found the back door, seeing bright white outside light spilling in around it. I had my escape route.

I was expecting an eerier environment back there, it being a monster store and all, but it just felt like a warehouse. Doubt crept in around the wisdom of the trespass. I didn't know where to start my search, or what I could find. I saw the staff out front; it was clearly not just Quebecois that worked there. I walked towards the only other light source, an open office.

The room was small, with a desk overflowing with papers taking up most of the space. There was a mini fridge on the floor between two filing cabinets, two chairs and a whiteboard. It looked like the site of occasional managerial activities and frequent staff lunch breaks. There was even a cup on the desk filled with plastic utensils.

The white board had likely been installed for announce-ments, but it was crowded with all kinds of writing and doodles. The whole thing had the gray dirty look that came from bad erasers and spare spray use. Most of the writing looked like squiggly marker tests with a few inside jokes, but at the top right corner there was a legitimately good sketch of a tentacle, with shading and everything. I moved further into the office to get a better look, the move making my escape more difficult.

The tentacle came from the side of the board and curled around about two feet across the top, twisting to show off the suckers on the underside. A closer look yielded some flaws. It got way too thick too fast, and the positioning wasn't entirely natural. I caught myself critiquing a doodle and scoffed, thinking I didn't need a degree to talk like an insufferable art school grad. My eyes drifted below the tentacle.

It was shaped like a normal list, with dashes representing each item, but it was written in bizarre, circular characters I had never seen before. I leaned in and looked to see if it was as simple as normal letters being half erased but didn't see any sign of that. The writing was seriously freaky, the letters were different sizes and I couldn't really tell if they read left to right or up to down.

I took a picture of the writing with my phone, figuring maybe it was coded language I could decipher. Success there was unlikely, as I was genuinely knocked back by the sight of it. It looked like an ancient, evil language people read out loud to summon a monster, the exact kind of writing I didn't need to see.

I couldn't figure out what I could do with the information either way. I was flailing, needing to do something to fix whatever I caused by coming back, but clueless as to what.

Because it was out already, I checked the time on my phone. I probably had two or three more minutes until someone came back and found me. I had spent too much time on the writing, which still had a pull on my attention strong enough that it took me a few glances at my phone to notice the time. I figured I should make my way back into the warehouse and look for something that could tie the Quebecois to the cut traps or the busted lighthouse. I didn't know exactly what I was looking for, but figured I'd recognize it when I saw it. Some water rope-saw or giant bulb hammer.

Besides the whiteboard, the desk had the most going on, all covered in food wrappers, paperwork and unopened mail. I brushed the wrappers off the table, to see the wood desktop. I only succeeded in uncovering a corner of a big tear-off calendar. Curious, I moved forms and mail off the rest of it and saw it was the current month. Nothing much was filled in, a few doodles, a shark the only thing close to on theme, in the square for the day after I arrived. The upcoming Friday box was circled aggressively, like the marker they used was pressed down hard. I couldn't imagine I'd still be in East Hook in four days. The three I had been in town felt like an eternity.

Nothing else on the calendar. I looked at my phone again and realized I was probably out of time. I checked out the forms, looking for French names I could tie to the Quebecois, potentially I could look them up for more info, but didn't see any of the telltale silent letters. The mail, however proved interesting.

Only about a third of the mail was addressed to The Splintered Mast, the rest was addressed to DW Inc. The first thing I thought was Detective Ward. East Hook was rotten with reminders of him. I decided it had to be whoever owned the store.

Thanks to a fight with our landlord the previous summer in off campus housing, I knew we could look up contact info for landowners and what other properties they owned. Even though it didn't connect to anything, it gave me something to do. I snapped a picture of the name, re-scattered trash over the front desk, and felt my way to the back door. The sunlight on the other side blinded me, but nothing was illuminated.

# Classicism

A s I walked by the Mayor's office on my way to the county clerk, I couldn't tell if *Leader of Men* still hung behind his desk. The entrance to his office had its own antechamber with a reception desk and waiting room. His door looked open and I could hear him speaking, but I would have had to walk into the reception area to see more than just the open office door. Five years before I would have walked right in, and everyone would have beamed at me the whole time. I was exactly who they wanted me to be then. I doubted I could even make the receptionist smile.

I should have been focusing more on the clerk's receptionist, and what I could say to get the property records of DW Incorporated, but I stopped just past the door. The mayor's voice was carrying, and I thought I heard him say "monsters." I took a step back and leaned up against the wall near the door, pulling my phone out of my pocket so if someone walked by, I'd look occupied.

"Well deputize some people then!"

Whoever he was talking to couldn't project as well, I just heard murmuring and maybe "can't trust."

"We just need people in uniforms, walking the footbridges and standing on the major launches. Making people feel safe

177

and making the lobstermen feel protected. I got Coast Guard support through the end of the week. Nothing's gonna turn up in the water." He must have been talking to the police chief. I wondered what was in the water they had to protect people from.

For the second time, I thought about walking in the office, to tell the mayor and his guest to have the Coast Guard looking out for something big on Friday. I couldn't think of a way to present it that wouldn't lead to all the questions I couldn't yet answer.

"Two weeks, Jim. June is in two weeks and this place is gonna have four times the people it does now, and twenty times the money. Something like this happens then, this town dies. Something like this happens to a tourist, boom, in one year, three-quarters of our stores, restaurants and hotels shut down for good."

As the mumbling man responded I thought about if East Hook as I knew it was really so fragile. Everything I'd seen that week had shown me the opposite; interest in the town was going up every time something bad happened. I figured East Hook wouldn't get less tourists, just a different sort of tourist. Everything, especially what has been with you since you were a kid, is always more fragile than you can accept.

"So let's get them up here earlier!" Whatever was said in reply was quickly interrupted.

"At least make it look like they're up here. Patrols, down-town, waterfront." The next reply was just talked over immediately.

"Lighthouses, Islands! Make it look like there's a lot more of you than there are! Inland can be the wild west for two weeks, it'll survive. At least on dry land people can see! We need a presence on the water."

The mayor's tone indicated that was the end of the discussion, and I heard chairs shuffling.

I didn't want to be there when some officer strolled out, he might recognize me. I started making my way down the hall to the Clerk's office.

The line wasn't too long, but all requests of the clerk apparently take a lot of time. I checked my email while in line and saw two messages, one from Guardado and one from Ivy. Wincing, I checked Guardado's first.

Ellis,

Surprised and sorry to not see anything from you. I feel I made it almost impossible for you to fail, yet you've managed. See you next semester.

-G

No more pleading for reason, no more bargaining, no more asking me for less and less, to give him something, anything just to show submission. He was desperate to prove that I still had to do what he said. Reading his message, I enjoyed the high of taking him down a peg but knew the comedown would be terrible.

Ivy's message was, surprisingly, about the same topic as Guardado's.

El,

Your Monster's teacher reached out, he's really worried about you and is going to fail you.

I don't want to be involved in this, but you don't want to fail.

It's not too late. Just take one of your five hundred paintings around town and send him a picture. They all have monsters in them anyway right?

You get to the bottom of your mystery yet? I genuinely want to know what you find. The East Hook Express doesn't have an online version.

IV

I read it a couple of times and caught myself smiling. Ivy was practical and a problem solver, even if she were no longer mine. Now I had an excuse to go into the mayor's office, I need to take a picture or the painting or I'll fail! I couldn't believe Guardado reached out to her, he was really being dramatic about this. If he had Ivy's info, he probably also had my mother's, which might necessitate me finding another place to sleep.

My wider support system in East Hook was crumbing along with my future. Rocco hadn't answered any of my texts, and Desmond was saying he hadn't heard from him either, but he probably had a million things to do with the boat and the traps. Desmond apparently also had a million things to do this morning, preventing him from driving me to City Hall. I took a taxi, rode silently with Caleb, which I appreciated. The car was cool and damp, but he was still the only one with goosebumps.

The guy in front of me was wrapping up, procuring some permit. He looked like he was a contractor, or someone that worked on dry land. I put my phone in my pocket and rehearsed what I was going to say. In big cities all the info was online, and I knew it was all available to the public. I just wanted to have an answer ready for why I wanted it, even if I had the absolute right.

The contractor put whatever got printed for him in a manilla folder, put the folder in a canvas bag and walked away. I waited for the clerk to make eye contact with me and nod before I stepped forward.

"And what can I help you with today?" She smiled as she asked, looking at me with my fresh haircut from mom like I was playacting at needing the clerk's help.

"Hi, I was hoping to look up the contact info and property records for a company." I had a story planned about wanting to send a painting to the friendly Splintered Mast owner, which replaced the story I came up with in the cab about doing research for a painting and wanting the owner's permission. As I made the request I realized I probably should come up with a third, believable story, but I never needed to.

"OK, what is the name or the company?" I avoided the interrogation, but her smile did go away.

"DW Incorporated." I wanted to ask if they would know someone requesting this information, but she hadn't asked my name yet, and it didn't feel like she recognized me.

She didn't move, and her eyebrows went up. "DW, like the letters?"

"Yeah D for Demon W for Water." My twin muses who were ganging up to ruin me.

She turned away from me to look at her screen and took on the slow tone people take as they type while they talk, making sure their mouth doesn't get ahead of their fingers. "That's easy enough. Then in-cor-por-rated."

Her focus narrowed, her brows furrowed a bit and I saw her lean toward the screen. "Huh." She started typing again and I prepared myself for some complication. Answers hadn't been easy to come by so far.

I was getting ready to ask if there was a problem when she emphatically hit the enter key and left the station to go deeper behind the desk. She wasn't gone long and came back with a printed page and laid it out in front of me.

"DW Incorporated owns three properties in East Hook, two residential and one retail, downtown. Now there isn't much contact information, the mailing address, email address and phone number are all through the retail location. It looks like it's right downtown."

I grabbed the paper, thanked her and walked out of the clerk's office before she remembered to ask me my name. I was holding onto the printout like it was some secret dossier. I realized I had no car or anywhere I could read over it quietly, but saw I did have a very private option when I walked by the entrance to the men's room. I plopped down in an empty stall, got my phone out and unfolded the paper.

The clerk lady was right, there wasn't much information, just a list of three addresses, two marked residential and one retail. The email was dw@splinteredmast.com and I looked up the local number, confirming it was also connected to the Splintered Mast. It was a match My heart sped up as I recognized the second residential address as probably the Quebecois house in Drydon. I didn't recognize the third address, and honestly couldn't come up with any guesses as to what it could be. 32 Westerly Way. I searched it on my phone and saw it was in Downhook, close to Lincoln Head on the West side. When I zoomed in I saw it was right on the water and seemed to have a good-sized lot. The street view from my phone showed just hedges and a gate, but judging by the neighbors you could see, it was an exclusive street. Too fancy for more staff housing. As I walked out of the bathroom, I kept my phone in my hand. I wanted to text Rocco to see if we could swing by on his boat, before remembering his boat was the source of some trouble, and he was choosing to be out of reach.

I would figure out another way onto the property, potentially with the help of my sketchiest friend. Before I called HK, I rode my temporary confidence spike directly into the mayor's suite and grinned at the girl behind the reception desk. Before she could ask how she could help me I introduced myself.

"Hi, when I was a kid I painted a seascape with a monster swordfight on it for the mayor's office. Do you know if it's still there?"

The receptionist took a second to take the question in, then smiled. "It is still there! Mayor Rossi tells new visitors about it every time. Are you Ellis Ward the student artist?"

I nodded with a genuine smile, probably the first since Desmond's party.

"Let me see if he's free, I'm sure he'd like to say Hi."

His door had been closed. She knocked, opened it and walked in two steps, keeping her hand on the frame. I heard her call me Ellis, the painter, and ask if he wanted to come greet me. He was projecting less than before, but his response indicated he didn't especially want to, but I heard his chair move and the receptionist turned around and gave me the thumbs up. Soon after followed the Mayor, with his arms outstretched and a folksy grin.

"The artist!" As he came closer he gradually pulled his arms together, so by the time he got to me they closed on my hand in a two-handed shake. "Ellis, it's good to see you. I point your painting out to everyone who comes in. I say, a local artist painted this, and when they compliment it, I finish with when he was sixteen." He leaned in and dropped his voice, even though it was only three of us in the office. "The summer folk eat it up. Always ask where you sell your paintings." He clapped me on the shoulder. "Telling them there's one thing in this town they can't buy helps keep me sane." He started walking into his office and gestured for me to follow.

We stopped in front of my painting, and I almost flinched when I saw it. It was an early work, but I couldn't believe I had ever been that bad. The monsters all had the same expression, even though their faces clearly had the musculature to show a huge range of emotions. The soldiers were ignoring all the beasts coming up from the deep, focusing their attention and fire on the one the captain was in the swordfight with. I couldn't figure out how far from the shore the jetty was supposed to be, and why the fight was so centered in the frame, like we were viewing it from some fifty-yard line in the middle of crashing surf. It had been so long since I painted it I was having trouble remembering why I made the choices I did. I was glad I didn't need to defend this in a seminar and knew I wouldn't try to grab it to mail to Guardado.

"Like the frame?" I looked at the mayor and he was smiling. I had been too focused on the painting to take everything in. He had re-framed it in maple, painted with one fewer coat than needed to give it a weather-beaten look. It was way too bright for the painting but did seem to match the rest of his office, where the vibe was almost a fifty-fifty combination of seaside cottage and fluorescent-lit corporate purgatory. It's not easy to make drop ceilings nautical.

"It looks great. Really fits the room." It was the first thing I said to him, and I wasn't in the mood to add to it. *We have no gift to set a statesman right.* I took in everything else that was hanging from the walls. Mostly maps and photos, but there was a seascape print in a heavier, darker frame and on the side of the lone window, two wooden word blocks, hung in a column, with about six inches between them. The top one read Duty and the lower one Wisdom. DW. "What do those mean?" I asked inelegantly, trying to understand their significance, I knew what they each meant.

The mayor was ready for that question. I saw his eyes glaze over as he shifted into politician automaton mode, gearing up to tell me why he had them up, in the exact same way he tells everyone who comes into his office. I felt sheepish, like I fell into his trap, as he launched into a somber opening about his duty as a citizen first, moving into the more hopeful second half about how impressed he is every day with the citizens of East Hook possess. He even personalized it, ending with "Citizens like you, Ellis, making our restaurants and stores and humble mayor's offices more beautiful. Not for money, but for East Hook. A mayor can't forget the wisdom of his citizens."

I thought I had never really painted anything for East Hook in my life, but probably just because I wanted to disagree with him. I just nodded.

He moved behind his desk. "You're still in school right?" He didn't motion for me to sit.

I wasn't still in school, but it was a little complicated, so I went with it, throwing out a line while I had him. "Yeah, back for Cadie O'Reilly's funeral."

He pursed his lips and nodded, showing how heavily it

weighed on him too. "Such a shame what happened." He looked beyond me at my painting. "The old East Hook bay is acting up again." The whole town really was infected. He made a show of moving his head back to the window. "The town's going to come together, Duty and Wisdom." It was painful watching the show, but I couldn't dismiss it.

Why was I doing all this? I guessed it was duty because I knew it wasn't wisdom. Just like what led my dad into the water to save that girl.

D for Dad, W for Water. D for Detective, W for Ward.

The mayor looked down at his watch and I got the message and started toward the door, amazed at how easily I followed his subtle suggestions. He'd had me on a string since he shook my hand.

"Thanks for stopping by Ellis. You're one of the good ones!" I was a few steps out his door when he yelled after me. "Oh Ellis!" I stopped, still beholden to his cues, and looked back in. He was staring at me. "I want another painting." He held my gaze then broke into a bright smile. My body and mind fought it, knowing it was wrong, but I felt the corners of my mouth turning upwards and to my horror, my lips parting. I returned his smile, then walked out the door, completing my embarrassing lesson in civics.

# De Stijl

ndy dropped me off two blocks from the address, too busy with a phone call to talk any more with me about East Hook. I didn't mind, the less he remembered about where he brought me the better. I was dressed in the darkest clothes I could find in the dresser at my mother's. A navy-blue zip-up hoodie and black skinny jeans that felt a little loose in the ankle. I waited until it was dark to head over, but the increased stealth may not have been worth the time I had to kill at home.

I had called HK with an update, letting him know what I found at the Splintered Mast and downtown. He was surprised it was so easy to get that kind of information but sounded encouraged by my progress. He had me repeat the address to see if it rang any bells, but ultimately didn't recognize it. He said he couldn't search the place with me, but to call him once I got there.

I was encouraged by my progress too, I started thinking I had a knack for investigations, and the thought so invigorated me I made a point to go look at my father's plaque, to share my success in person. It was easier and less incriminating than going back to his grave. His eyes looked through mine, taking it all in, giving away nothing. I thought about what he'd say to me but could only hear his voice saying: "Don't go in the water."

My mother was even less helpful, coming home around four pm like she was fired out of a bazooka. Guardado had gotten through to her. She finally had her confirmation I didn't know what I was doing, and probably her confirmation that everything, the scholarship, the degree, the getting me out of East Hook, was too good to be true. I was back home; the same failure she'd always had a feeling I was. As big a bomb as Guardado threw when he called my mother, he did give me small lifeline out of the conversation. He told my mother he'd think about not failing me if I gave him something that night along with the best excuse and apology he ever heard.

I went back downstairs as quickly as I could, away from her, promising to work on it and salvage what I had worked to destroy. I went down, flipped through the Yeats book, skipped dinner, and once the sun set, called for a cab and snuck out the basement door when I heard Andy's tires on the driveway. I saw my mother stand up from the kitchen table through our front window as we pulled out. The front door was just opening when we went out of sight. I turned my phone off.

I waited for Andy to drive out of sight as I put the hood over my head. As the taillights faded into the fog I checked the map on my phone and followed along the map to Westerly Way. It was cooler out there, and I could hear the surf against the waves. There wasn't much wind, the air was thick and briny. I hadn't been near the open water at night, and I forgot how different it feels. It looked the same though, fog covered everything.

Westerly Way was a small dead end with only six houses. Two on the high dry side, with a similar view of the bay that the road had, and four backing up to the water. Number 32 was the third one down, and the only one with full privacy hedges and a matte black iron gate. I could make out the gleam of a metal call box hidden in the bushes on the driver's side. I skulked up to it and saw it had a keypad and call button. It didn't look like it had a camera, but it was way too much for East Hook.

I wondered if it would have been easier to come by water. If Rocco were answering his phone he could have dropped me off right on the private dock. In the fog none of the neighbors would have seen a thing. I looked around and saw, unsurprisingly, that there were no neighbors to snoop. None of the houses had any lights on. I was in the heart of summer folk town, and real summer folk knew to stay out of East Hook until June.

The emptiness on the street reaffirmed my choice as the safer one. I heard the mayor talking about how carefully they had to watch the water, and even now, I saw dim lights creeping slowly across the bay. It had to be the coast guard or harbormaster, patrolling the water. We would have had to think of a damn good excuse if one of them spotted us, there's not much to paint in impenetrable fog.

I walked up to the gate. It was about seven feet tall and the metal solid, at least two inches thick, without any footholds. The top was smooth and straight. I backed up, taking eight long, careful steps and stopped just about at the end of the driveway. I took in another breath of that heavy, salty air, and sprinted toward the door, jumping up right in front of it and grabbing the top edge. I pulled myself up while pushing off the sticky matte finish with my feet, and once I got one foot over, sat on the edge like a squirrel on a branch. It wasn't comfortable, but I felt like I conquered something. I could see onto the property now and didn't see any flashing lights or hear any alarms, so I stayed up there, breathed in the sea again, and hopped down onto the grounds.

I landed on the driveway, which looped to the house and back around, dividing a well-maintained lawn sloping to the water. I had to take it all in by the shine of the clouds, no lights were on. I couldn't tell the color, I knew it was dark, probably a one or two on the Munsell scale, but it could have been mauve or dark moss green. It was the shingle style, and built into the slope, one of those houses where it was hard to tell which story you were looking at. Even in the darkness though, it was impressively designed, maintained and sized.

I walked up the driveway, wincing at the sound of each step. I knew the surf would drown them out. I really couldn't hear much else. There was some rustling of leaves and the occasional cricket song, but it was a quiet night out on the Western Bay. I walked up the steps to the side door and tried the knob. It was locked.

I looked under the welcome mat, looked under all the rocks near the entry path, even jumped up to look over the door frame, but couldn't find any keys. I debated throwing a rock through a window but decided to check the other entrances first. Rare as it was to lock your front door in East Hook, it was even less common to lock your back and side doors too. I started walking the perimeter, watching my feet the whole time to not trip on the sloping ground, keeping an arm's length from the outer wall of the house. I trod on some sprouting annuals and stepped through some blossoming bushes but kept my footing on the way to the back door. A patio ran underneath a deck I could access via stairs, but there was a sliding door I could try first. That was locked as well. I used the flashlight on my phone to check if it was just the lock but saw the wooden rod at the base of the non-sliding door, wedged to prevent any sliding.

When I leaned up against the glass and cupped my hands I could see inside the room, but I couldn't find anything to focus on. The room was empty, devoid of all furniture or anything on the walls, except a carpet. I leaned back from the door and felt my way to the stairs, keeping my eyes down at my feet, afraid to look into the mist or out at the water I could hear crashing behind me.

I heard every creak on my walk up the deck stairs, but the whole thing was well constructed, and I didn't hear anything once I was up there. It would have presented a great view of the water, but at night, even on a clear day, the water is just darkness. Sometimes you can make out the flash of a lighthouse, or the red blink of a buoy, but in May weather it was just a vague dark gray wall.

The deck had some built-in seating, and a tree grew through a designed hole in the decking, sure to provide shade during the sunny season, but still a cool effect in the dark. The quality of the whole thing made the emptiness stand out so much more.

I walked up to the door, blinds ran the length of the glass, pushed up against the outside like it was between another pane on the inside. I couldn't see anything. The windows that looked out on the deck were covered on the inside too. I tried a few of them but everything was locked. I started to understand that I wasn't getting into the house without breaking something.

I turned back out to the deck and noticed something not

keeping with the line of the deck railing. I walked closer, waiting for it to move or reveal itself as some decorative gargoyle. But it was just a coffee mug, with what looked like the waterlogged dregs of a drink in the bottom. I stuck my nose closer and thought I might be smelling the remains of an earthy tea, but it could have been actual earth and rain or collected mist, depending on how long it had been out there. The dregs weren't stained on the bottom though, and the outside was clean as far as I could tell, so it looked like it was used recently. I turned back up to recheck the side of the house, seeing if anything moved in the windows. I closed my eyes, listening for anything besides the surf and the distant clang of a shallow water buoy.

My eyes were starting to adjust to the darkness, and I was able to take in more details about the house and the yard. The lawn sloped toward the water gradually up by the driveway but turned down much more sharply by the water's edge. There was no seawall, but there was a small square poking up from the rocks, too clean and perfect to be natural. After ten minutes walking around a dark empty house, I was almost relieved to see something I could investigate, something to make my trespassing worthwhile. I walked down the stairs onto the lawn, following the slope down toward the water.

I felt my foot step on a smooth surface and focused my phone's light down at my feet. It was a flat oval stone so smooth it looked polished, buried in the ground so the top was level with the dirt under the grass. Nothing was etched into it or written on it, I supposed it was decorative. I tried swinging my light around to see if I could catch any others, but nothing reflected except the dew on the grass blades.

Continuing down toward the water, I felt the grade becoming steeper and made myself stop. In the wet grass my footing was anything but sure, and I didn't want to build up enough momentum that I couldn't stop myself tumbling into the sea rocks. Stopped, I looked for the square to reorient myself. It looked more ornate the closer I was to it; some design had been carved into the sides and the top jutted over what looked like a base. I shone my light below me to plan my descent. It was another ten feet down, in less than ten feet horizontally, but looked relatively flat near the shore. I sat down on the wet grass and slowly slid down, digging my heels in to control my speed.

Once I reached the bottom, it did flatten out, into kind of a bowl. The steep slope came in from all three sides, blocking the area off from views of everything but the roof of the house. Panic started to set in as I wondered how I'd get back up any of those banks with the grass being so slick, but as I waved my light around, it caught the same smooth stone I'd seen and felt under my shoe above. Like the other one, it was buried into the side of the hill, but instead of being flush with the slope, it jutted out from the grass, about two inches thick and almost perfectly flat. I moved my light up to see if it was part of a path up but couldn't find anything until I slid the beam to the left. There was another stone about two feet away and a foot higher. I followed the path and counted 6 more, spaced to form a curved, probably unsteady stairway up the outer edge of the bowl. My panic was replaced with wonder, as the design struck me as so simple and elegant, nothing like my paintings, so filled with detailed textures and the strained illusion of movement.

The tablet in the rocks, once I turned around and took it in, was much more like one of my paintings, it even had tentacles on it. It was stone, or treated cement, almost four feet tall, three feet across and looked to be at least six feet deep, long end toward the water. Twisted branches and screaming faces were carved into the sides. Monsters claws and talons held up the top plank, which had a simpler diamond pattern carved into it. I had never seen anything like it before, but on the rocks in the mist surrounded by crashing surf it looked like it belonged.

I recognized it as an altar; a monument to the death, pain and mystery on the water it looked out on. Suddenly my hoodie felt like it wasn't warm enough.

I forgot if it was high or low tide but judging by the small pools and seaweed strands on the rocks next to it, the altar was probably within the waterline. I shone my flashlight at the base and saw the telltale salt stain about four inches from the bottom at the front, and two inches up at the back near the grass. It was impossible to see the bay through the mist, but I wondered how close boats could get to it, and what it would look like to a lobsterman setting his traps. I wondered how something like it could just exist in public without prompting a lot of conversation.

As eerie as the design was, and how appropriately it fit the area didn't spook me half as much as the dimensions. It was the perfect size for a human body to fit in, or lie on top of. The painting came in my head, a robed man with his arms raised, violently shouting an incantation above the crashing surf, while a girl in white lay on the table, restrained and terrified. At the edge of the painting, over the water, I'd show glimpses of the unholy creatures with impossible anatomy being summoned through the fog to

194

feed on their sacrifice. The entranced, more drably robed followers would be watching from the grass bowl, maybe joining the incantation.

The robed man leading the incantation was my father, DW, the girl Cadie.

I stared into the fog and started to see movements, like flashes of the monsters in the painting I was composing, but this time not in my head. I blinked and they went away, then blinked and saw something else. I had to look away but found no soft landing place for my eyes. The sacrifice was still happening on the rocks and the altar, the sloping lawn was filled with bloodthirsty acolytes, chanting: *Go gather by the humming sea, some twisted echo-harboring shell.* Closing my eyes didn't prevent me from seeing any of it, only made the colors more vivid. I was starting to come adrift, spinning in place on slippery rocks, alone at a place no one checked, and nobody knew where I was. I wondered if this was how people ended up in the water, and hoped it wasn't my last thought.

I thought I saw a flash, like a beam of light, that slowed my spinning. My vision had changed to a cop leading the incantation, my father in another form. My eyes caught the peaks of the house roof, whose blessed plainness anchored me to the real East Hook, or at least the one I had always thought I lived in. I focused on the roof, seeing for the first time a light burning, and something in the window. Too woozy to take a closer look, I focused on my breathing, noticing how heavy my panting was. It was drowning out a fainter sound.

The flash came back at the side of my vision and I turned toward it, blinding myself against the beam. I heard the same noise repeated, not faint at all this time.

"Stop moving and put your hands on your head. You're

under arrest for trespassing."

# VII

# Wednesday

# Cubism

I t was about four in the morning when something rapping
on the bars woke me up from what couldn't have been a
deep sleep. I spent the previous five hours lying on a thin
strip of foam, fully dressed, under the harsh fluorescent light
of my cell. Sleep wouldn't have come easy in a deprivation
tank, or one of those frightening nap pods, I couldn't get my
mind to slow down. It was my first time in jail, my first time
getting arrested, and I was still seeing the storm, the alter and
monsters when I closed my eyes. Exhaustion is a powerful
thing though, the fifteen minutes or whatever I got in that
cell, in those conditions, is a testament to just how ragged I'd
run down my body. Maybe the visions were a testament too.

The officer who arrested me cuffed me down in the lawn
bowl, emptied my pockets and led me up the stairs and across
the lawn. As we walked, he kept asking questions about what
I was doing there, but I couldn't respond. It was as real a
situation as there is, but it still felt like part of a hallucination.
I tried blinking, to wake up, but kept seeing the lawn and
the house, and feeling his hand on my back, pushing me up
the hill. I was able to nod that I understood him a few times.
I remember the gate was closed when we got to it, and the
officer pushed a button or punched in a code to open it so

we could both walk back through to his parked cruiser. No flashing lights were on and he had no partner. He gently put me into the back of the car and once behind the driver seat turned around before we started moving.

The streetlights and LED lit dashboard were helping pull me back to reality, combining the relief of being away from the water with the growing panic of being in the back of a squad car. He was asking a question, but it still felt muffled until I spoke.

"Did I trip an alarm?"

He flinched when I started talking, stopping whatever he was saying. He looked back at the house.

"What do you think? Why were you there?"

Once my mind restarted I tried to use it to think quickly. "I was scouting a location for a painting I'm doing. The final for my art class." After it was out of my mouth, I wondered if I should be drawing attention to paintings and my work. I didn't know how much the police knew or saw. He didn't seem to recognize me, just furrowed his brow.

"A painting? Bullshit, what were you looking to steal?"

I didn't expect that question, "I wasn't stealing anything. You saw me, I was down by the water. Nothing to steal down there."

He has started shaking his head halfway into my explanation, and when I finished he pointed at the gate. His headlights illuminated the black front gate, my eye was drawn to a single, sandy half-footprint three quarters of the way up. I had left my mark.

"How would you know what to paint? Can't see the water from here." He turned more towards me, so that both hands were on the back of his seat. "What were you looking for? You

200

had your flashlight on! Who told you there was something here?" I started to protest, and he cut me off. "What are you on? Right now?"

He did find me swaying, and verbally unresponsive until just then "Nothing! I wasn't even drinking." I was really getting grilled for someone trespassing. I flashed back to the discussion I heard the mayor having, maybe this had to do with extra water patrols and maybe he thought I might be tied to the vandals. I thanked God I didn't have my spray cans on me.

He looked me up and down. "We'll find out down at the station."

I decided my best bet was to stick with the artist story, maybe also gin up some local sympathy. "It's empty! All these places are. They aren't using them." I was chalking up the light in the upper window as a part of my hallucination. It didn't feel like part of it, but the place being empty was convenient for the story I was telling.

He turned forward and shook his head, almost laughing. "Doesn't mean they're your playground. You jumped a fence; these people obviously don't want you here." So whoever was there didn't call me in.

I took my chance to learn more about these people who didn't want me. "Do you know who owns this place?"

He snapped back around. "Do you?" he almost shouted. I recoiled then stayed still. He collected himself. "Hope it was worth it. No water to paint where you're spending the night." He put the car in reverse, and we drove off together towards the police station.

I took in the back of the squad car, looking around with a sense of unreality. It was like being in the back of a taxi, with a cage instead of a plexiglass barrier, and it was lulling me into a sense of normalcy I needed to fight. I went through different things I could say to stop heading toward the station. I couldn't tell them everything I knew, because that was almost nothing, just several pieces that I couldn't put together but were starting to reveal an ominous mosaic. I was similarly incapable of telling the truth because that's what I was looking for, so far unsuccessfully. I could, however, still be honest, providing one compelling fact.

"My dad was a cop in East Hook."

The officer up front sounded skeptical. "Oh yeah? What was his name?"

"Detective Logan Ward."

He recognized the name. His eyes flashed up to the rearview mirror, analyzing my face for similarities to a plaque down at the station he probably walked by every day. I'd done the same analysis a few days before, with Ivy, I knew the results.

The officer looked more annoyed than anything once he knew I was telling the truth. Hopefully, he was thinking about defending himself from all my dad's old friends, whoever was left, for arresting the hero cop's kid. If I were lucky, one of them would be at the station, one of the officers who knelt next to me at my father's funeral, swearing to look out for me. It was looking like now was my chance to cash in that chip.

"What would he have thought about you trespassing at night?" The officer's question caught me like a slap. I never thought of myself as especially sensitive about my father, or protective of how people talked about him, but that cop got my blood way up. I wondered where he got the nerve to speak on my dad's behalf, some wannabe fascist D-student thinking he could speak from a real hero's perspective.

"I think he would have been proud of me." I said, more in defiance than insight. I never had any idea what my father wanted for me. The last few days had me doubting if I had any idea about him at all.

Only one other cop was in the station when we got there, he looked old enough to have worked twelve years before with my Dad. The place looked empty, while also feeling small. There were four desks and an office out front. I found the picture, the same one that we had at my house, of my father. The actual photo was blown up to a bigger size there, and instead of mounted on a plaque, it displayed under clear plastic or glass, with just his name: Detective Logan Ward. His eyes weren't looking right at me, but I still felt seen by him, trying to wonder what he actually would think of seeing my walk in there in handcuffs. I still couldn't see it through the mist. Maybe that was a good thing.

The officer who brought me in, a little more roughly than he needed to, was in a hurry to get back out of there. The one behind the desk tried protesting, mentioning all the paperwork they needed to do.

"That's what you're here for Mendel. We're under attack out there." And he walked out the door.

I saw Officer Mendel mouth asshole under his breath, then look up at me, seeming to take in my general shape at first but doing a double take on my face and increasing the intensity of his focus on my face.

"Jesus Christ, you're Logan's kid."

Officer Mendel was nice enough and a little apologetic about everything but said he couldn't just let me go without getting

Officer Methot, the asshole, or some detective to sign off on it. They were in a state of high alert, dealing with ten times the calls they usually got before tourist season, and they were under a lot of scrutiny. He did, however, hold off on some of the formal booking processes. I called my mother, who only stayed on the line long enough to find out what I was there for. Saying she'd get more rest at least knowing where I was as she hung up.

There was only one cell, built with four metal shelf bunks and a toilet in the middle of the room. I sat on the bottom bunk closest to the door and watched Officer Mendel lock me in and walk away with my freedom. He came back within five minutes, not to correct a mistake but to throw me a blanket, he said from his car. Apparently he had to stay out front on the radio with how crazy things were but made sure to say that he'd be back to check on me when he could. He didn't come back, leaving me with my dreams.

After waking me up hours later, Officer Mendel took me down the hall into a small room with two chairs and a table. He didn't handcuff me. I saw a small mirror on the side wall, which I figured was two-way. I was in the interrogation room.

I assumed it had all caught up to me, that the cops had followed all the clues pointing in my direction. It was impressive they worked that fast, maybe all of them were enough like my father. The chief must have listened to the mayor and brought in an elite squad.

I wasn't sitting long before an older cop walked in. He wasn't in uniform, but I could tell from his haircut and how his shirt was tucked in that he was a cop.

"Hi Ellis." He said as he slowly made his way to the chair.

He threw down a notebook and a pen on the table and stuck out his hand toward me. I shook it without standing up. "I'm Jim Potter, I'm a detective here. I worked with your dad." He sat down and crossed his leg. "Sorry we kept you here so long, we're running a little thin, with everything happening."

I was too self-conscious to nod, scared of giving anything away. Detective Potter noticed. "You know what's going on, right Ellis?" His tone was gentle, and he was trying to keep it conversational. I knew that I still needed to be careful.

"Yeah the vandalism." My eyes were treating the calm, gentle detective like the sun, holding eye contact with him made my whole head hurt. I alternated between seeing the table, my hands, and the floor as we slowly made our way towards wherever he was dragging me to.

"You know I was going to talk to you yesterday about it, even talked to your mom. Then today I come in and you're just here waiting for me." I didn't join him in his laugh.

"Hey, Ellis, don't worry. We're gonna let you go on the trespassing thing. It's a first offense, we got a million things going on here and like I said." He winked at me. "I worked with your dad."

I figured a real friend would have gotten me out of there a lot sooner but was certainly relieved. Relieved for the hoops I wouldn't have to jump through, and relieved to be talking to someone who could do something about all I'd seen.

"So let's start with last night? What were you doing on Lincoln Head?"

My relief evaporated. A trespassing charge was the least of my problems. I couldn't start from the beginning, with my tag on Cadie's grave. I couldn't start on the Quebecois property on Drydon, or my pictures in the buoy. I couldn't start with my other break-in, at the Splintered Mast. I couldn't really say anything.

*Though I'd a finger on my lip, what could I but take up the song?*

"Everyone knows it's the Quebecois! They're obsessed with sea monsters and want to bring them back. The lighthouses and traps are to keep people off the water. They're planning something big and more people are going to get hurt! It's at their house in Drydon, it's at this house on Lincoln Head. That's why I went. It's owned by the same people who own the Splintered Mast. There's a creepy altar. Go there! Everything must be there!"

I had not been prepared for the sophisticated dissection my choice of story required, sloppily trying to carve myself out and leave all the important pieces intact. Instead I totally shredded everything.

"OK, OK!" Potter made sure I stopped talking, both his hands were up in the air waving me down. "Take a breath, Ellis." I noticed with his hands up that he hadn't been taking notes. He looked disappointed, like he expected more from Logan's son. I hadn't seen the details he wanted. I couldn't spot the difference between what it looked like and what it was. "If you want me to look somewhere, you need to give me a lot more than that."

I must have had a dumb look on my face because he shifted his posture like he was addressing an idiot, and he affected the kind of patience normally reserved for kindergarten teachers. "We can't just crash open the gates of a house like that. Our summer residents contribute a lot to the community and have the loudest fucking voices when something doesn't go their way. I have a couple of my guys break in and search the place, it doesn't matter what we find, I'm out on the street, and the mayor cuts us off at the knees, halves our funding and our headcount."

I couldn't care less about DW Inc's civil liberties, we had a good chance to stop whatever was going on now, to keep people safe. My brief spell of authoritarianism was quickly followed with the inevitable next step, accusations of racism that I didn't take well.

"What you are giving me, is a lot of the same anti-foreigner crap I have been hearing since the Quebecois moved here." My eyes narrowed and I was pulling inwards, ready to get real defensive. He sensed it and put his palms up, showing he wasn't accusing me of anything.

"They're not from Quebec, they're from Algeria." He shook his head and chuckled. "No one ever leaves this town; they hear someone with a French and accent and immediately assume Canada." I wondered if they spoke a third, Algerian language that could explain the weird symbols I had seen.

"They're in town to run the Splintered Mast, we got one of them on speeding and a little bit of weed, but otherwise they're clean. Yet every other day I get some complaint about them being involved in some conspiracy." I felt cowed, but still had traces of self-righteousness running through my blood.

"It has nothing to do with where they're from! They are..."

"Different." Potter cut me off almost immediately. "They wear those stupid pincers and listen to loud weird music. They work at a monster store!"

I was shaking my head and he started nodding. "You're not wrong to think it, ok? A lot of shipwreck stuff starts happening in town, getting everyone worked up about monsters. Couldn't it be the monster store? Couldn't they have something to gain? Wouldn't it be worth looking into the people who dress like sea monsters?" His eyebrows were up, and his mouth was a little open. "We thought it was. So we did." Potter was kind of sounding like Guardado, telling me just because something looked a certain way, didn't mean it was that way. As hard as it was for me to accept, I thought I knew what was coming.

"There was a late-night event hosted at the Splintered Mast the night the lighthouses were vandalized. They were all there the whole time; forty people can attest to it." I didn't expect it to be that clear. How could I have been so wrong about them?

"Even for the traps, where nobody has an alibi because it was at three in the morning, they do. One of our officers responded to a noise complaint and broke up a party at three thirty, and again, they were all there. Witnesses we talked to confirmed they had been there since eleven." I felt like a few of the legs on my chair were taken away, the world was wobbling. "The only ones out on the water even around then were the harbormaster, your buddy and you."

Detective Potter's expression and posture hadn't changed. He still had an easy smile, was slouching a bit in his chair, but even if he didn't look different, he was. The interrogation had finally arrived.

"What were you doing out there?" He asked with fake curiosity. It was pitch black with a cement fog when we went out, I couldn't imagine someone seeing us then. It was more likely someone saw us come back, either tie up at the dock or saw us at the Porpoise. Maybe it was MyKayla.

"Rocco wanted to get out early and I haven't been around lately." Maybe it was Rocco, then the truth would come out fast, but until then, there was no reason to be honest with the police.

"His smile got a little deeper, but his eyes looked sadder. "So you woke up at four AM to join him on a trap run?"

"Yeah we hadn't seen each other in a while, I go to school in the city, in town for Cadie's funeral."

"Yeah Ellis I know. You're a great painter."

"Thanks. And he wanted help in the mist. He's got to keep an eye on the GPS and right in front of him to find the pots. I just figured why not."

He nodded, like it all made sense to him. "You pull up anything?" He could eat shit.

"Not a lot."

"But something, right?"

"Yeah."

Now he moved, sighing and tilting his head back.

"Here's the problem, Ellis. No one bought lobsters two days ago in the morning. Everyone was panicking about their lines being cut and no store or restaurant took anything in." Apparently he'd done the legwork. I thought about coming clean, about the graffiti and the paintings. If it came to it, I could cop to the Splintered Mast break-in and explain why I was at the DW house. I couldn't see any way that would get me out of there faster though. Detective Potter had all but dismissed suspecting the Quebecois, or whatever they were.

"I don't know about that, we kept them in the tank and stopped for breakfast, then Rocco went back out." He didn't move, like he expected more, and I was more willing to go on since I was back in the realm of truth. "After breakfast, he went out and I walked over to the harbormaster and heard about the traps."

"Rocco's traps weren't cut?"

"Not the ones we tried." Back in the realm of lying.

"Where were you? What part of the bay?"

"Out by the Stains."

"And you didn't see anything? No floating lines, no other boats?"

I shook my head. "No." I had been wondering myself why I hadn't seen anything. We were focused on a specific buoy and it was foggy. I remembered the boat I thought I heard. "I heard a boat, sounded like it was farther out than us. But never saw it."

For the first time, he started writing in his notebook. Without looking up, he said, almost to himself, "Could have been the harbormaster." He finished writing, capped his pen, and looked back up at me. "What about last Friday, what were you doing?"

I wasn't exactly sure what day of the week it was, so it took me a minute to figure what I was working backwards from. After a few seconds, I remembered Cadie's funeral was on Saturday. Friday night I was driving up, and someone was smashing lights in the lighthouses. Someone else, no matter what it was starting to look like.

"I was driving up from the city with my girlfriend. I got to my house around four, and we stayed in with my mom." He was writing again, but not much.

"So just your mom and girlfriend could confirm it?"

I knew where he was going and wracked my brain for other ways to prove I was there. I heard some commotion back toward the station, fast footsteps and loud voices. We both looked up and Detective Potter shrugged. The commotion got louder, and the footsteps closer. There was knock on the door then it opened before Potter could respond. Officer Mendel stuck his head in, his face didn't betray anything, but he was breathing hard. "Detective" was all he said, and he nodded his head to the side while looking into the hallway. Universal for Get out here. Potter understood it. He stood up to walk out, not forgetting to say "Excuse me" as he did.

All I heard were hushed voices in an obviously concerned tone; I couldn't make out any words. I thought about getting up and listening at the door, but my pragmatism outweighed my curiosity. I didn't want to be hopping around when Potter came back in, and I could use the time to think, get my story straight. Whatever was happening out there had nothing to do with me.

If the Detective knew what lobsters were sold, there was a pretty good chance he knew about the graves being defaced. Depending on who he talked to, there was a good chance he knew the EH tag was mine. He mentioned he knew I was a painter. He was keeping what he knew close to the vest, but I would be stupid to assume he didn't know more than me.

I tried to step back and tell myself that I didn't cut the traps, destroy the lighthouse bulbs, spray paint any graves, or put my paintings in a metal box by the water, so that I couldn't be hurt by the truth. I only let the thought of sharing everything sit in my mind for a fraction of a second before dismissing it. When had the truth ever not hurt?

I started thinking about what lawyers I knew and how I could get in touch with one when the door opened back up again, and Potter stomped back in. His easy movement and casual smile were replaced by tense, halting steps and furrowed brows.

"When's the last time you heard from Rocco?" he almost shouted at me. I tried to think, looking around the room while I did.

"Uhhh" I dragged it out while I remembered it was at the Porpoise. "Two days ago!" I was screaming back. "He's been avoiding everyone."

"You're sure?" My head caught up to my heart and I started wondering why he was shouting at me.

"Yeah. Why? What's going on?"

He didn't answer me, and the tension left his body. "You can go, Ellis, but do not leave town. We need to continue this conversation." He started walking out. "And don't go anywhere you're not allowed to be. You get picked up again, we'll charge you."

Just like that. He was gone and left the door open. I wasn't sure if I was supposed to just walk out. They still had my phone. Whatever happened, looked like it got me out of some trouble. Officer Mendel walked in and waved me towards the hall. "Let's go."

"What's going on?" I said to him as I got into the hall and started following him to the front. He didn't answer, instead turning around and waving again. "Let's go, come on" and started walking faster. I sped up to match him and walked through the door to the front. It was almost as empty as when I came in the night before, except not at all silent. All the phones on the desks were ringing, staggered, so all parts of the ring were playing at the same time. I followed him behind the desk, where he unlocked a drawer, opened it, and got out my phone, keys and wallet. He handed them to me, then looked for a form in a tray on the desk. He found the one and presented it to me.

"Mr. Ward. Have all your possessions been returned to you?" They had, and I nodded. "Ok, sign here, and you're free to go." I signed and started walking away. Out of habit

I checked my phone. It was dead. I turned around and he already had a receiver to his ear. I heard "Officers are on the scene and more are incoming. Thank you." When he hung up I got his attention before he grabbed another ringing phone. He looked annoyed but stopped reaching.

I realized how busy he was and felt sheepish even asking. "Can you call me a cab? My phone's dead." He looked at me for a second then gestured for me to look around. "Sorry." I said automatically while he went to answer the phone again. "Yes, just off West Hook, keep the coast guard off it for now... uh huh." He looked at me while he was listening, looked at the desk and waved me over. "As long as no one can get through." When I got to the desk he pointed at a phone charging cord coming up from the floor.. I mouthed thank you at him and plugged in.

While I waited for it to turn back on, I tried to piece together what was happening based on what he was saying. It sounded like there was a crash, maybe in the water, near downtown. I had heard him mention an ambulance, but not fire trucks. My imagination was filling in the details, with the same unholy figures I was seeing the night before, and the bright fluorescent-lit room started feeling a lot darker. My phone buzzed that it was back on, and soon after started buzzing constantly for almost a minute. The short, single dot buzz of text messages, hundreds of them. I grabbed my phone and the first one I saw was.

He's alive, for now, they are putting him into a coma.

I started scrolling down, saw Rocco mentioned enough to know it was about him. Most of the messages were from

213

Desmond, with a few from MyKayla, MyKenzy, and my mother. I opened Desmond's and scrolled until something made sense. Right after the "now you don't answer either?" from the night before I found it.

Rocco's boat exploded an hour ago in the water just off downtown. He's not doing good.

# Rococco

I called Desmond and he answered on the first ring.

"Holy shit. Ellis, where have you been? I thought you were dead."

I told him I'd been in lockup, and it took him about a minute to believe me. I explained how I was picked up, how they questioned me and then all ran out when the Rocco thing happened. I tried to go through it quickly so I could hear the latest about Rocco. I could hear movement in the background then a thump. I asked what was going on and Desmond said he was coming to pick me up, but we could talk while he drove to me.

Turns out he had been diligent about texting me, a potential dead man, and the last thing he heard was that they induced a coma.

"So they found his boat blown up?" My focus had been on the present, so I hadn't had time to think about the past, the how of it all.

"No, it didn't blow up. I thought it did, but apparently they didn't think it was explosives, the boat was just torn apart like it was thrown into a rock or a.."

"Or something bit through it."

Desmond wasn't seeing the same pattern; his previous

215

forty-eight hours were less illuminating than mine. He didn't answer for a while and when he did, his tone got stiff, like he was scared. "How did you know that Ellis?"

"I didn't! I was hoping you'd tell me I was crazy."

"Do you know something about this?"

I wanted to spill everything to him, like I did when I was trying to get with Cadie in high school, relying on his experience and cool to make everything feel more normal and attainable. I wanted to tell him about cults and sea monsters and my destiny at the center of everything. I held off, possessing enough self-awareness to realize I was likely working on less than an hour of sleep, and knowing he wasn't the same Desmond to me anymore. No one was. I looked back at Officer Mendel, who was turned away from me and still fielding phone calls, but he could probably still hear everything I said. "No, nothing. I'll tell you in the car."

Desmond just replied, "Cool I'm almost there" and hung-up. I kept the phone at my ear and called home.

My mother also picked up on the first ring but didn't seem as excited to hear my voice.

"How was your night?" Suggesting she hoped it was awful. She must not have heard yet.

"Mom, Rocco is in the hospital, they put him in a coma." Right after I said Mom, my voice started cracking. I had to take a big sniff after I finished.

Her energy changed at the tone of my voice. "Oh my God! What happened?"

I told her about his boat getting destroyed.

"Oh Ellis… Can I come get you?" She didn't say it, but I understood it. I'm sorry.

I was too. "No Mom, it's fine. They let me go. Desmond is

coming to get me and we're going to the hospital."

"Oh that's good you'll both be there." We stayed quiet. "Poor Francesca. I need to call her. Tell her how sorry I am if you see her."

Desmond was calling me on the other line.

"I will. Desmond's here, I gotta go."

"Ellis! Wait!"

I unplugged my phone from the charger and waved at the officer as I walked out. "Yeah Mom?"

"Be careful. I lov…"

I hung up before I got to the door. Desmond was idling in front of the wrong entrance. I got his attention and waved him over. When he pulled up I hopped in before the car came to a complete stop, but he waited to start driving.

"It was the Quebecois." He was staring straight ahead.

"I don't know." I looked at him for a second, then looked straight ahead through the windshield, trying to see what he did. "The police investigated them, and they have alibis for stuff." He started to shake his head. "They're not from Quebec either. Algerian."

"Nice haircut. They give that to you in there?" I didn't respond. "No, it was the Quebecois." Now he looked at me. "Last night, Rocco wasn't answering, so I went to his house. Too many people go quiet here and just keep getting quieter. He didn't want to let me in, but I pushed past him. He was drunk, high, hadn't showered, his place had old plates everywhere. It was scary. I tried to talk to him, but he was fixated on the cut lines. Like five of his pots were cut, he's gonna lose ten k or something like that."

"Shit." That's a lot of hundred-dollar paintings.

"He was convinced it was the Quebecois." I didn't correct

217

him. "I hadn't heard it from anyone else, but we saw they have a boat, so I told him it made some sense and I..." He pursed his lips as if in disgust and shook his head. "I told him where they are, where they live in Drydon."

"He went there?"

"He must have! He was pacing around, talking fast, like he was about to explode. You should have seen him. He's scary when he's pissed, he's so big." I knew, I'd seen it a few nights before in the cemetery.

"So you think he went there, confronted them and they blew up his boat?"

"Crashed it. I don't think it was explosives." He looked down at the cupholders than back up at me. "I shouldn't have told him where they live."

"He could have found out from anyone, and we don't know what happened." It felt like we had it pretty close though. "We going to the hospital or Drydon?"

His eyes widened and he almost grinned. "Fuck Ellis, the hospital." He scoffed. "One night in jail and look at you." He put the car in gear and started forward. His smile got wider, then reset to a frown "How did you know the boat would look like something attacked it."

Because something probably did. "Anything that would throw Rocco from the boat must have also torn it apart. Was there a surf advisory?" I wasn't ready to share my theory with anyone. I wondered how quickly you could go crazy not telling anybody anything. The current experiment suggested it was only a few days.

Desmond shook his head. "I asked. It was just a fog advisory. No strong wind or waves." I shook my head too. It didn't make any sense. We drove on, silent in the car, internally both screaming at ourselves for causing it to happen.

I couldn't help but focus on the Quebecois, the Algerians. Why would the detective dismiss them so fast? It got me thinking about the detective, and how he basically accused me of both cutting the traps and destroying the lighthouse bulbs. It sure seemed like he only let me go because Rocco's boat accident happened while I was in lockup. If so, that meant he was operating under the assumption, or he had proof, that they were all related. If they were related, then the pattern was real, and heading toward something bad. The events kept getting more and more destructive. A series of plagues on East Hook to atone for some sin I felt guilty of committing. Things were only going to get worse.

I caught myself breathing heavier and tried to calm down by admitting there were a lot of ifs, I was focusing on the worst-case scenario and no matter how it looked, I hadn't actually done anything. Plus, even if I was in bad shape, I was better off than Rocco. For the moment.

The hospital was just south of downtown towards Lincoln Head, tucked away in the woods at the bottom of a hill. The main building looked like an old colonial house, but sleek newer wings had been added in the last few years, each named after a different generous summer family donor. It didn't take us long to reach and when we arrived the parking lot was mostly empty.

Going through hospital doors is like breaching a membrane between best case scenario and worst-case scenario. No one is doing well at a hospital, more than a few are having the worst days of their lives. Some unlucky ones are there day after day, trying to make the best of some nightmare phase, or fighting to see another one.

219

I wondered for a second if I was living the worst day of my life. I spent the morning in jail, and my best friend had to be put in a coma after his boat blew up, and I maybe caused it. My stomach clenched at the thought, like I was going to throw up. But I knew that no matter what happened to Rocco or to me, this wasn't the worst day.

My Dad never made it to the hospital on my worst day, probably his worst day too. Paramedics came with the police, but there was no reviving him, nothing a doctor or machine or fancy new wing could help with.

Rocco didn't look like himself, lying on the bed covered in bandages with tubes snaking in and out of him. Machines dominated the room: beeping, releasing and intaking air, blinking ever-changing incomprehensible measurements.

Rocco's mother sat next to the bed, scratching out part of the solution on whatever puzzle book she had. She must have been close to cracking it, we got three steps into the room before she even noticed us.

She looked up startled, but her eyes lit up when she recognized us, and she put down her puzzle and stood up.

"My boys!" She whispered in a ragged voice, like we were going to wake Rocco up. Desmond entered the room ahead of me, so she greeted him first with a hug and a kiss on the cheek. After breaking the embrace with him, she came to me and put her hands on both my shoulders, looking me up and down. "Ellis!" she looked me up and down, then came in for a hug warm enough to shake some of the mist from my bones. I squeezed my arms tighter around her because it felt so good, and as she pulled away she held eye contact, like she was the one who felt sorry for me.

Desmond put his arm on Rocco's shoulder, without any delicacy or apprehension. "How's the big guy doing?"

Rocco's mother pursed her lips and looked back at her boy: a warm, beeping statue, and kept looking there as she talked, in that same ragged whisper that gave away just how much crying she'd been doing.

"They put him in a coma, and they thin..." She was too choked up to make it any farther into the prognosis. I moved to go to her, the true north of a real mother attracting me when I most needed one and hugged her again.

"He's gonna be alright. He has to be." I wasn't sure how loud I was talking since it was really meant for me.

Desmond joined the hug, but it only lasted a few seconds, Rocco's mom was regaining her composure. When we were standing on our own again, she dabbed her eyes with a tissue Desmond provided, and nodded. "He was lucky. There's a good shot he'll pull through."

A consequential amount of tension left my body, like all my muscles exhaled at the same time. Tears started welling up in my eyes as she continued.

The Coast Guard found Rocco floating in the wreckage. He was still breathing but not responsive. Apparently the cold water had kept his blood pressure low, so he still had enough left in his body when the harbormaster fished him out. They tried to remove pressure from his brain and decided to induce a coma to let it heal on itself. He also had a broken collarbone, fractured ankle and a handful of bruised ribs. The hope was that once swelling subsided, they could wake him up and confirm his motor functions weren't significantly impacted.

He was far from out of the woods, but there was a chance the East Hook water had given one back from the deep. One

221

all my nonsense had probably put in there.

"Do they know what happened?" Desmond acted like he'd never doubted Rocco would be fine.

Rocco's mom just shook her head. "One of the officers suggested it was some mechanical failure, and another officer said it could have been a whale breaching. They have no idea!" She wasn't whispering any more. "I can't get a straight story from the police. Nearby witnesses heard a boom or a series of booms and went down to check it out, but the Coast Guard say they were responding to a distress call." I felt the familiar sting of lacking answers, and the familiar pull to do something about it.

A quick look at Rocco reminded me how destructive that pull can be, like a riptide. If I had just waited for answers, or been fine with not knowing everything immediately, everyone in the room would have bene better off. Someone was trying to send a message for me to leave it alone, maybe spiritually Someone, maybe literally someone, and at some point I would have to heed it.

The pull didn't go away so easily. The pattern of events still revolved around me, in tighter and tighter revolutions, and if I didn't figure out what was really going on soon, it was likely to pull even tighter, right around my neck.

It wasn't just me who was getting lost in their own thoughts. Everyone was quiet. Rocco's mom returned to her seat between the bed and the wall. Desmond stood over Rocco with his hands in his pockets. I leaned against the wall closer to the door. Footsteps, staccato clacks getting louder then fading away, joined the piercing beeps and aspirating inside the room to break up the silence. They all kept a mostly steady beat, eventually smoothing into the quiet, until something got out of rhythm. A set of footsteps, slower and a little squeaky, increased in volume then instead of decreasing, stopped completely. We all turned around at the same time to see a short, tan, middle-aged man with styled salt and pepper hair in a lab coat looking down at a clipboard then checking his giant shiny watch. He flipped a few pages, and looked up to see us staring at him. He gave us a gleaming white smile that reminded me of Mr. Sinclair's and nodded toward Rocco.

"How is everything in here? How is…" his eyes flashed down, almost imperceptibly, to the clipboard then smoothly back up "Rocco coming along? Any changes?"

I didn't know what change we could see, other than him waking up. Rocco's mom seemed to have the same question. "What are we supposed to be watching for?"

The doctor kept smiling generously, like we were too simple to follow his obvious logic, but he admired our salt-of-the-earth straightforwardness. "Nothing, at this point. Just make sure nothing on the monitors spikes." He looked down at the clipboard again. "We'll scan him again this afternoon to see if his swelling's going down on its own or if we have to go in there. But really we can just wait at this point." He walked further into the room, clapping me on the shoulder as he passed and doing the same for Desmond. A woodsy, charcoal aroma trailed behind him. When he got to Rocco he checked one of the bandages then clapped him on the shoulder too, a little harder than necessary. "Another one in the water." He looked out the window. "Less and less time between each one." I cleared my throat, preparing to ask a follow-up question, but the doctor kept going like I did nothing.

"He may have gotten lucky, and he's a strong dude. We're gonna do our best for him." His voice had gotten deeper, and he had been directing everything at me and Desmond, like he was trying to impress us. He was even leaning against Rocco's bed, trying so hard to look relaxed he was practically sweating.

"Honestly, it's harder for you, just here waiting." He pushed his hips off from Rocco's bed and walked back past us. I saw his tag: Dr. Wainwright. When he was right between us he slowed down and lowered his voice. I'm sure Rocco's mom could hear, but it wasn't meant for her. "You need something to take the edge off, help you sleep, let me know." He raised his fist for Desmond, the real target of his attempted bromance, to bump. Desmond complied, looking a little impressed and a little more confused. "Dr. Leo." He turned to me and did the same thing. I bumped it, and immediately started looking for hand sanitizer. "Dr. Leo" He winked, "Ask for me, they'll page me."

He put his arm on Rocco's mother's shoulder, modifying his energy down so it wasn't a clap. "He's in good hands." He put his hands up as he started walking out of the room. Before he got to the door, he said "I'll be back for the scan in a few hours" without turning around. He walked out, dropped the clipboard back in the tray and left us staring at each other as his footsteps got quieter. The smell lingered.

We left soon after. Rocco's mom wanted to focus on Rocco, and we felt like we were taking her attention away from him. Our speed leaving the room increased with every step down the hall and down the stairs, only to halt just before the exit waiting on an older man being wheeled out ahead of us. From the back he looked like a gift-wrapped skeleton, his clothes hung off him and he had tube running up from a holstered oxygen tank running under his nose.

If we went single file we could have passed him. I had already been in the hospital too long. I started drifting to the right to try a pass, but Desmond nudged my arm. He wasn't being the rudeness police, he wanted to show me something. He pointed to the oxygen tank.

"They have explosions without fire."

I wasn't following. "What?"

"Rocco's boat. It exploded but there wasn't fire. It can happen"

"How?" I was skeptical, it seemed like Desmond was still in the rationalization phase. Trying to convince himself there was a normal explanation for what had been happening. I blew past that stage when I found my paintings in the buoy. And things had gotten a lot stranger since then.

"Pressure. They're always pressurizing beer in kegs at the warehouse. You pump enough air or something else into a contained space it can burst. I didn't see it, but someone lost most of their nose because they weren't careful."

The man in front of us was getting raised up into a van on a hydraulic lift. I pointed to the tank. "I thought oxygen blew up all the time?"

"Not oxygen! You can pressurize like any gas or liquid. Something pierces the shell, or some chemical gets in it, boom! No fire, just boom!"

My skepticism went down. It seemed reasonable enough. "What's pressurized on a lobster boat?" We were almost at the car.

"I don't know. I've only ever been on Rocco's."

"You know anyone we can ask?"

Desmond didn't answer. He made a show of digging into his pockets for his car keys as we approached. He found them, clicked it unlocked, but stopped outside his door. I opened the passenger side but saw him still just standing there.

"Ellis, I don't…" He looked like he was having trouble getting it out. I raised my eyebrows, trying to coax it out of him through body language. He shook his head, then opened the car door and sat down. I did the same. When our seatbelts were buckled I said "What, Desmond?" didn't need more people holding out on me.

He looked straight ahead, again not looking at me. "I don't know." Not very helpful.

"What? You don't know any lobstermen? So what. We can go to literally any restaurant and wait on the dock."

He reached to put the keys in the ignition but stopped and put his hands down. He turned his head towards mine but kept his eyes down. He opened his mouth once and nothing came out and he did a quiet sigh. He seemed to be exercising some restraint, at war with himself. Finally he found his voice, wavering but clear.

"Shouldn't you go back to the city?"

# Mannerism

I didn't immediately take Desmond's advice. He dropped me at my mother's after an uncomfortable ride and I let myself in through the unlocked door. I knew she wouldn't be home and was thankful for it, I wasn't ready to share my story. I didn't know what the story even was, it had so many missing parts, I just knew the ending wasn't happy.

I couldn't guess what Rocco had stumbled on that would make him such a target. The last I had seen of him he got on his boat, warning me he couldn't keep my secret forever. The last time I had thought about him, it was to worry he'd cause me a headache, expose my involvement. My sense of what was possible had expanded at a frightening pace over the last few days, so I couldn't dismiss that what happened to him may have been somehow willed by me or made happen by someone on my behalf.

I had only caught a very small part of what was really going on in East Hook, and my feeble mind couldn't grasp it. Whatever monster the murderous death cult was summoning to East Hook, I knew the community was powerless to stop it. They had infiltrated every level of East Hook, wrapping their insidious tentacles around the city tighter and tighter until we all choked. Since I spent the ride back with Desmond on my phone avoiding conversation, I noticed yet another, angrier missive from Guardado in my inbox. As I had with the others, I ignored it, but became angrier as I thought on it more and more, imagining the blissful, naive life you'd have to live to tell people not to be afraid of monsters. Thinking like that made me righteous, like failing his class was principled act: I rejected its entire premise.

I knew I should sleep, but also knew I wouldn't be able to. I looked around the living room until I found my mother's laptop, thinking I could do some research and formulate some kind of plan to stop it, or at least get the message out about what was going on in my town. My father's warning rang out in my head, an admonishment really, as I had not heeded him, to disastrous results. I told you not to go into the water, you don't know what's down there.

My father. Unlike in real life, in my head he kept coming to the surface of my thoughts, refusing to stay under. I couldn't explain why I saw him in everything, how he had ties with the signs on the water, the cemetery, the lockbox, the initials: DW. I went over to his plaque by the bathroom and really looked at him.

The face staring back did look like mine, except for the eyes. My eyes kept seeing him in everything, but were they seeing the truth? What would his eyes tell him? Something disturbed me much more than how often I saw him: how much I felt him out there with me. I was being guided, maybe even protected by some force out in the water, where he died and where he always warned me not to go. What if he stayed down there when he drowned, becoming something more permanent and scarier while the limp husk of his body was pulled ashore. I felt a paternal presence guiding me, asking

228

me to spot what was wrong, and at the same time protecting me, all from down there.

"What are you trying to tell me, Dad? What is this test?"

Those eyes. I imagined them narrowing in annoyance, like they always did when he had to repeat himself, when I just wasn't seeing what he wanted me to. His guidance was leading me somewhere and had been leading me to the same place since long before Cadie died. Don't go in the water. The solution became clear through the fog.

Not the solution to save East Hook, not the cure for monsters, but a solution. Whatever the Algerians were doing, it seemed to be orbiting around me. The tagging, the paintings, the monsters, Rocco, all only had me in common, and they were always one step ahead. The more I dove in the more people close to me got hurt. My father went in the water to save people in the town, and he couldn't have wanted the same for me.

I had to go back to the city, away from the water, towards my foggy, but dry, future.

I went downstairs to collect everything I was taking back with me and one thing I wasn't. I had one more thing to do before I left town, hoping not for the last time.

When Mr. O'Reilly opened the door he looked thinner, more withdrawn and about ten years older than he did at the funeral. As he got a look at me, I saw him take in his breath, ready to sigh away another condolence-giver.

"Mr. O'Reilly?" I'm not sure why I asked it like a question, he probably remembered me from the funeral and his brow furrowed in either confusion or concern. He opened the door wider but stayed behind it.

"Yes… What can I do for you?"

I was holding the Yeats book against my left hip. I brought it up, flipped the front cover around so he could see it. "I stole this from you, like seven years ago, I'm sorry."

He kept his eyes on me as he opened the door wider and stepped out onto the porch. He reached for the book with both hands and took it from me. He studied it for a few seconds, ran his hand over the indented writing, then looked back at me, more confused than before.

"I'm Ellis Ward, I was a friend of Cadie's."

He kept the same expression for a beat, then his eyes widened fractionally.

"Oh, the artist." I got hot, waiting for his retribution for vandalizing Cadie's grave. But instead of tension and growing anger, his body relaxed, and his face settled on something more like bemusement. It looked like to him I was just a book thief, the thing who had taken the least from him that month.

I just nodded, and he nodded back. He held up the book.

"Why?"

I wasn't going to give him the real reason, but I worked out a story on the way over. Again thankful for Caleb's silence.

"I don't know. I read a couple of the short poems and really liked it… I figured I'd give it back later that week… and time just…" I started out looking him in the eye but was looking firmly at my feet by the second excuse. Had I always been so pathetic? I straightened up and looked back at Mr. Reilly. He had a gleam in his eye.

"Do you have a favorite?"

Of course I didn't, Yeats just fluttered around in my head, rhymes and stanzas catching on a branch now and then. In fact, as I was knocking on Mr. O'Reilly's door The Folly of Being Comforted caught. *I have not a crumb of comfort, not a grain.* I knew I should say something though.

"I liked To a Child Dancing in the Wind." I almost winced as I said it, but to be fair, children and sadness come up more than a few times in Yeats.

He seemed too numb to be stung by a word. He nodded, like it was an acceptable answer. "I always liked Two Years Later, maybe because I'm a teacher. You know that one?

I nodded, *"I could have warned you, but you were young, so we speak a different tongue."*

Maybe he wasn't too numb, his eyes started welling up, but he caught himself, sniffed and wiped his hand across them, unashamed. "Do you want to come in?"

I wasn't sure, but I followed Mr. O'Reilly inside.

"Art and poetry, you really are a cultured young man." He sounded surprised as he was closing the door behind me, as if drawing and liking words that rhyme can only be taught by a governess, like they belonged to the summer people. I had the urge to tell him I woke up in the police station that morning.

The house looked different than I remembered, more open concept, like it went through the common empty-nester renovation after Cadie moved out. Far from looking like a design magazine spread though, mail was piled up on the key table, clothes were draped over the furniture, flower arrangements, still in their plastic wrap, were piled on the dining room table. I noticed a box of tissues on the arm of an easy chair in the living room.

Mr. O'Reilly let me take it all in and I was relieved he didn't apologize for the mess. His house should look like that. When

I turned back toward him pointed upstairs. "I want to show you something." He was still holding the book as he started up the stairs. I followed, wondering if I left behind some embarrassing evidence in high school, but wondering more if I'd feel Cadie again when I walked into her room.

We didn't make it that far though. Mr. O'Reilly stopped in the hallway and gestured toward a small framed painting. "You remember this?"

It was the drawing I made in high school, of Cadie's dog by her feet. Not only had Cadie keep it, the family had it framed. I felt flush of shame, knowing why I did it, but the colors looked good in the frame they picked out. The lines were bold, the light and depth were consistent, and the dog looked so lively and playful. Maybe I had been better than I thought in high school, or maybe I was happy to see something without a fucking sea monster in it.

"Our dog, Shasta, died a few years ago and it broke our hearts. We found this in one of Cadie's drawers and it just captured the way she was, how happy she made us. We actually had it framed and hung before we knew you did it. My brother-in-law used to joke that it raised the status of the house. We read about your paintings in city hall and the doctor's office and yacht club, it put us in good company." He had a pained smile; every memory of his family was now a sad one. "Do you remember doing it?"

"Yeah, in high school art class. Cadie brought me a picture of Shasta and I did it after school."

"I've seen a few of your paintings around town, of course. You're in school now for it, right?"

"Just finished." It was true whether Guardado failed me or not. With or without a degree, I had attended my last art class.

"Well you had great talent even in high school, I'm sure your work now is very impressive."

I had braced myself for the inevitable question about what I'm planning to do with my life now, but Mr. O'Reilly was just being robotically pleasant. He was still looking at the dog painting, I imagine thinking about the patron instead of the subject. We stood there together for a beat, looking at Shasta, not knowing what to say. It felt like time to leave, but I was starting to learn to not trust my feelings.

Mr. O'Reilly sighed and broke his gaze at the painting to look down at the Yeats book. He had been holding it at his hip and he sort of shrugged to make the book bounce. "Yeats." He looked at me. "I quoted Love and Death in Cadie's eulogy. Were you at the funeral?" He hadn't remembered me after all. He was working his way through a fog thicker than anything in East Hook.

"Yeah, it was a good speech."

He looked back at the book. "It was, thank you. My daughter is dead, and all I can do for her is fucking poetry." It was time for me to leave after all.

I took a step back, but he looked back up at me, almost glaring, and his tone stopped me in my tracks. "When is the last time you saw her?"

I thought about lying to pass whatever this close friend test was. Rocco's words came back to me, who was I anyway?, but I just told the truth. "Maybe last summer in passing, but I think it was longer than that."

His expression unexpectedly softened. "That's good. You'll remember her like that." He looked down at the book again. "Probably would have been good for her to have kept hanging around with you though." I wasn't sure if he was trying to

233

make me feel guilty, but he continued, "Eh, I know parents can't control who their kids are hanging out with." He looked down at the book and choked out a sad chuckle. "At least you were just a book thief."

Not a killer, I thought to myself, wondering what he knew.

"I think I would have liked you; you might have been my favorite of Cadie's friends. Certainly, my favorite artist." I had no idea what he was talking about, and he was starting to get more animated. "I know one thing; you're not going to see any paintings in this house by Oliver Sinclair.

"Mr. Sinclair?!" I blurted out, feeling the world tilt under my feet. I thought I might fall backwards down the stairs, so I instead leaned forward against the wall. What the hell did Mr. Sinclair have to do with Cadie?

"I know!" He looked up expecting solidarity but instead saw me bracing myself against the wall, looking like I'd been punched.

"I forgot, you must have known him well, he was your art teacher. Cadie's too, the sick bastard. I had a parent-teacher conference with him back then. Seemed normal, bright, someone who cared. My instincts are broken, always have been."

I leaned harder into the wall as visions of a skinny Mr. Sinclair in the parking lot at the church, a glint in his eye when he saw me. Rumors of Cadie dating an older man. The painting laminated in the buoy, an amateur version of my own style. The sea monster cult knowing my art, my tags, my friends. Someone looking out for me like a father, with mine already claimed by the deep.

"Are you alright Ellis?" He put his arm on my shoulder, his touch was gentle and reassuring. It made the visions stop.

My heart and head were still racing, but I could feel the wall against me. I pushed off it and Mr. O'Reilly helped steady me. My voice came out ragged, and much softer than I intended.

"Did he kill her?"

Mr. O'Reilly's eyes got wide and with his hands on my shoulders, looked like he considered shaking me. Instead he just gave a light squeeze and pursed his lips.

"He might as well have."

I was coming back to the world, but the world didn't make any sense. Why didn't the police mention this? Thinking of the police, I thought of one more question, tact, good manners and comfort be damned: "Do you know how she ended up in the water?"

Mr. O'Reilly let go of my shoulders.

"Ellis, Cadie died of a heroin overdose. Police think she rolled into the water after she was already dead."

# Pointillism

I double checked the number, even the street signs, to make sure I hadn't taken a wrong turn. The addresses matched, but the house I remembered going to, for art club parties, studio work and sometimes just to get away, did not match what I was seeing in front of me. The yard was overgrown and patchy at the same time, with weeds in the place of grass. The paint wasn't yet peeling, but the facade matched the shabbiness of the yard.

I hadn't come there to feel sorry for Sinclair, I came to confront him, but seeing his house in that condition floored me, and filled me with shame. How could I not know how he had been living? Was I so self-involved that I missed all the signs? People would talk about Mr. Sinclair around me, but I never got the subtext. He needed help. Whatever he did to Cadie, maybe even to me, he did it out of desperation. I didn't know how passionate my confrontation could be. I was heading towards just another victim.

I walked up the cracked, uneven stone path to the front door and paused before ringing the bell. I stood on his stoop and looked out at the neighborhood. It all looked shabby now, out of focus and poorly maintained. Sinclair's house was the worst, but it either brought the rest of the street down with it, or I had been remembering the whole place with skewed nostalgia. Monsters wouldn't pop in a place like this, they would fit right in. They did fit right in.

I took a mental picture of the view from the stoop, wondering if I could make the street look even more run down, and paint some overgrown hedges and hanging vines into the shapes of monsters, suggesting their hidden presence. Guardado would probably find something thematically wrong with that too. I turned around and rang the bell, looking to speak to the art teacher who was never disappointed in my work.

I thought I heard the bell chime but didn't hear any movement in the house. I opened the screen and knocked on the door a few times.

"Mr. Sinclair!" I said a few times, increasing the volume with each repetition. Still nothing. I tried the doorknob and felt it spin. No one locks their door in East Hook. I stepped in, cautiously, no longer knowing exactly whose domain I was entering.

Inside was so much worse. Half the walls in the entryway had holes punched in them, with pulverized wood in a pile of powder on the floor beneath, the other half had wallpaper almost entirely peeled off. It wasn't destroyed the way HK's house was, ransacked, looking like a tornado came through. Sinclair's house looked destroyed piece by piece over years. It had been awhile since anything had been cleaned, repaired or replaced.

The outside suggested a squalor the inside more than delivered. The outside also had the advantage of open, moving air. It smelled so bad I almost choked. I went back to the front door to open it wider, see what could circulate in and out through the screen.

The house seemed empty, besides whatever dead animal I was sure I would step on as I checked each room. I called out Sinclair's name a few more times, and still heard nothing. That didn't mean he wasn't home though, I'd come in before stomping and yelling, back in high school, and get no response. There was only one place he could be if he were there, his studio. I turned left into the kitchen.

It was even more torn apart than the entryway. The sink had a tower of dishes and the refrigerator door had rust creeping onto the front from the hinges. Cardboard cereal boxes and plastic chip bags lined the floor and coated the counters. A small, six-inch break in the trash wound its way through the room like a path, stopping at a door.

Mr. Sinclair always used his basement as a studio, and it wasn't one of those walkout basements, it got zero natural light. It also suggested, at least to me, that he kind of wanted to keep that part of his life hidden. I never knew which of those two hurt his art more.

The door to the basement stood like a pure monolith against the destruction of the rest of the kitchen. It was untouched by decay, probably even recently repainted. A familiar symbol stared back at me from eye level. Hand painted in stark black against the white door, not stenciled and spayed: an oblong O with a circular S inside. The symbol from the lock box and the painting at the Splintered Mast. Sinclair's tag.

I staggered a bit as I tried to piece together what he would have to do with the lock box and the Quebecois. I kept moving though, toward the scary thing, and knocked on the door. No answer. I turned the doorknob with a shaky hand, slowly, it wasn't locked. I inched the door open, staying behind it until it was perpendicular with the frame, then stepped behind it and looked down the staircase. It was pitch black, no sign of anyone.

Luckily, there was a light switch at the top of the stairs and when I flicked it, the darkness went away. I listened to hear if anything scurried off or moved with the light, then flicked it on and off four or five times as a signal I probably meant no harm. With the lights firmly on, I made my way down the stairs, not for the first time, but likely the last.

The floor was littered with paper. Mostly tossed aside sketches and some makeshift palates. A lot of swampy greens and slate grays. I had to duck my head under some driftwood nailed over the entrance to the stairwell. I turned around to look at it once I passed under. It was painted white, with the same O and S sign on the left. Next to it was block script, attempting to look like a typewriter font but clearly hand painted, spelling out in all lowercase: original sin. I had officially solved the mystery of the OS tag. I couldn't help myself from scoffing. Some things are more impressive as a mystery.

The room was a small semi-finished walled off section of the basement, painted the same white I remembered, with a teal carpet where you could see it. The ceiling was exposed wood and insulated pipes. A door across from the stair entrance lead to the unfinished section with the boiler, washer/dryer and storage space. It was eight or nine feet across, and about twenty deep, with the lone tiny window above the far end at the back of the house.

A few paintings hung from the walls. Seascapes and East Hook landmarks mostly, with a few blank places where a painting had been taken down. I found myself breathing easier, while this room was a mess, it looked like someone lived and worked here. It didn't have the decay of the upstairs, and smelled like paint and paper, instead of rot. I saw food containers and an overloaded trash can. It felt like Sinclair basically lived down here, which was a relief after imagining he lived in the rooms I had just walked through.

At the end of the room, right under the small window was an easel with a painting near completion. I noticed the greens and grays from the palates and as I got closer, more details started to emerge, each one eerier than the last.

A great old monster, with a tentacled beard and a biped dinosaur body, stood astride downtown East Hook, in the middle of a great storm. Boats were capsized in its wake and the lighthouse towers at the entrance of the harbor were crumbling or cracked. The footbridge between the two sides of downtown ran across the bottom of the painting and in the middle of the bridge on the water side was a pedestal, the only real departure from the actual downtown layout.

The monster was looking at the pedestal, where a thin figure splayed out, in the same posture as the subject in the Wyeth painting in the field. I couldn't tell if it was a man or a woman, it looked like Sinclair hadn't made up his mind, the freshest paint was all in that area, around the head.

I had kept walking closer as I took in the painting and when I got right up next to it I leaned in, trying to see everything. Ropes wound around the monsters, coming out of the water catching it above the knee. Most of these ropes were attached to buoys and lobster traps, some pulled out of the water by the monster's progress toward shore, some cut free. My eyes moved to the lighthouses. I noticed them cracked and crumbling before, but now that I was close I looked at the lamps to see what detail he'd added. Neither lamp was on and both had shadowy, and clearly broken bulbs.

I could have probably found more clues in the painting's details, but my eyes drifted back to the figure on the pedestal. The human sacrifice. I looked at the hair, I looked at the hips, I looked at the clothes. It was skinny but I really couldn't tell. The prescient elements in other parts of the painting turned this into new mystery. Was it Cadie? A sacrifice the deep demanded? Or was it me?

The smell got worse with each step I took back up the stairs. I took my time going up, suddenly feeling like prey that had walked into a trap. Ancient survival instincts took over and I listened to every sound, identified and cataloged every smell, and felt for subtle changes in air pressure. I couldn't focus on my career and the next steps in my life, nor my reputation in town and avoiding difficult conversations with the police and my family. All I could focus on was getting out of there.

I padded up to the kitchen. All the lights that I had turned on were still burning, and the trash was strewn around the floor and counters the same way I remembered it. Sinclair made me dinner once, after some summer art exhibit in town. It was a foreign spicy noodle dish he whipped up on the stovetop while talking to me. I thought he was so worldly and grown-up. I looked over to the table I ate at, only to find it gone. There was a folding chair by the stove, but nothing else. I wondered if the stove even worked.

I didn't bother turning any lights out as I left the room. I kept going down the hall toward the front door when my senses caught something. It wasn't quite a sound, more of a vibration, of a thud upstairs. I stopped, not even breathing, to try and listen for anything else. Instincts were pulling me toward the door, but my mind turned back on and added a bunch of complications. What if someone was planted at the top of the stairs ready to pick me off when I ran by? What if nothing's there, it's just a beat-up house, and I regret not going upstairs forever? What if I charged upstairs, surprising whatever's up there and gained an advantage? What if I stayed perfectly still, except for my hand, which could silently slide my phone out of my pocket and call 911?

Bravery and stupidity are so similar sometimes you can't even tell the difference with a microscope. I did the brave thing. Instead of running for the door, I slowly bent down and picked up a two-foot broken section of floor molding. I did a few quick quarter swings until I was satisfied with the heft. Staying slow and quiet, I started tiptoeing toward the stairs, ears up, waiting for some shift of weight or creaky floorboard to give me more direction. Everything stayed silent.

I'd never been upstairs at Sinclair's house. It probably would have been weird if I had been. Most houses in inland East Hook were variations on like three or four designs though, so I was confident I knew what layout to expect. A bathroom right at the top of the stairs and a bedroom to the right and left, maybe two to the left if he didn't have a master suite. The first stair creaked.

I winced and stopped to hear if anything reacted, but still heard silence. I took a breath, deep and slow, then went up another step. It creaked too. I was amazed the basement ones were so quiet, it really was an oasis in the rubble.

My plan of a sneak attack was shot. "Hello?" I yelled and leaned back down and flicked all the light switches at the bottom of the stairs. The hall light turned off, but the upstairs landing lit up. Whatever the third switch turned on or off must not have been working. I took another step up. It creaked. No response, no shifting posture, nothing indicating life upstairs. I kept the club and started up again more steadily, still wincing at each creak.

The top landing looked like I expected, a battered bathroom straight ahead and a battered door to the right. There were two doors on the left, so it was a three bedroom. Upstairs was carpeted, but still covered with a layer of trash and crumbled drywall. The smell, which I had successfully pushed out of my consciousness while trying to locate my combatant, was too strong to ignore.

Despite having some nicks and dents, all four doors were closed, but only the back left bedroom door had a faint glow spilling out of the base onto the dusty carpet. The lights were on.

"Mr. Sinclair." I yelled through the door. "It's Ellis." One time Ivy snuck up on me when I was listening to music with headphones on and drawing. I was so startled I came within a centimeter of stabbing her with my pencil. I did not want to surprise Sinclair. I dropped the piece of molding and walked to the door. I turned the knob and pushed it open.

It had the same damage as all the other rooms, but a bit more furniture. There was a dresser barely holding itself together and a folding beach chair with cup-holders in the arms. A bedsheet was nailed to the side wall covered with different spray paint designs, and the other walls had some graffiti too. It didn't look like anything Sinclair would have done, was even more amateur. Everything surrounded a double mattress, lying directly on the floor, with blankets hanging off the side.

On top of the mattress, in a tank top and boxers, was Sinclair, lying, unmistakably dead, with a syringe poking out of his foot between the toes.

# Abstract Expressionism

I could tell when I saw him but went through the motions of checking his neck and wrist for a pulse and held my phone beneath his nose to see if he was breathing. His body wasn't cold yet, but colder than it ought to have been. He was so unrecognizable that I couldn't even be shocked. That Mr. Sinclair was not the person I knew, not the person who cultivated my talent and taught me how to be a man, not just a painter.

The suspicions I always carried with me moved to the front of my brain. I must be a fraud. This is the only kind of person who would vouch for me. Of course Guardado didn't think my paintings were any good, he had all his faculties. I was always going to fail. I almost got away with it, came withing an inch of grifting my way through school. I didn't care what this Mr. Sinclair thought about my paintings, but I still regretted he was gone. Just when I got to know the real him, he died. All the questions I had come to his house to ask would never get answered, they'd stay with him, wherever he was, forever.

I found Sinclair's phone on the carpet next to his mattress. I pulled my sleeve up around my hand and picked it up, seeing if it had any juice left. When I saw it did, I held down the button to place an emergency call without leaving any prints.

I touched the speakerphone button through the sleeve and held it in front of my face. When the operator picked up, I got right to the point.

"A man died at twenty-seven Larkspur Ave. Looks like a drug overdose." The dispatch replied asking for more information, but I was distracted by a drop of water that appeared on the phone screen. Before I really recognized what it was, another drop splashed in front of me. The dispatch's voice rose, yelling for my attention, but I just watched the screen, which had become really blurry. I was able to make out another drop fall onto it, right after it rolled down my nose.

I hit End Call, threw the phone on the bed and got the hell out of the house.

Sinclair's place wasn't too far from downtown, and I headed that way, letting the mist wash away the tear tracks on my face. I still had questions, but my main one was if everything was all over now. Did the person who killed Cadie, and frame me just get executed for his crimes? I didn't feel like it was over, but something definitely was.

I got to the main road before I heard sirens and saw flashing lights zoom by. It was just one police car and an ambulance. I put my head down as I walked, not needing any more police attention, but realizing I was being foolish. Had I done anything? I worried that was another question I'd never really get an answer to. Even without a definitive answer, I couldn't ignore the body count I was leaving in my wake. I figured I was better off sticking to back roads and pulled my hood tight around my head.

I had no destination in mind, just distance, and I covered

ground fast. I was totally lost, but luckily there are only a few main roads in East Hook, so only existentially. Before I knew it, I was on the outskirts perched above downtown, a mix of old houses turned Bed & Breakfasts and old convenience stores turned provision shops. I descended into downtown proper, making sure to stick to back streets and alleys where I could. I knew these alleys well, I had marked them with my tag back in the day, a symbol that had been thoroughly corrupted. No doubt feeling morbid, I turned down the small alcove that ran between stores on Main street and stores on the boardwalk to see if any of my tags were still there.

I noticed a lot of fresh paint, like really fresh, probably applied in the last few weeks on most of the buildings. I couldn't figure why they would pick the wet May days to do it, but I guessed it was an annual task most of them did right before the busy season. At one point I had four different tags back there, three done by me and a fourth, slightly sloppier one done by H.K. He had stood too close, moving the spray can with his wrist and elbow instead of arm's length, getting a straight line using just the shoulder. Now it looked like just one remained.

As I got closer to it, everything felt less familiar. It was sloppy, but it wasn't in the same place H.K. had done his five years ago. It was near the end of the alley, behind the last store on the boardwalk side, Harbor Pizza. I had never put one behind Harbor Pizza, and it was about eight feet off the ground, higher than anything I had done back there. I got on my tiptoes to look closer, and the paint looked fresh, even more fresh than the wall paint on the rest of the buildings. It could have been done around the same time as Cadie's headstone. I wondered if Sinclair had done it. He would have needed a stepladder.

I couldn't understand, why had all my tags been painted over only to have new ones crop up in different spots than I painted them? I was too freaked out to continue onto the boardwalk. Even on a foggy Wednesday, it was more people than I was willing to deal with. So I walked back the way I came, down the alcove onto a side street. I looked to one side and saw the harbor, shimmering but still so dark, the looked the other way and saw the Splintered Mast looming halfway up the hill, all the lights turned off. I knew answers probably existed in both, but I wasn't ready for either of them. I darted across main street and ducked behind the stores there, to a small employee parking lot with a community dumpster.

Two of the stores were new, or at least hadn't been there when I was in high school. One was a boutique canvas bag store, the other sold sandals. The third, the middle of the three, was a candy shop, with a taffy puller in the front window, The Sugar Shack. They had a painting of mine at one point, a small one, one I hadn't even titled, featuring a top-down view of a whirlpool, much bigger and forceful than in real life. White churn spiraled around the vortex, with two abandoned kayaks, a broken surfboard and other flotsam spiraling below with it. Underneath the spiral was a white stick, turning the whole thing into a big lollipop. I remembered sketching out a monstrous, tentacled hand holding the sucker, but erased it before I started painting. Hard to believe, but there were times even I was sick of painting tentacles.

Thinking about the painting drew my eyes to the Sugar Shack's back entrance, but as far as I could see the wall was blank. I stepped back to check out the whole back wall of the three attached shops, and saw it, a little further towards the sandal shop than I would have thought. The harbinger of everything this town was gonna take from me, my tag, on the back of a fucking candy store.

I heard footsteps and voices in front of the Splintered Mast. I couldn't make out much in the fog, so I walked closer to see what was going on. It was way too late to be a customer, and too late for normal staff too. I kind of hoped it was one of the Quebecois thugs, I still had a lot of energy I wanted to get out. I also kind of wanted to avoid them totally. It was my town, and I'd spent enough time being chased in the fog to have a few favorite hiding spots and getaway routes.

The footsteps slapped the ground and were getting louder, heading down the hill towards where I'd come out onto the sidewalk. I saw the feet first, decked in sandals with a toe ring. Then the legs, in shiny tight-fitting pants, impossible in the dark to tell if they were leather or stretchy yoga material. Marika was wearing a satin bomber jacket over a dark turtleneck. It was the first time I had seen her without her shoulder and that hammerhead tattoo exposed. Her strides were still confident, as if any part of her could not be, and soon she was close enough to see me too, without the sound to guide her eyes. Her steps slowed for a second, her head tilting down to take in my whole body. I must have passed the once-over, because her pace picked back up almost right away, walking right in my direction.

"You're out late, artist." Her eyes reflected the glare from a streetlight and glowed for an instant as she closed the distance. She had that same smile as she got in close. "I like your new hair."

Everything primal in me pulled my lips up towards a smile, the same parts that quickened my pulse when I saw it was her and she was headed my way. I couldn't manage it though. It wasn't a night for smiling.

"What were you doing at the Splintered Mast? Isn't it closed?"

Her smile only widened, though some of the warmth evaporated. What replaced it was more feline, a more predatory showing of teeth. Her posture shifted, the weight on the balls of her feet. "I know the owners."

Of course she did. Up close I saw a white logo on her turtleneck, poking up from the collar of her satin jacket. Her hair was wet, the curls leaving a droplet trail where they caught her shoulders.

"Yeah, so do I." I should have been peppering her with questions, finally get to interrogate someone as part of my totally botched investigation. But I knew answers wouldn't fix anything that I broke, and the more I got, the worse everything looked. Sometimes it's better if the fog never clears.

I think she was expecting some questions too, and when I could only offer weak agreement as conversation, her posture relaxed again. "I am going to walk across the bridge there." She pointed significantly Southeast of the actual inner harbor bridge, but I knew what she meant. "I have been here one week and haven't done it yet."

We were going to pretend everything was fine. I was more comfortable playing tour guide than interrogator anyway. "The views aren't so impressive this time of year."

She rolled her eyes. "Ahh, painters, so focused…"

I waived her off and said what I was never in a mood to hear, much less that night. "Focused on what something looks like, not what it is."

Without noticing, we had started walking towards the harbor. She spread her arms, "The breeze, and the smells, and the sounds" she looked at my lips "and the taste." The primal feelings weren't as dormant as I thought. I reached out and brushed her elbow with my fingers, then slid them down her forearm to clasp her hand. She made a point to look around. "Your haunted little town does not feel like anywhere else."

"It's only a matter of time. It's turning into everywhere else." Mad as the mist and snow.

Her eyes stayed on me as we walked. "Not tonight."

We walked through the mist, past the shops and restaurants with my paintings in them, past the alleys and dumpsters spray-painted with my EH tag. Past a wet white sign with big red letters, telling me something I had known forever.

Marika seemed lighter; her footsteps didn't fall with the same force. She wasn't bouncing anymore, she was gliding. Her head kept tilting up into the mist, watching it fall, so fine it was almost a shimmer, past the few streetlights on Main street.

She squeezed my hand and I noticed her smiling at me, less alluring and more playful, like we knew each other better than we did. My muscles weren't going to produce a matching smile, but I still met her eyes. "Tell me about the snake."

It wasn't what I expected to hear. "The snake?"

Her smile kept growing. "The water snake..." She squinted, working her brain, then her eyes got wide in recognition. "Fang!"

My mouth muscles were starting to forget everything that happened and were on their way to matching her smile, stopping just short. I looked back ahead, not trusting myself to keep looking at her eyes. "Foamfang?"

"Yes! Foamfang." I stayed looking ahead, and she squeezed my hand again. We were almost at the bridge. "Tell me about him."

I wanted to ask where she heard that name, making her tell me it was the Splintered Mast, bringing the topic back up. But instead I just assumed she heard it in one of the other hundred places in town that only knew how to talk about sea monsters, especially that week. She probably knew more about him than I did by then, but I told her anyway, same as I told Ivy and everyone else who really wanted to understand my hometown.

"He was a dinosaur, one of the few survivors when the asteroid hit a million years ago. He was at the bottom of the sea at the time, and that's what spared him. He saw a bright flash, but by the time he made it up to the surface all he saw was fire and ash and all his friends dead.

"Dinosaurs were rough customers, all they knew was battle, all they respected was strength. Foamfang thought whatever happened to his friends was something stronger than he could imagine, but instead of respecting it, he grew to hate it. He mourned his friends by obsessing over the great death-bringer, attacking everything still left under the sea and getting stronger, swearing that when it came back, he would win the fight, get revenge for his friends."

I hadn't been looking at Marika, so I just heard her snort, then giggle. "I am very glad I asked." We stepped onto the bridge, surrounded on both sides by the fog. I was right, there wasn't much to see, but I knew what was out there. "Does he get his revenge?"

"No, he gets confused. He's so focused on getting stronger underwater that he doesn't notice the environment above the surface changing above him. Humans arrive on the shores, later visitors from the new world start building towns on the banks. Ships start floating over his head, but he stays under, focused on an enemy he'd never see. One day, he gets what he's been waiting for, what he's devoted his life to, he sees a bright flash above water. His training and will drive him up, fangs out, towards the monster, and when he breaks the surface he sees something moving quickly, big as some dinosaurs he remembers but with no noticeable head or teeth or claws. Running on instinct and training, he dives again to come up at it from underneath, coils and strikes from below, smashing this thing to pieces, causing little squirming parasites to fall off the side. He swallows most of them whole once they hit the water, and swims away, disappointed this great enemy didn't put up more of a fight, but satisfied he prevented another apocalypse."

I was picturing it out in the fog, a battle at sea between a fearsome, hateful, trained monster and an unsuspecting prey. Marika was looking out into the fog too, leaning against the bridge railing. "But he was confused."

I nodded, wanting to wrap up the story before I saw too much else in the fog. "The flash wasn't from an asteroid or an explosion, it was from a newly built lighthouse. Horn Light, out that way." I pointed Southeast. "And Foamfang tore through a ship carrying a cargo of mostly corn with a twenty-person crew."

"He ate them? They were the parasites?" Marika looked back at me, hoping she was wrong but knowing she wasn't.

"Yep. And he did it three more times. Thinking he was

saving the world every time."

"So many shipwrecks in this bay. Have you been in one?" She probably meant to tease, but now I was seeing another wreck in the fog, looking much more recently into the past than anything Foamfang caused.

"My friend was in one yesterday."

Marika didn't gasp, didn't straighten up, didn't even ask if he was ok. I wondered if she heard me, she was looking out into the fog, transfixed, seeing something as clearly as I had. Keeping her eyes focused on it, she said, in a quiet voice, "I have been in two."

"Did a giant sea serpent cause them?"

"Some monster fucking did."

We stood together, transfixed by the fog, and the histories we saw in it. She broke first, turning to look at me. "Why are you out tonight Ellis?"

"My friend died tonight. And maybe he wasn't my friend." I couldn't explain what I saw at his house, and how it fit together with my paintings and the Quebecois, but some shapes were forming from the gray.

Marika's posture stiffened, and her eyebrows went up. "In a shipwreck?"

"That one's in a coma."

"You were here for the funeral of a friend Saturday?" She shook her head. "It is a bad week to be your friend."

No kidding. "Are we friends?"

She laughed. "No, certainly not." She gestured down the bridge. "You are no friend! Walk that way, across the bridge! I want some water between us."

"Don't blame you." I put my hands up in surrender and started backing down the planks, waiting for her to call my bluff. No part of her moved. I turned around to start walking in earnest, feeling like the slight sting of the mist on my face was well earned.

"Only thing is…" Her voice rode on the fog, it sounded like she was right next to me whispering. I turned around to see her leaning in the same spot, fifteen feet away, shoulders back. "My place is on this side."

I shuffled back trying to keep a look on my face like I didn't hear or didn't understand, but the pace surely gave me away. When I got close I grabbed the railing on either side of her, leaned in until I could smell the cinnamon, and stared into her eyes. I watched tiny mist droplets fall onto the pale green and disappear, like light Florida rain falling onto a lagoon. Marika blinked and I heard her, barely, more feeling the breath of her words on my lips. "I am not your friend Ellis." I tilted my chin forward to meet her mouth just as she finished saying my name. I liked it better when she called me the artist.

Her kisses consumed me, every inhale took in a part of my soul, whatever parts remained. I returned her passion, but in a more scared and desperate way, clinging to her like a life preserver. I was afraid that if I let go, I wouldn't touch anyone else ever again. Since the last time Marika and I kissed, short as it was, my human physical contact was practically zero. My mother cradled my head as she cut my hair at the salon two days before, Rocco's mom hugged me to share her grief at the hospital yesterday, Cadie's dad put his arms on my shoulder at his house earlier. I ached for Marika, everything about her was pulling me closer, but even holding onto her physical form and feeling her heartbeat through her skin, she made the world feel less real, not more.

I didn't break away though, I didn't even ease my grip. After some time, who knows how long, she gave me a gentle push and pulled her head back to whisper in my ear. "We can walk back to the store."

The world felt real again, the world where I was in real danger. "The Splintered Mast?"

She didn't pick up on my vibes. "Yes, I believe they have a back room."

"I know for a fact they do."

Her eyebrows went up, like she was impressed. "Let us get out of the rain."

Even with everything I knew, I thought about it, tried to find some loophole and some way I could be smart enough for it to work. I got really smart. I called the taxi company to bring me home. Caleb was already downtown, so he was able to get to the bridge in a few minutes. Marika looked even more impressed when she realized what I was doing, and a little hurt.

"So we are friends." I could still see her eyes through the mist, but they no longer glowed. "Fuck."

"No." I shook my head, completely sincere. "You're something else entirely Marika." I'd probably never know what.

I saw her posture stiffen, the tension returning to her body as she gathered herself. She ran her hand through her hair a few times and straightened out her clothes, casting glances at me throughout. "Take care of yourself, Ellis. The world needs more artists." I took one more look at her eyes, the mist made it look like she was crying.

"East Hook doesn't." Caleb pulled up next to us and I felt my phone vibrate.

We kissed goodnight in the road next to the car and I got

in. The windows were too foggy to see her once I shut the door, but I thought I saw a dark outline wave.

When I got back to my mother's place I was disappointed to see all the lights off. I had hoped she'd be up waiting for me. I debated waking her up, I wanted to talk about Dad. Instead I went downstairs to my room, not turning any lights on, making my way through the familiar pitch black to my bed.

I slept. I didn't dream about anything; I was way too tired. I could have slept twelve more hours, and intended to, but the peel of my phone broke through. It was loud enough to wake me, and I noticed it, but was too groggy to figure out what I was supposed to do about it. By the time I realized it was my phone ringing, it was too late to answer or look at who was calling me, or even what time it was. I wasn't looking to move too much, it felt like the back of my head was chained to the pillow, so I figured I would let that mystery wait until the morning. The top suspects were a spam call, wrong number or a pissed off, high Guardado.

The comfortable fog started swirling in again, ready to take me back to dreamland when the phone beeped, not a ring, but a message. The fog burned off and about twenty seconds later, it beeped again. Without lifting my head, I slapped my hand on my desk until it found the edge of the phone and I grabbed it to look. I was holding it about eight inches above my face while I tried to focus on the message. It was from Desmond. It was a picture. It didn't make sense to me at first but as I slowly figured out what was going on I almost dropped my phone on my face. I sat up and took a closer look.

In the picture, Desmond was sitting down in a short-sleeved

shirt, his eyes almost all the way closed. Around his right arm was a tied-off piece of rubber tubing. His face was blank, his mouth was hanging open and it looked like the back of the chair was the only thing keeping his head up. There was a message below the picture, I hadn't bothered to look at it and just zoomed into the image, but when I noticed it I saw just three letters: SOS. Frantic, I didn't know who to call, but figured 911 was the best choice. I took another look at the picture, disturbed by everything I saw, but probably most by the fact that both his hands were in the picture. This wasn't a selfie.

The phone started ringing. It was Desmond.

"Desmond!" I only heard breathing on the other end, slow breathing. A muffled voice was muttering in the background, and then I heard louder groaning.

"Huh?" The same muffled voice came back, but I couldn't understand a word. "Ellis?" Desmond practically shouted. "Ellis are you there?"

He could talk at least.

"Yes Desmond! I'm here! Are you ok?"

He didn't answer for a minute. I heard rustling then the muffled voice came through, clear as a restored masterwork. "Ellis, are you listening." Un-muffled, the voice was deep, with some accent. "Confirm you can hear me."

Maybe I was still asleep. The nightmare I've been in wasn't over. "Who is this?"

"Your friend took too much, just like your other friend Oliver." Sinclair. "I have a dose of Narcan and a dose of fentanyl, you choose which one I give him."

"What do you want? Keep him alive!" My voice broke into a yelled sob.

The voice on the other line was bloodless, continued in its monotone. "You have fifteen minutes to get to the Splintered Mast."

The Quebecois, not from Quebec, and not interested in bringing an Elder God up from the depths, wanted to meet. They'd taken their shots and hit everyone around me, now their aim was true.

# Brutalism

I rode with Andy to the Splintered Mast. I had waited for him in my mother's kitchen without turning any lights on to make sure I didn't wake her up. Looking out from the darkness I saw his headlights sweep into her yard, cutting through the mist like a lighthouse, its beam again finding something dead in the water.

Andy was too alert and energetic for the hour, I wondered what kind of stimulant he was on. I didn't see any coffee in his cupholder. "Hey Ellis, how's it going?" All I could do was shrug. He grinned. "I know you're a morning person, but this is a little earlier than normal." It was three AM.

He was still looking at me, so I just nodded.

"Going back to the same place?" I'd taken so many cab rides, I hadn't realized that I was, and I was having him drop me off at the same location: the street behind the Splintered Mast. I tried to remember what kind of mood I was in on the last trip there, what long-term plans I had, and which friends weren't in mortal peril.

"Yeah, getting an early start."

Andy and I had shared some deep conversations that week, so he felt more comfortable prying. "Nothing open down there now."

I remembered last time I rode with him I didn't want to lie to him, this time I didn't give a shit. "Yeah well I'm leaving tomorrow and dropped my keys at Shanty's when I was there earlier. I actually rode back with Caleb a few hours ago." Andy nodded; he saw every call that came in. "One of the bartenders found it during close and is still there, not gonna wait forever for me to come grab them." Shanty's was always the last bar to close, but I knew three AM was pushing it.

He seemed to buy it, laughing to himself. "That would have sucked if you didn't notice until you went to leave."

"Yeah I was lucky." I almost couldn't get the last word out. What was the point of pretending to be someone with a future to worry about? I could no longer imagine a life where calling a locksmith was some great tragedy.

Andy tried to start a conversation a few more times but I wasn't present enough to hold up my end. My head was in the future, what I could do or say at the Splintered Mast to stay alive. I started thinking through what a plan would look like, realizing that I was way too late. I didn't know anything, much less enough to have anything on the Quebecois. I tried to come up with something I could have on them, some leverage or surprise. Nearing the end of the trip, I broke a few minutes of silence for some last-minute desperation cramming.

"Do you know where to get heroin here?"

Andy looked even more alert than before; his eyes almost left his skull. He looked back a few times through the rearview mirror and turned around to look at me to see if I was serious. I met his eyes each time, ready to repeat myself if I needed to.

"No, Ellis." He kept driving, shaking his head every few minutes until we arrived.

In the alley behind the Splintered Mast, I noticed Sinclair's OS tag to the left of the store's rear entrance at about shoulder height. It wasn't stenciled, and I could see bulges in both letters where the trace wasn't precise. I was always too hard on Sinclair's work, it felt too transparent what he was trying to do, and what kept him from being able to quite get there. I knocked on the back door and reached out and touched my palm to the tag, letting it linger there until I heard the lock turn.

A familiar face greeted me on the other side. Officer Methot, my arresting officer at the Lincoln Head estate, out of uniform, waved me inside.

"What's in your pockets?" He wasted no time in patting down my sides, slapping into my ribs a little harder than he needed to. I knew this was going to be rough as soon as I got off the phone, I just didn't know what I'd be able to stand.

He found my phone and lifted it out of my pocket. He waved it in front of my face before dropping it inside his jacket with one eyebrow raised. Once it was secure, he patted his chest over it and said "We're gonna take a look through this in a minute." He finished patting me down, taking time on the ankles and wrists, then finishing by touching every part of my chest and stomach. When he was satisfied he mumbled under his breath, "No gun, no knives, no wire, guess you just came to talk." Both his eyebrows were up as he grabbed my shoulder and started marching me through the dark storage room towards the lit back office.

"Where's Desmond?" I said as we walked.

"Sleeping it off at his house. I'd recommend he drinks lots of water tomorrow." They were never going to kill him. Part of me knew that all along. I had come because I needed to know, even if it was only for the night.

What I could see of the objects stacked on the shelves was only enough to make me walk as close to the center of the aisle as possible. There's a lot of eerie stuff in the backroom of a shipwreck store in the dark. I wrapped myself in my fear of the darkness and the unknown like a security blanket. It kept me distracted from my fear of what was waiting for me in the light, what was really happening to me. If I didn't think I was better off being snatched up by an inter-dimensional being and pulled me into the void then, I was sure I would prefer it in five minutes.

There were four of them in the room, two sitting behind the desk and two standing behind them. None of them were wearing the fake pincers. All the clutter littering the office when I had been there two days before was gone. Everything was cleared and polished, all the paper was organized in trays, cabinets and drawers. I wondered if all the bills for DW Inc were filed in a D folder somewhere. All the writing on the whiteboards had been erased.

No one moved much when I walked in with Methot, though their eyes all lifted towards me. He guided me to one of the seats in front of the desk and put pressure on my shoulders to sit me down. He took his hands off my shoulders but stayed standing close behind me. One of the goons standing behind the desk walked around to the door, shut it and stood in front of it with his arms clasped. The room felt smaller and at the same time the entirety of my world. I knew there was a chance I'd never leave it. I had resigned myself to pay the piper, but now that payment might be due, I knew I wasn't ready for it.

One of the sitting goons, presumably the leader, or the

one with the best English, looked around the room, as if confirming everybody was in position, then pushed a button on a round white device on the desk. The smooth static of white noise filled the room. I wondered who they were worried was listening. Satisfied everything was ready, he slowly looked back at me and spoke in a low purr, with somewhat of a French accent and none of the flourish.

"What do you know?"

He might as well have been sporting real pincers, I was scared stiff. I tried to find my voice and squeaked out, "I know..." I cleared my throat and tried to sound normal, despite all the moisture evaporating from my mouth. "I know I want to live." It was pathetic. I caught the goon leaning back against the wall on his elbows smile when he heard it. Nothing demonstrative from the two sitting down, but their eyes had a crinkle. The same one spoke as before.

"That depends what you know." He looked behind me at Officer Methot then the goon guarding the door but didn't change his expression. I considered what I did know and considered what they knew I knew.

"I know you've been using my paintings as waypoints to distribute heroin."

Two of the three in front of me frowned in confusion. The speaker caught the look and showed a thin smile, like he was amused. "Waypoints, like on a chart. Very nautical." His amusement faded quickly, and he motioned for me to go on. He wanted more of what I knew.

"I know whoever owns this building and your Drydon place owns a mansion out on Lincoln Head." The interrogator flicked his hand up off the table, like this information was nothing to him.

I was floundering, I decided to switch strategies, start using the forum to try out my theories, at least get some answers before I joined the deep.

"You're signaling someone with those pincers you all wear."

"What pincers?" A few of them laughed.

"You killed Sinclair, you tried to kill Rocco, and your heroin killed Cadie O'Reilly and probably the other two who ended up in the bay."

This one made more of an impact. Everyone looked around at each other with just their eyes. Their bodies were perfectly still. The speaker looked to his left, trying to telepathically confirm the right approach, and apparently got his answer, because he sighed deeply and spoke.

"Your friend Sinclair is not your friend, and your friend Rocco is not your friend, you know this right?"

"What do you mean?" I jumped in almost before he finished talking. I was caught between not quite believing him and needing to know what the hell he was talking about immediately.

"It was Oliver Sinclair's idea to use your paintings as a waypoint, once we couldn't use cell phones," he paused to allow me time to appreciate his use of my word. "And his idea to frame you for all the vandalism. A performance art project for your final at art school." Now I believed him. I should have known at the first sign, the sloppy spray paint on Cadie's grave. The mist had lifted, only to show the monsters more clearly. The desperate ones with no choice, and the indifferent ones making a choice about me.

"What about Rocco?"

"The big man confronted these two, telling them you had been on our property and pulled up our buoy." He turned to the others and said something that sounded like Arabic, and they all laughed. When they finished their chuckle, he shrugged at me and said. "We noticed our last delivery was a little light, now we know why."

It took me a minute to get the joke, but when I did I leaned forward and almost shouted. "You think I took some? There were no drugs in there when we pulled it up, just laminated paintings!"

This didn't draw any laughs, though it did bring a smile to the interrogator's face. "We do not trust artists here anymore. Your friend Sinclair stole from us, tried to buy on credit, owed us, and made things right by giving us overly complicated solutions to simple problems, like your friend Cadie O'Reilly."

During his speech about artists, the goon leaning against the wall in front of me coughed and when he moved his arm to cover his mouth with his hand his elbow slipped off the wall and he lost his balance. He slid down to the right about a foot before catching himself and straightening out. Both the seated the goons turned around, almost at the same time to glare at him. He looked embarrassed, then nodded and stood up straight, his eyes scanning the room for a comfortable place to settle.

I relaxed a little, finally understanding the weird energy in room. Everything was a show with these people. The costumes, the paintings, whatever intimidation this tableau was supposed to inspire, all came up just short of being convincing. They were well matched with Sinclair, the same tacky aspirations, and the inability to quite reach them.

After the short interruption, the speaker continued. "We gave him too many chances, and he almost cost us everything. So we did the simple solution. Now, we have a new artist, and a new, simple solution.

I had it backwards, I hadn't come up just one credit short in Art School, I'd been there far too long. Seeing through their facade and picking it apart was not a victory. I was trapped in a room with dangerous killers who could kill me a hundred different ways and intended to and I had convinced myself that they were the real fools.

"I know what you want the final act in the performance art to be." As if he hadn't already just told me.

The interrogator looked glad he didn't have to say it. "What is it?"

"My human sacrifice suicide in the water." Saying it out loud made it truer than it had been before, and I started looking around the room for sharp objects and other ways I could make my last stand. The place was spotless, by design.

The speaker spread his hands and nodded like I guessed right, and it pained him. He was about to confirm it for me out loud but him saying it would have made it even more real, and I wasn't ready for that. I cut him off as his lips started forming the death sentence.

"It won't work though. I've already said your name to the cops."

The group looked up behind me at Methot. I tried to tilt my head back enough to see him too. When he laughed, my head went back down. I was running out of places to look.

"He accused you of being a sea monster cult and cutting traps, nothing about drugs."

I was running out of cards to play. Remembering Methot was in the room sprung another option to mind. A card I had saved for a long time.

"My father was a cop here, who drowned in the water when

I was nine." I looked back at Methot. Now he was looking at the ground. "He died saving someone's life. The cops aren't going to just back-burner his son dying the same way. They'll come after you."

They looked back at Methot. I kept looking forward. "He's right. His dad was a cop who drowned saving somebody." He went quiet, probably trying to think through how the investigation would go. "You guys are clean. You'd have alibis and you aren't anywhere near anything tying you to it. I'll be there…"

"Walking by my dad's picture every day, covering up his son's murder." I had been looking to cut him off once he mentioned my dad. I had finally gotten too bold. I felt a blow come down on the crown of my head, bit through the side of my tongue and felt my neck compress a few inches. My vision shimmered and I was having trouble focusing. I heard shuffling behind me, like someone was keeping Methot from hitting me again. Iron-tasting blood was filling my mouth and I knew it would just be the start if I spit it over the pristine desk in front of me. I brought my arm up to my mouth, heavy as it was feeling, and basically just drooled my blood onto the sleeve, hoping it would absorb.

Before I got a good look at the damage to my clothes I heard multiple gasps. Apparently people were watching me. I heard yelling in the same twisted Arabic and heard the door open. I turned to follow the sounds but was still moving to slow to catch anything more than the door closing again. A hazy drumbeat got steadily louder. A fast one-two repeating until it started to form, from hums, to sounds, to syllables. "Ellis!" Someone was yelling my name "Ellis!"

I was coming out of the fog, but it lingered in the corners

of my vision, like I was living in a wide aperture photo. My mouth was filling up with blood again, but I recognized at a slower pace. Still, I reached my sleeve up to repeat the draining process when something grabbed my bicep and forced it down.

"Ellis! Stop. We are bringing towels and water for you." I think it was the normal speaker who said it, but his voice was softer.

"Yeah keep your mouth shut. Should've done it in the first place." I knew who said that, and I followed everyone's directions, more aware of what would happen to me if I didn't.

By the time one of the thugs came back with a mug filled with well water and five paper towels, there was hardly any fog. In fact, the silence was a gift. I wasn't reacting to something every second and could think through the situation and what they wanted. I drank what I could and swished the last sip around my mouth and spit it back into the mug. I wasn't bleeding anymore, but my tongue was a little swollen. Not too swollen to try a new approach, but too swollen to make my point clearly.

"You have it backwawdsh." Everyone looked up at me for breaking the silence, confused about what I was getting at. "You are getting more thweathening, when you should be getting lesh." The softness I was treated with after the hit persisted, allowing me to keep going. "I know how people pershieve art like this. If you get more intensh and end with a death, you're a psychopath. If you get more whimshical, then the bad stuff gets chalked up to going to far." My tongue, and my head, were feeling lighter, it was like I was back in class, critiquing the latest installment in the park, or planning a group project.

Even the interrogator made for a fine lecturer, challenging my viewpoints. "We told you. We are done with artists. They comp..."

"Oliver Shinclair is not an artist!" I yelled my interruption, surprised this of all things is what made me snap. I knew it had more to do with gradually reaching a breaking point than extra sensitivity to the topic.

I stood up, wobbly at first, but my footing held. Methot took a step towards me to force me down by my shoulders but I swiveled under them and took three unsteady steps to the whiteboard. By the time I got there all four of the Algerians were standing as well, but relaxed when I grabbed and uncapped a purple dry erase marker. They didn't have indigo or eminence, but I knew it would more than serve. I drew a horizontal S curve with a curl embellishment at one end. I drew a second curve starting at the end of the embellishment following the first curve while slowly widening the space between the lines. Then I drew a third curving line in between them, never quite halfway and disappearing before the curvy end. My lines were steady, I would have to take a much harder blow to the head to throw off my sketching. I drew quick circles, ovals and cylinders in between two of the lines for suckers, then started crosshatching shadows assuming an upper left corner single light source, like the moon, instead of a boat's headlamp, and how they reflected off the various curves and surfaces. I left spots near the top of the curls white, to suggest moisture reflecting, and added shading and depth to the suckers. The tentacle was a little too horizontal, I'd need to add another curl to have it coming up from somewhere or add the kraken head it could be originating sideways from.

Needing to make a decision always stopped me in my tracks.

When I knew what I wanted to do, I could go for hours without looking up. I never needed Ivy's headphones to block out the world when I needed to concentrate. Once I had to figure something out, solve some problem, anything could distract me, especially a room full of drug dealers I had to convince not to kill me.

I had some idea that only a few minutes had passed, and when I turned around, I saw their attention hadn't yet flagged. Those standing had inched behind me, leaning as close to my shoulder as they could. The seated thugs sat forward in their chairs, tilting their heads to try and see around me. It seemed like the sideways tentacle coming from nowhere was enough.

"Something else I know. I know you had a tentacle Sinclair drew for you right here." I pointed to the board just a few inches over where mine was. "How long did it take him?"

No one answered immediately, kept looking at the drawing. I looked at the one who had been speaking for an answer, but it was the one by the door who spoke up, with an almost no accent and higher voice. "A whole day." Everyone's attention followed mine and he moved his head to address the two seated. "And he had a picture open he was referencing the whole time. He kept looking back and forth." He smiled as he finished the story, and a few of the others snorted. I wondered if there was another way I could have proved my point without humiliating Sinclair one last time.

"I'm a trained artist. I can do higher quality work in a fraction of the time. I know what people are looking for. This is how I can help you."

The Algerians were able to settle back into practicality quicker than I had hoped. Their leader spoke for them. "How does art help us."

271

I looked back at the tentacle, wondering what I could have done differently to impress them for longer. "We do one more event. Less destructive, less in the way, something the town can show off when the summer folk arrive next week." The idea had been forming in my head since I saw Sinclair's Cthulhu painting in his studio. I just needed to refine my pitch.

"Then this whole episode gets chalked up to a disturbed, but well-meaning artist, not a murderer. And Sinclair was right, at the end, it has to be me." Whatever the penalty for cutting all those traps and destroying federal lighthouse property, it was better than getting found in the bay by the harbormaster or a lobsterman. I wasn't planning on taking the rap for blowing Rocco's boat up, but I still didn't know how that happened.

Most of them were shaking their heads, but the one by the door stepped forward and started speaking in the language only they understood. It seemed like he was trying to convince them of something but wasn't gaining much ground. It never got too passionate, but these were cold blooded killers, so it probably took more than artistic disputes to get them riled up. After a few minutes of back and forth that had me completely tuned out, the other seated thug, silent the entire time, switched to English and looked at me. His voice was soft, his accent thicker, and his tone so completely without emotion it shook me. "What is the event?"

# VIII

# Thursday

# Synthetism

The preparations didn't take long. The Algerians followed direction well, especially from someone who was basically their prisoner. Completely their prisoner, I hadn't left the Splintered Mast for a full twenty-four hours. They supervised a few texts I sent responding to my mother and Desmond. I was glad I blocked HK before entering the store.

They kept me fed, running to different stores to get me all three meals while I worked. One of them was always on hand, like a butler, except in addition to making sure I had what I needed they stayed close enough so they could quickly stab me if I tried to scream loud enough for the customers out front to hear me. Even though I hadn't slept, the day went fast, I had a project to distract me.

At first they were skeptical of my idea, supposing it lacked the danger to connect it to the other stuff in people's minds. I kept repeating the need to tone things down. I also sketched out how in the right wind it could be lethal, something none of their events, including blowing up Rocco's boat, had accomplished.

They agreed to go ahead, but with a patience that reminded me of how you agree to go along with whatever a little kid wants to do in the last hour before naptime. It was the same way with the takeout they brought me; they asked what my favorite dish at my favorite breakfast place was, then the same for lunch. For dinner they went to my favorite restaurant, a little Italian place miles from downtown, on the river, ordered the risotto, then immediately boxed it and brought it to me. I kept resisting, telling them was I wasn't hungry, that I just wanted a sandwich or pizza, but they insisted, pulling out all the stops for my last meal.

As we planned and put together what materials we'd need, I tried to nonchalantly ask about how they accomplished the other earlier ones. There wasn't so much mystery around smashing lighthouse bulbs, but I was legitimately curious about how they cut all those lobster pot lines in a few hours, and especially how they exploded Rocco's boat without a fire. They never bit though, almost always just ignoring my questions. Occasionally I'd get waved off and one of them would point to the plans, urging me to stay on task. I wasn't given free rein to walk around the store, and the only potential clues I could see were a black wetsuit and four or five handguns.

Our plans weren't ambitious, and no one would wonder how we did it. The only part that could trip us up was the actual installations at the sites, but I wasn't worried about getting caught. Running into a cop, the right one, was looking like my best shot at getting out.

The materials were easy to gather; two of the thugs went to two separate superstores, both about thirty minutes away in opposite directions. Each bought four sets of green King size bedsheets. One bought a sewing machine and the other a fabric scissors and an Exact-o knife. We put a couple tables together for a workstation and laid my sketches on top.

Once everything was set up, I manned the sewing machine, rolling the sheets into a tube with a little less than a two-foot diameter. I had to sew two seams in each one because I wanted the fabric to make two loops, to give the tubes at least a little structure, and they weren't wide enough to make it all the way around twice. I cut the fitted sheets in each set and turned them sideways to make shorter, wider cylinders. For the pillowcases, I took half of them and just sliced open the top seam and they became easy tubes. The other half I folded the top corners together and sewed a seam down vertically and diagonally, making a closed off triangle end.

Before sewing the tubes together I slid a piece of cardboard, no need to send out for that as the Splintered Mast backroom had plenty of it, down the center of the tube. Then I chose a side and started cutting holes of varying sizes into the sheets with the Exact-O knife. No circle was perfect, but better and faster than it would have been with scissors. When I joined the first batch of tubes together, I realized they weren't nearly long enough, so I sent a few thugs back out to buy eight more sets, at different stores if possible. The greens didn't have to match exactly, they just needed to be longer.

The plan was to hang one of the tubes with the pointed ends on each side of the centers of four bridges around East Hook: the two into Big Hook, the inner harbor bridge downtown that connected East Town and West Town and the outer harbor bridge that connected just north of downtown. Even though only the inner harbor bridge is primarily for pedestrians, there were sidewalks and railings on all four bridges. The plan was to tie the top of the tube to the top rail, and the bottom side to the lower rail. I assured them it would take a special knot to tie them off with the right level of slack and couldn't describe the knot whenever they asked.

The tubes were sewn together at angles, so when they hung limp they should look kind of like tentacles. Maybe a little too geometric if someone were close enough, but they wouldn't be confused for anything else. They would never hang limp though; ocean breezes would whistle into the sucker shaped holes I cut and keep them squirming and writhing like real tentacles. Gale force winds, like the ones that were coming to drive the fog out, would fill the whole structure and send them waving around, potentially above the bridge line and maybe even into the road. This was the lethal scenario I suggested was a possibility, maybe a strong wind would send one of the tentacles onto the windshield of a car and it would spin off the bridge.

I wasn't too worried about beating a manslaughter rap in that scenario. Partly because I knew my odds of making it to that point lessened every minute I stayed with the Algerians. But mostly because none of them would ever actually get tied to anything.

We pulled up to the Island bridge and I told Officer Methot to pull over right in the middle of it. When the car stopped, he stayed behind the wheel, wondering whether to leave his headlights on or not. The fog that night wasn't just pea soup, it was cement. The bridge was narrow, a tight squeeze when cars passed each other going different directions and had only four feet of shoulder. I knew he wouldn't want to draw any more attention than he had to, and a car with its lights on pulled over in the middle of a bridge would prompt any well-meaning, unhurried and not especially fearful driver to at least look twice.

Leaving the lights off in the fog was more likely than not to cause a collision with any car that passed. Also less than ideal on a narrow bridge.

"Change of plans." Office Methot said as he put the car back in gear and slowly drove us forward until we were off the bridge and onto Big Hook, never leaving the shoulder. He went about a hundred yards onto the island before pulling over where the shoulder was a lot wider, entirely off the road. "We'll walk it" he announced as he shut the car off and popped the trunk. He patted his chest, where he'd already showed me he kept his gun. "Wait here. I'll open the door for you."

After he got out, he came around the front of the car, keeping his eyes on me the whole way through the windshield. When he opened the door he grabbed me by the arm and pulled me out of the car. I didn't make it too tough for him. I stepped out and let him shut the door behind me. He pushed me forward, back towards the open trunk.

"Grab 'em." Is all he said into my ear while standing so close behind me we were almost touching. He wasn't going to give me an inch. I bunched up one of the fabric tentacles into my arms then spooled a second into my arms. Nothing was too heavy, so I was able to reach for the zip ties and grab six of them. My hands full, Methot pushed me aside while grabbing a fistful of my jacket. And shut the trunk with his other hand. His grab on my jacket turned into a push, in the direction of the bridge. So that's where I went, the crooked cop with me step for step.

D for Deadman, W for Walking.

He clicked on a flashlight, and the beam illuminated nothing but a wall of gray. We only needed to see down to our feet, making sure we stayed on the edge of the road. It was slow going with my arms full of sewn bedsheets, and my hands full of zip ties, but we didn't have far to go.

Pretty soon the ground turned from pavement and dirt to the block cement of the bridge sidewalk. The gray was different on the bridge, brighter and emptier than on land. I felt like I was in the middle of it, that every step was just a platform suspended in the eternal mist and one misstep and I'd dissipate fully, finally joining it. The platforms kept appearing though, and we made it to the middle of the bridge.

I put down the fabric and two of the zip ties, keeping two in my hands. Methot was still not giving me much room, if anything he was even closer, trying to watch what I did so I wasn't needed for the other seven. I figured he was planning to let me put the first one on and then the second on the other side. I tried to obscure what I was doing with my hands with my back, hunching over the two bars I was supposed to tie off.

I wouldn't get to the second one, once he saw the secret knot method. I looped a tie through the B hole I'd cut in the base of the fabric, then wrapped it around the lower railing and ran it through the clasp. I saw the beam of the flashlight Methot was shining on my hands move up and away, like he was surprised that was all there was too it.

"This is the hard part, keep that on me." I scolded him, trying to act like a temperamental artist at work. When he adjusted it back towards me, I shook my head and my hands. "No keep it focused on the second rail there. I stood up, keeping a hand on the top rail, to more clearly point to where I needed the light, telling him to move a little farther back so I could see more.

Though clearly annoyed, Methot took direction well, and took a step back. He was still only eighteen inches from me, but his momentum was on his back foot and both hands were on the flashlight. Free of his touch for the first time since we left the car I jumped back, turned and put both hands on the rail, and threw myself over it, into the omnipresent mist. I had finally ignored my father's advice and all the signs, I was going in the water, ready to find out exactly what was down there.

The bridge was high enough that I had time to notice the mist droplets hit my face as I fell. When I hit the water, which I was almost certain would be deep enough to prevent a major accident, my whole body clenched from the cold. It was difficult to concentrate on anything else, then my foot hit something moving.

I couldn't be sure which way I was oriented, but I figured I stayed facing the same way since hitting the water. When I started swimming up, I also stroked forward so when I popped up there was a little distance between me and the bridge. Not that Methot would be able to see me either way, the fog was too thick. He would be able to hear me though. I broke the surface and when I opened my eyes I was in the middle of a cloud. I couldn't see more than five feet in any direction, and what I did see was too dark to make any sense of.

I could hear Methot yelling my name, surprised by how faint it was. He couldn't have been able to distinguish the noise I made when I surfaced from the surf washing on the rocks. I treaded water as I located the direction the shouting was coming from, and once I located it, started paddling in the other direction. I had to keep swimming away, even though every molecule in my body was screaming to get me out of the water.

It felt like my body temperature went down one degree every minute I was in there. I hadn't swum since high school, and even then, it was never for long. My arms were a different kind of tired than I was used to, and my lack of form was causing me to overuse them. I started kicking my legs more to share the load, conscious of the sound but understanding it probably didn't matter. The higher legs kicks pushed my face down into the water, and I had to start turning my head.

Putting one arm in front of the other wasn't just difficult because of muscle fatigue or cold shock, every movement I made had me fighting my body, as all my muscles were petrified with fear. Seeing nothing gave my imagination too much to work with. I was seeing movements on the water and in the sky and feeling things below. Every piece of rope or seaweed I brushed past could be the tentacle that pulled me under. It made too much sense for me to die in the bay, just like my father, just like Cadie, just like all the innocent, unlucky people in my art. If the cold was slowing my brain, it wasn't doing it fast enough to keep the thoughts away, and I felt myself struggling in place, losing my sense of orientation in the mist.

An earsplitting bang brought my focus back outside my head, and I thought I heard a splash a few feet away. Before I knew what was happening, another bang rang out followed by more muffled shouting. Officer Methot was shooting at me. If I had really heard the splash next to me, it was probably the bullet just missing my body. I heard my heart through the water and started kicking my legs and punching my arms faster. The shock of the cold was canceled out by the shock of getting shot at, and I started making progress further into the mist.

There was nothing pleasant about doggy paddling through freezing water in less than three feet of visibility, but I felt vindicated by my choice to put myself there. I suspected Methot would shoot me or drug me once I installed the tentacle pieces, or even before. After the shot I knew it. This was my only way out, and after wrapping myself in so many layers of East Hook's problems, any way out couldn't be easy.

My foot hit something hard and after reflexively pulling it back up, I sent the other foot down to probe if I was on solid ground. It found a rock. I swam toward it, feeling around for any of its friends. I found purchase on another rock, and a seawall came into view. I didn't recognize the wall but decided to follow it, North, away from the bridge. I was on the Pequod Point side, where the houses were closer together. It wouldn't help me, as Methot would have easier access to the water from the road and the houses were empty. It I were on Big Hook he'd have to hop a fence like I did to get to the shoreline, meaning he'd have to guess the exact right house. Still, I was happy to not be swimming, even if I was half submerged.

A wooden pier came into view jutting out above the wall, hanging above me like a gallows rack. I pushed off the wall and swam under it for forty feet until reaching the plank coming down towards me and towards the dock at the end, a blissful two feet above the waterline. I stayed hidden by the plank for a minute, taking in the sounds around me. I certainly didn't hear footsteps and figured if I were lucky enough to avoid a bullet, I was probably lucky enough to not be at the exact dock Methot was.

I wasn't lucky enough to come to a dock that had a permanent swim ladder, so I had to hoist myself up. It took two tries, but eventually I flopped over the dock, bruising my side on a tie cleat, and lay there catching my breath for a minute. The heavy air felt great after the freezing water, but I knew I should find a towel. I looked up the pier into the mist, seeing only the start of the plank, and considered what risks I wanted to take.

Up the pier would lead to a house or landing, which might be empty, and I might be able to get into to get warm. But I would have to do it with all the lights off if Methot was looking at me, and eventually I would have to get on the road, which he could be patrolling in his car. As cold as it was, it was less risky in the water, at least until the night was over.

I looked back out into the mist over the bay, toward where I assumed downtown was, but couldn't see the telltale orange glow the town's lights cast. It was probably deserted at this hour with everything going on. I took a step towards it and caught a darkness, instead of a glow, at the bottom of my vision, like something was obscuring the water to the North. I took a few more tentative steps towards the dark blob before recognizing it as an upturned rowboat. I touched it and felt plastic, not wood. I tested lifting it, my muscles weary from the swimming, but it went up easy. Underneath were two plastic oars. I didn't need the deep sending me any more signals. I tipped the boat over and pushed it into the water without much of a splash. I picked the oars up and stepped down into the boat.

I wasn't thrilled about heading back into the fog, but I had to risk the monsters in my head against the monsters prowling the shore. The boat would let me cover a lot more ground, putting more space between me and Methot, and greatly expanding the range of possible landing spots. I used the oar to push off against the side of the dock and started rowing. I tried to use what I thought was the faint yellow glow of downtown as my heading, but I wasn't aiming for anywhere too precise, and I was facing the wrong way to do any serious navigating. Into the mist, as little as it cheered me, was the only direction I could go.

# Orphism

drenaline carried me through the row. I set my heading in the general direction of the Bucks Island lighthouse, as faint as the beam was in the fog. I knew I wouldn't be able to stay straight on my own, with the tides, wind, currents and the fact that I rowed more powerfully with my right arm than my left, pulling me off course with every stroke. As long as it was and how little the scenery changed, I was never bored. Just after pushing off, every stroke made me feel freer. My back and arms started hurting after five minutes, and the lights from Pequod point weren't looking any farther away. I thought about Rocco, how he rowed out to his boat every morning, he could have crossed the bay in half the time. He wasn't there, I was all I had.

Frustrated by the slow-going and growing pain all over the top half of my body, I decided to take a break and pulled the oars into the boat. I closed my eyes and smelled the salt, felt the mist of my face and the up-and-down rocking of the waves, heard the foghorn sound a few times, in between the slapping of the water against the boat. I should have kept my eyes closed. Even though I had jumped into the heart of it, I couldn't bring myself to stare into the mist for too long. I couldn't convince myself something wasn't going to jump out of it. If monsters exist anywhere, then it's in places like where I was, far from witnesses or anyone who could help. If I focused on what little I could see, the water immediately surrounding me, it became clear that even though I wasn't rowing, I certainly wasn't staying still. I looked back towards my way star, the dim flash of Bucks Island light, and saw I had already drifted more than ninety degrees off course. It looked like the tide was pulling me back towards Pequod Point, back towards Officer Methot and all the other monsters hidden by the fog. I ended my break and didn't take any more.

My muscles didn't exactly relax as I got into rhythm, but the pain became more manageable, or at least more normal. Every ten strokes I would turn and adjust back towards the faint beacon. I had been adjusting every other stroke but found that every row took me a little sideways and correcting so often was slowing my momentum. I moved up to five, and when I saw I wasn't that much further off course than after two, I went up to ten. Slowly, too slowly, the light started getting brighter.

Staying on course only kept my mind partially occupied. To distract from seeing movement in the water and mist, I started thinking of what I would do when I landed. If thirty minutes had passed, Methot had probably admitted that he lost me. A smile broke out on my face, thinking one of the thugs would bash him on the top of his head and make him bite off half his tongue. The smile went away fast, as these were the same people looking for me, and any discomfort visited on Methot would be paid out onto me.

If he had told them, then they were probably spread out over town, either at major landing spots or locations I'd be likely to go. Thinking of them at my mother's house made me grit my teeth, but as I started to think it though it wouldn't do them any favors to threaten her now. They needed everything under wraps for the next twenty-four hours and doing something to the local hairdresser is the surest way something gets out. They'd be more likely to stake out the place from outside, not bothering her.

The same was likely true for Desmond's house, and when I thought more about where I wanted to go they'd for sure be in a position to cut me off before I got to the police station or harbormaster station. I stopped rowing thinking about the harbormaster, at least one of them should be patrolling the bay, especially with the increased presence. While I had heard engines, I hadn't heard anything close by, and wasn't ready to yell or slap the oars on the water just in case it wasn't the coast guard or harbormaster out in the fog. It was a stupid thought when I first started the row, but after thirty plus minutes, it was feasible they got in their boat to search the bay for me.

I didn't want to row right into the crosshairs of one of the guns I saw at the Splintered Mast, and if I headed to the Harbormaster station, that would be the only way they could really defend it. Sit someone on the end of the dock with a silenced rifle.

The harbormaster and the police didn't present the easiest solution to my problems. I would be back to where I was two days before: telling a wild story to the cops about the Quebecois with no evidence. Methot might even have them looking for me. He could show them the tentacles and say I was out on the water finding the next bridge to set up with new tentacles. I knew I had to land somewhere out of the way, because I had no idea what I could do once I got on land. Everything I thought of just eliminated possibilities.

As I got closer to the growing beacon, I heard something splash near me and heard the caw of some nocturnal seabird, I laughed to myself, thinking it was probably squawking about whatever it just dropped that caused the splash, a crab or a fish. I started wondering if that was the case, where the bird picked it up, and how far it had been carrying it before it escaped. Hopefully, it was something the bird found on the water; a chipmunk wasn't much better off in the ocean than a hawk's beak.

The quiet of the row helped me start paying attention to the quiet parts of my mind. An idea had started forming as soon as Mr. O'Reilly told me Cadie died of a heroin overdose. Still small and almost silent, compared to other, more immediate and violent thoughts, it took up almost none of my consciousness. At Sinclair's house then downtown a few nights ago it started growing, into a barely audible whisper, when I realized what my paintings were actually being used for. Over the previous twenty-four hours, getting acquainted with the Algerians, their plans and their upsettingly vast support network, the idea started speaking more plainly. I still ignored it, too busy maneuvering to stay alive, but it never went away. Thinking about the bird and the food chain couldn't have raised the volume too much more, but it was so damn quiet I couldn't ignore it any longer.

I intended to get closer to the lighthouse then turn North towards downtown and land on the rocky beach nearby, but once I saw the rocks, and knew I was across, I realized how badly I needed to get out of that fucking boat. I kept rowing towards them until the rowboat ran aground, wedged in tightly between the rocks.

They stretched too far for me to be able to see the land

proper. I didn't know if I was landing in someone's backyard, a private warehouse or public land. I knew I was far enough away from downtown to have a good chance of landing unnoticed. I couldn't think of anything near Buck's Island the Algerians would have been smart to stake out.

The boat was wedged so tightly that I couldn't even rock it sides to side, making my step out of it much less treacherous. I needed every bit of steadiness, because my tentative first step up onto the rock couldn't find any surface that didn't feel totally coated with Crisco. If I had to put any weight on that rock, I would have slipped and broke my head open, or at the very least sprained my ankle. And I needed my legs to get me out of this.

Straight ahead of the boat was a little channel I tried to row into before I got stuck. At the end of the channel, and my vision, it looked like the start of a more gradual slope up. I tried getting out of the boat on the other side, even though I was stepping into water.

It only came up to my shin. It was cold, but whatever was going on with my body and mind dulled the shock. I took a sluggish step and didn't slip. The resistance of the water kept my progress slow and helped my balance as I climbed toward dry land. I saw a more jagged rock I could get my hand around and when I grasped it there was some slime, but my grip held. I hoisted myself up by my hands, pinching my feet between two rocks so they wouldn't slip as I moved my hand holds.

I was able to stagger up the rocks mostly in the same manner. There were a few slippery steps I had to use my momentum to get across, but always found something to grip or fall onto. I got close enough that I could make out a seawall through the fog, which meant I had guessed right, and was on a private property. Given the location, there was almost no chance the owners were home, but even if they were, they weren't seeing me through the fog. I was so heartened by the glimpse of dry, safe land I got sloppy, and an ambitious step on what looked like a flat rock sent me sprawling. After a terrifying split second of falling, I caught myself on my wrists to save my head from crashing. My hands and wrists were already torn up from the earlier climb, and this didn't help. I was able to get myself up on my feet and shuffle, like I was walking on ice the rest of the way to the wall.

The sea wall was only three feet above the rocks, but I couldn't find a foothold steady enough to push off from, so I had to force myself over with my torn-up hands and worn out arms. I flopped more than sprung, rolling over the wall and landing sprawled on my back in the grass on the other side. The fall was only about six inches, so it couldn't have knocked the wind out of me, but I lay there for a long time catching my breath. I went to lift my neck off the ground first but it was way too much effort. My arms felt like stones and my back was throbbing.

Twenty-four hours before, playing amateur detective had caught up with me. Lying there, the effort of playing Houdini caught up with me, but that price I was happy to pay. I lay in the wet lawn aching, bleeding, soaking and freezing and I laughed. I turned my head towards the water, seeing only the stone of the wall, and felt insulated from it. I turned the other way and saw no lights burning at whatever property I was on. I kept laughing, even though every movement hurt, while I waited for a second wind. I knew if I made any wrong turns or had any bad luck I wouldn't laugh again, but it made me laugh harder. I knew Rocco was still in the hospital with his mom, and Cadie in the ground, without her dad, and how remarkably unfunny and unfair it all was, but I laughed anyway. It was either that or fall asleep. When the delirious hilarity subsided, maybe ten minutes later, I was able to roll onto my side and shakily work myself onto my feet.

HK got a new door, apparently at a company that makes safes, because it was solid metal. When I knocked on it I felt like I was knocking on the side of a battleship. It hurt the side of my fist, but it had a satisfying, resonant sound. I couldn't hear shuffling or anything afterwards, so maybe it was soundproof too. I knocked again and stepped back.

After less than a minute, I heard a series of clicks indicating the door was about to open. It swung inwards, an impressive three inches wide, and HK stood behind it, in a t-shirt and athletic shorts. I wasn't sure if they were his pajamas or he always dressed like that. He was surprised to see me.

"Ellis! Shit man, what happened to you?"

I had been cold and wet so long I hardly noticed it. "Just a late-night swim." I nodded into the house asking him to invite me in. He stepped back and let me walk through. He must have had the heat on, because I felt the thaw starting as soon as the huge door shut. It had great insulation too. I'd have to ask about it, the next time I was over.

"I was worried about you. I heard you got arrested. I called like ten times; all went straight to voicemail. I thought..." He looked around, like the door wasn't soundproof. "I thought I led you into the lion's den." It came out a little too fast to be touching, but it helped he was feeling guilty.

A minute back in the heat, and my brain finally got the

292

message how cold my body was. I started shivering with my teeth chattering so much I could barely talk. HK leapt back when he noticed what state I was in. "Are you alright? Let me get you something."

"C-c-c-of-f-f-ee" was all I managed. I went to sit down on his couch and felt the ice-cold wetness of my clothes. "D-dry c-clothes." I wasn't concerned about getting the couch wet, this sea water coming off my ass was probably the closest it would ever get to cleaned. HK moved quickly back into his bedroom and returned a minute later with sweatpants and a sweatshirt. My convulsions had abated into a low-grade full body tremor.

"Sorry I don't have any coffee." He looked in the direction of the kitchen, "I have food I can heat up for you." HK was so skinny I wondered if his clothes would fit me, but realized I'd be fine. Us city art kids wore everything with a tighter fit than up the coast. In three years or whenever they caught up, I'd be in trouble.

"It's fine. Thanks for these." I got up, struggling to get my legs to move again, and limped into the bathroom to change.

Peeling my clothes off sapped what remained of my strength. Once I had the dry sweatpants and sweatshirt on, I sat on the edge of the tub and yelled for HK. He could come to me.

He almost ran in, thinking I'd fallen or something, but saw I was ok and stood leaning on the doorframe. "What happened Ellis?"

I wanted to tell him everything, because I wanted to tell someone everything, but stopped myself. "You're right, it's the Quebecois." My words were breathy, I was still winded. "We can pin Cadie, the lighthouses, the traps and Rocco on them. You were right about everything." I was laying it on nice and thick for him. "I can take care of it all tonight."

He looked impressed. I could see the wheels turning behind those normally vacant eyes. "Did you really get arrested?"

I waved it off like it was all in the course of business, like I wouldn't hold onto the trauma of my back to back nights of confinement forever. Even being behind HK's thick door was locking me in a little tight, and I didn't close the bathroom door while I changed. "Yeah, but they let me go pretty quickly once the older cops, who knew my dad arrived."

HK's head tilted back, remembering my father. "Ah. Nice connection to have." He pursed his lips, remembering something else. "I've been arrested before. It's not so bad." He spread his fingers out in front of me. "Now they have your prints though." We were reconnecting, lawbreakers together in high school, still lawbreakers. It's a lot less cute in your twenties.

The reconnection was exactly what I came there for, I seized the opportunity. "I need your help for the last part, we take it from them, and they get put away forever."

Even as connected as we were, HK shrank back at the idea of confronting them directly. His voice took on a shrewd, wary tone, "Take what from them?"

I didn't answer, instead looked at him for a long time without blinking. Moving only my mouth, I said "Might be better if you don't know." I got up, ignoring the ache in my legs and the black at the edges of my vision, presenting the picture of capability. "It'll be easier if I go alone." His posture relaxed, he looked a little relieved, but not convinced. He nodded, but before he could say whatever he was planning to I continued. "I just need to borrow your car, and some cash to buy one of those refillable phones."

He was even less convinced. "What?!"

It was time to mix in a little truth. "My phone and wallet are the bottom of the bay. That swim I took was to get away from them. They know I can prove it. They tried to stop me from getting the proof."

"Prove it how, Ellis? I need details if I'm gonna get involved."

"It's at their place in Drydon. A 3D model showing where they were going to strike when, hammers, rope clippers, pressurized gas canisters." Basically what I saw combined with what I was looking for when I was there. "Sinclair told me where everything is in their garage. Desmond and I unlocked a window last time we were there." I was making the task sound distasteful as possible to HK, but I knew I could clinch it. "I'm going to take pictures with the phone, then call the cops from inside the garage so they have an excuse to search it when they arrive. I'll say they locked me in there."

HK's brow was furrowed, like it wasn't the best idea. "Are you just gonna drive in the driveway? How do you know they aren't home?"

He was perched on the edge of the trap entrance; another step and I'd just have to pull up the pot. "They're running all operations out of the Splintered Mast now and…" I had to pause for effect. "They're all out looking for me."

It was HK's turn to pause. He ran a hand through his greasy hair and looked down at the bathroom tiles. "Where are you leaving the car." Nothing left to do but pull up the pot. "The public landing across the street and down a few houses. Lots of cars park there overnight."

"How much are those phones?"

# IX

# Friday

# Naturalism

H K's car was almost out of gas, so my first stop was the station by the Y a mile inland. It seemed like a safe place to stop away from downtown, and not on the way to anywhere the Quebecois would expect me to go. I kept the hood up on my sweatshirt and my head down as I filled the tank. I asked HK for a good chunk of cash, and he didn't hesitate, spinning the dial on his new safe and pulling out the bills from a much bigger stack. In the station store I used a fraction of it to buy a prepaid cell phone that could take pictures, a car charger adapter, notebook paper, colored pencils, a box of one gallon double seal clear plastic bags, a shammy car towel and a waterproof flashlight. The gas stations in East Hook were like superstores.

Once the phone had enough charge to turn on, I texted HK a picture of myself with the message Reach me here. I looked at the clock, it was almost one AM. I turned the heat to the highest setting, pulled off the sweatshirt hood, put the car in gear and drove off towards my only shot at staying alive: leverage.

I tried to choose my route carefully, to avoid any patrols looking for me. Maybe it was just being warm and dry, but I was feeling like my odds had shifted. HK's car windows had a dark tint, and not a lot of East Hook roads had streetlights. The worst-case scenario would be running across Methot in a patrol car, and my plan in that situation would be to not pull over, instead drive right into the police station with a lot of witnesses and try my luck there. It would be less than fifty-fifty, but better than I had been dealing with.

I didn't have far to go. I followed the main road for less than a mile back towards town and took the first exit of a roundabout that lead me down a narrow winding road that ran along a stream. I was on that road for a little over a mile, turning down a public access turnoff and taking it slowly down a hill, parking in a public parking lot at the start of one of the many East Hook hiking trails. I didn't see a single headlight or taillight the whole ride.

The drive was too quick, I wasn't ready to leave the heated car. I checked the phone to see if it had an alarm feature, thinking to recharge a little with a nap, but quickly realized it couldn't get loud enough to wake me even if I did set it up right. I knew if I fell asleep, the only person harder to wake in town would be Rocco. Be in a grim situation long enough you can't help having grim thoughts.

As tired as I was, I couldn't lose my shot. If I didn't guess right, I'd have forever to sleep real soon. Instead of napping, I practiced my own form of meditation. I took out the notepaper and colored pencils, and I started drawing.

Once I finished I flipped the paper over to jot some notes on the back and put the completed work into one of the plastic bags, making sure I pressed all the air out and closed both seals completely. Concerned about the quality of the plastic, I doubled up, putting the bag inside another one, performing the same excess air removal and sealing activities.

Satisfied, I slid the paper and plastic into the front pocket of the sweatshirt and put the hood back up, then I turned off the engine and stepped back into the wild.

When I shut the car door and the light inside turned off, I realized how dark it was. If there was a moon, I couldn't locate it through the fog and the trees. It could have been blocked by the hill I was on too. I reached into my pocket and flicked on the flashlight. The beam was strong, catching the mist drifting, floating through everything. I took a deep breath in, feeling that mist go down into my lungs, and started down the hiking path. Hearing lakewater lapping with low sounds by the shore.

The path was marked by arrows on trees every thirty or forty yards, so I wouldn't have been able to stay on it long even if that was my plan. I veered off to the left, down the hill toward a spot that looked clear, but with plenty of trees to slow my momentum on the way down.

I stepped down through the trees, careful of my footing in the dark. Still, my feet crunched through things I knew weren't twigs, and slid on things I knew weren't wet leaves. The whole area was much quieter than I ever remember it being, and if I was right, I knew why. When I reached the clearing at the bottom, safely away from the road, I finally turned my flashlight on. I scanned the waterline of Sherman's Pond, and the beam caught at least five dead animals. Two squirrels, a weasel, a robin and a rabbit, in various states of decay. I didn't need to sweep my light across other areas to know I'd see more of the same.

The animals were dead because the biggest freshwater source in the region had been poisoned, just like the lobsters out by the Stains. I cast my beam across the surface of the pond to the middle, and with the fog much lighter inland, it caught a dark, matte object not bobbing, but shaking a little bit in place out in the middle of the pond. A black buoy. I had a pretty good idea what was attached to it below. I had bet my life on it.

I had learned from my last trip into the water, mostly that I wasn't going to enjoy it, but also how I could shorten the duration of my discomfort. I started by taking my shoes and socks off, then HK's pants, which I still needed a belt to keep up, despite outweighing him by thirty pounds. I had to remind myself of the logic when the breeze kicked up and the cool air found my exposed skin. The plan was to dry myself as much as I could with the car shammy towel, then have dry clothes to change into. I would warm up in no time that way, it didn't hurt that I also had a car with a blessed heater just up the hill. I told myself as I took off the sweatshirt that in ten minutes max, I would be back in that car, warm and in a new, likely safer phase in my life.

I put the clothes and towel together, between a dead skunk and a dead crow, and got right up to the water before remembering the notepaper inside the bag. I jogged back to fish it out of the sweatshirt pocket, then kept jogging into the pond, knowing any hesitation would just add to the time before I was back in the car.

The water was warmer than the bay, but not by much. Between the fog and the trees it didn't get a lot of sunshine to heat it up. I was able to make small progress with my steps, but as the ground sloped too far beneath me I switched to an awkward sideways doggy paddle. I was barely keeping my head above water and making headway at a painfully slow pace, the hand holding the baggie and flashlight wasn't creating much pulling force.

I felt my teeth chattering after less than a minute, and I looked just as far from the buoy as before. My skin was no longer being stabbed by the cold; it had moved into numbness. I wasn't worried about freezing, I kept telling myself I just had to last another nine minutes, then I'd be dry and warm. In order to make that schedule, I would have to pick up the pace. I stretched out my right, free hand in front of me and kicked out my legs and switched to a modified side stroke, getting my head wet, but covering more ground. I felt water going in and out of my ear, but I made sure none got into my mouth. I didn't want to end up like all the other animals around me.

There were no currents or waves to deal with, so the going was smoother. The fog wasn't as thick on the mainland, and I was better able to orient myself. Still, every stroke made me more tired. I avoided looking up towards the buoy to avoid getting discouraged. The pond wasn't big enough for me to get too far off track. I worked on controlling my breathing, trying to turn my ragged gasps into something steadier. The fact that every breath, along with every stroke, entering and exiting the water, rang out over the otherwise silent pond, helped me focus. No katydids or crickets chirping, no leaf crunching from some nocturnal forager, no buzz zooming into then away from my ear. Nothing was moving here, except the idiot splashing his way to the middle of the pond, only half certain what he'd do when he got there.

Eventually I did. I risked despair by looking and saw I was within fifteen feet of something darker and steadier than the water. I had to maneuver around to shine my flashlight over it to confirm, but I had reached the buoy. I came out of my side stroke and started treading water, pulling slightly in the buoy's direction but saving energy. When I was close enough to reach out I grabbed the top handle and tested just how buoyant it was, checking if holding onto it would keep me afloat. It sank with me, but much slower than I would have gone down on my own. I still had to tread water, but only needed to kick once every few seconds. It was like taking a break, one my body needed, and my brain didn't.

Allowed to think about more than just moving through the cold and staying afloat, I was able to consider the next step in my undercooked plan, everything that could go wrong with it, and all the reasons to swim back, run into the car and think of a better plan. What I was doing was nothing like my painting, I didn't have any of the details, I was just making single broad strokes, no idea where the next one would start, what color it would be or what it would look like at the end, just hoping it would all come together, turn into something.

My breathing had slowed since I'd grabbed the buoy, so I started hyperventilating. After three big fast breaths, I sucked in all the air I could, and sank under the surface.

As soon as my whole head was under water, I tilted my upper body forward and kicked my legs out behind me, trying to point my body facing down. I opened my eyes and after the initial shock, found the beam, faint in the grimy water. I swung it back and forth until I found the rope connected to the buoy and followed it down as far as I could see. The beam couldn't penetrate all the way to the end of the rope, but I wasn't too put off, it only illuminated five feet. It did mean I had to move faster.

I grabbed the rope with both hands, just the thumb and pointer finger of my left hand, which also held the flashlight and baggie, and started reverse climbing down, pulling myself deeper while kicking to support my descent. The flashlight was slowing me down, I couldn't generate any pull on the rope with only two fingers, and I still couldn't see anything. I switched gears, moving so the rope was on my right side, and kicked harder, pulling with only my right hand, pointing the beam straight down with my left.

I knew I was making progress seeing the grit float up towards me, but the beam still hadn't found the bottom. I wasn't struggling for air yet, but I had a lot more to do down there. I was starting to panic, probably the least helpful thing to do underwater, when the light caught a square edge, the metal reflecting the light right back out at me.

By the time I got down to it my ears felt like they were being pressed into my skull. I was less than twenty feet down, but the pressure was still intense. It was too murky to tell if the corners of my vision were starting to darken, but I trusted my body to tell me when it was time to go. It was in fact telling me, quite directly, but I was going to wait until it screamed.

I tried lifting the box by the handle but couldn't make it budge. So I felt around the side of the box for clasps, finding one on the side, and yanked at it, remembering the mechanism from the same box we found out by the Stains, that Rocco and I opened what seemed like years ago. It was stubborn on his boat, and it was stubborn down there, likely made worse by the water pressure. I used my left hand to steady the box and the top half of the clasp, pulling the lower part with my right hand and even swinging my body around to push off the box with my legs.

The screaming I was waiting for started, and I gave one final pull, putting my left hand, or at least my finger and thumb with my right fingers and pushed off with my legs. I felt it start to give then spring open, my momentum carrying me off the box and up. Thankful for the momentum, I swam and kicked like crazy for the surface, racing the instinct to breath in. When I broke the surface I felt dizzy, my gasps for air and aching muscles not able to kill my sense of accomplishment. I got the clasp; I would get the other three. Maybe my ten minutes were up, but that feeling sustained me more than heat could, for the moment.

Not waiting for the fog to clear enough for me to be rational, I dove again, surer of my method and adjusting my approach slightly. I hardly needed the flashlight, I could just grip the rope straight down, but I had nowhere to set it, so I kept it in my hand with the paper in the bag. It didn't impede my progress too much, I got down to the box much faster and shimmied the front two locks open before I came back up. I started working on the fourth and final one, but gave up before I had to, there was no need for close calls so close to the end. My broad strokes were coalescing into something, maybe coming together into something beautiful, definitely something monstrous.

My break was shorter on the surface, and I again improved my time down to the pond floor to open the last lock in no time, probably because I'd loosened it before. I'd expected the water pressure to keep the lid shut, but as soon as the last clasp was free, it almost floated up. It had been filled with water the whole time. No wonder it had been so heavy. I panicked for the second time down at the bottom of the pond, worried I was too late, that my lifeline was already out and dry and ready to poison a different East Hook animal.

Through the panic, I opened the box wider and the flashlight beam caught four rounded bricks covered in plastic, white as fresh packed snow. I wasn't too late. The Quebecois should have killed me in the Splintered Mast.

I swam back to the surface to plan how to bring them all up and out of the pond in a space I could breathe.

It didn't take too much thinking, I figured it out before I got back above water. They weren't precious cargo to me, I would just try to squeeze everything between my arm and stomach, and if one of them dropped, it still did the job, as long as it wasn't in the box, or somewhere they couldn't get it. I did need to proceed with some care though, the animals of East Hook had been poisoned enough.

I held onto the buoy while I caught my breath. I took a minute to look around, though a second of looking around would have been enough, fog surrounded me. I stared into it, watching the subtle motions along the surface, and the rising vapors. For the first time since I'd been home, I was seeing the fog, not what it could be hiding. Sure I couldn't see my destination, couldn't see and prepare for all the challenges that lay ahead, but it was fine. I still knew which way to swim: down into the water.

I dove, for what I hoped was the last time, bringing up four plastic wrapped bags, surprisingly easy to carry, loosely wrapping what I knew to be tens of thousands of dollars' worth of either cocaine or heroin.

In their place in the newly re-closed leaking iron box at the end of the black buoy floated a water-sealed bag containing a newly created Ellis Ward work, not an original, but a colored pencil reproduction of one of my best paintings, with a note on the back.

The calm and relaxation I felt sitting in the car with the heat on full blast was almost entirely mitigated by the stress of having kilos of drugs with me. If I were pulled over, I'd probably be better off if it were Methot, so much product would put me away for a long time. I understood why the Quebecois kept the bulk of it on public land, so they never carried to much of it at once. I waited in the dirt parking lot for thirty minutes before summoning enough courage to start driving. It helped that I knew all the cops in the area were focused on the water, as the Quebecois planned.

I had four hours or so until sunrise, and nowhere I knew I could go, so I decided to drive North along the coast. Driving South, all the way to the city, making things right with Ivy and Guardado, re-entering my life had a gravity I wasn't expecting, and I changed my mind. I would stop and pitch the contraband on the side of the road, take some pictures and send them to police. I would be warm and dry and out in the sun, and the people close to me would stay out of danger.

When I had to make a final decision, at the main coastal route junction, I kept switching between my right turn signal and left turn signal. I started a left turn then violently swerved right and made my way North. Real life could wait another day.

Only three miles up the road, I saw a sign for a motel, one I'd passed in the car with my friends and parents a thousand times, but never noticed how the parking lot was in the back, cut into a forest behind all the rooms. It was a road motel, far from the coast and the quaint towns to the East, but every summer it was fully packed. That night, I wasn't the only car in the back lot but there weren't many others.

I parked as far away from the other cars as I could, then

made my way into the office and bought a room for the night with cash, half price since I arrived so late. The guy behind the counter shrugged when I said I didn't have my ID.

I left the drugs in the trunk of the car. If someone found them there, it wasn't my car anyway. I worried about HK having car tracking software, or the Quebecois somehow finding it, or the motel night manager getting a little too curious. There was plenty to worry about, and as I stepped out of HK's shoes, stripped off his clothes, and crawled onto the mattress made of what felt like Styrofoam, I worried about all of it. Until my head hit the pillow. Then I didn't do anything until around noon, when the banging on my door got too loud to ignore.

# Synchronism

It was just the motel manager, a different guy from the
night before, angry I hadn't checked out already. He said
he was less than a minute away from unlocking the door
and bursting in, and that I had to pay the late fee, or pay for
the next night. I wondered why he was enforcing the rule so
tightly; there wasn't a rush to get my room cleaned. From
the looks of the parking lot, I was the only occupant at the
whole place, and didn't expect an afternoon rush. I guessed
that was exactly the reason he was being such a hardass, he
had literally nothing else to do.

I went to the money HK lent me and gave him twenty of it,
asking him if I could have ten minutes to shower and then I'd
leave. He stood there for a while, thinking I might give him
more just to make him go away, but I never looked back at
the door, instead moving to the bed and looking at my phone
on the nightstand. Eventually I heard him shut it and mutter
about kids and rudeness in a volume not normally used for
muttering. He could have said whatever he wanted, nothing
was pulling me away from the phone, and the twenty-nine
messages, two voicemails and eight calls I had missed.

Seven of the calls, and both voicemails were from HK. There
wasn't much to them, the first one told me he'd tried me a few

times and to call him back, he needed an update. The second one was a little more frantic, saying he wanted to make sure I was ok, but reminding me I had his car and he gave me a lot of money. The texts, all but four from him, covered the same ground. I'd update him once I was on the road.

The other call was from a number I didn't know with an East Hook area code. That same number sent two texts, and the last two were from a blocked number. One set, the one that also called me at seven AM read:

ur dead

It was followed by:

u have to know that.

The other set, sent around the same time, read:

We can track this number idiot, we know where you are

It was followed by:

bring it to us and we can figure things out

It appeared the Quebecois had gone to Sherman's Pond at seven AM. Early risers, but six hours too late. They also got the message I left for them inside the lockbox, protected by a clear plastic bag. At least they got half of it, the part with my new cell number. I smiled thinking about how confused whoever opened the box must have been, and how it had to have dawned on them what happened slowly. Thinking of them raging in the Splintered Mast or the Drydon compound kept me smiling as I put on HK's clothes for a second time, slipped on his shoes, and walked out the door.

The car looked the same as it did the night before, and I risked looking sketchy to the manager, who surely was watching, and checked the trunk before I got in. The four bags were still there, every gram accounted for, except for what had leaked into the pond. I shut it and hopped in the driver's seat, thinking about whistling to seem nonchalant. I was maximally chalant. If I made any mistakes over the next twelve hours, I was in for a quick death, and so many other locals would follow me into the deep, much more slowly.

I took off, South again, a few errands to take care of, the wheel in a death grip.

I parked the car at the end of a secluded residential street a few blocks up from the church. It was far enough outside the church's radius that no one would park there for services even on Easter Sunday. While my main focus was avoiding the Quebecois and their lackeys, I didn't want HK stumbling across his car either. He'd been pressing me every hour since I've been awake, asking when I'd have it back and what I found, but I wasn't answering any of his calls, and being as vague as I could be through text. I alluded to the fact that we'd meet up at Sinclair's service, which was where I was headed once I parked, in the cheapest black suit I could find in a shopping center north of town.

While I walked the pants were chafing my legs and the shirt was cutting into my neck. I had to look up a few videos on tying a tie before one turned out ok. The whole suit was soaking up all the humidity in the air and seemed to weigh more with each step. I cut through someone's backyard and walked along the side of the church to the parking lot. Taking a wide angle so I could see around the corners.

They were waiting for me just off the side of the entrance. Three of them, dressed in designer black clothes, free of their pincers, and anything else that would call attention. Except from me, the day I spent with them had seared all their silhouettes and postures into my head. I would have recognized them from a lot farther away, in much thicker fog.

I acted on instinct, diving behind a car, and duck-walked deeper into the parking lot, where the church walls blocked their view. I looked back at the small residential woods I had come from, and thought about taking off towards them, hightailing away like some small furry prey. After a few deep breaths, my higher motor functions resumed, and I started thinking how I could get myself through.

I had known they might be there; I had come in through the back knowing they might be there. But seeing them standing out front, waiting to see me, made me realize that I didn't actually know anything. The scenes I played out in my head were all out of a comedy of manners, relying on those monsters not making a scene in front of the funeral crowd, and maybe having enough respect for Mr. Sinclair to not try anything during the service itself. There were a lot of reasons for them to think twice about grabbing me in public, but maybe they would react like I did, with panicked animal instinct. I couldn't take that chance. If I were wrong I'd be dead. I looked back towards the woods.

There weren't many cars in the parking lot, despite the service scheduled to begin in fewer than five minutes. I compared it to Cadie's funeral, only a week before, and how so many people were packed on the church's front lawn, everyone was bumping elbows. Despite their coupling, the funerals only being a week apart, and how they both died the same way, Cadie and Sinclair were laid to rest in opposite circumstances, in two different East Hooks. The charming fog of last week had turned poisonous, and I wondered if word had gotten out about what the police found in Sinclair's house. Cadie was also a twenty-three-year-old local with a lot of friends. Sinclair was thirty-nine, from away, and spent the last few years shedding friends as quickly as pounds and teeth.

As I stood in the back of the lot waiting to make a move I watched a few more cars pull in, the stragglers. A sleek, gunmetal sports car glided into a spot, and I saw my new friend Dr. Leo hop out in a tight dark suit and shades, moving fast to the church entrance, remote locking his car with a beep over his shoulder without breaking stride. I wondered who else I knew that was already inside. I couldn't find my mother's car, but she could have come with friends. I did see the Mayor's car, parked in almost the same spot as it was for Cadie's funeral. The car I was leaning on had a Kraken pride bumper sticker, which was given to each student every year but exclusively displayed by teachers. HK wouldn't have driven, he didn't have access to his car, but I wondered if he was inside too.

I had no idea how long the Quebecois would wait out front for me, and if they'd go in for the service. I hoped so, not just to get a thick stone wall with no windows between us, but I felt Sinclair's service could use the boost in attendance. The bells rang their mournful tone, and I didn't check back out front. I took another look at the woods across the clearing, then walked around to the back of the church, wondering what I'd be able to hear through the wall.

Inland, there was always less fog at night. You could see a small halo of falling mist around the park lights if you looked up, but at ground level, the view was pretty much clear. The ground was still wet. My pants had soaked through an hour before, to the point I was starting to worry about diaper rash.

I didn't get up though, I sat in the trees and sipped from my second thermos of coffee, looking out on the cemetery where my father, Cadie, and now Mr. Sinclair were buried. I was paying tribute, on guard, but mostly on a stakeout.

The part of the service I could hear focused on forgiveness, not for what he had put the town though, but for everything else we need to forgive drug addicts for: lying, stealing, wasting potential, for being sick in a way we couldn't understand. I wasn't at the forgiveness stage, it was really a coin flip whether I made it through the night, but I was glad I stayed for a part of it. It helped put some pieces together.

Apparently everything had started with the car accident. It lingered with Mr. Sinclair, in his muscles and bones, making every breath hurt. The fix for his pain lingered as well, and when the oxycontin he was prescribed, probably by that asshole Dr. Leo, got too expensive and weak, he found heroin a more than capable substitute. Until that too became too expensive, and he got in bad with his dealers, the Quebecois, or whoever they were. He used what brains he had left to try and dig himself out, making himself valuable with his knowledge of monsters, his knowledge of my works, and his ability to make a spectacle. There were a few pieces missing though, or ones that didn't quite fit together. So I sat on the cold wet ground and hoped the fog continued lifting.

Cadie's pain was harder to pin down. I'd never know where it came from, and her funeral wasn't as direct at answering those kinds of questions. Her father seemed nice enough. I doubted he made it to Sinclair's funeral. I hoped Sinclair and Cadie were a comfort to each other at the end, no matter how it ended. They played a massive part in my high school experience, and, as it turned out, my college experience.

I was having trouble accepting how wrong I'd been over the last week. Not just about Cadie, and the wild goose chase that kept me from everything I'd been working toward, casting my future even more into doubt. It's one thing to be a shit detective, but it's another to be a shit friend. Rocco was in pain when Cadie died, everyone tried to tell me, but I assumed I knew him best. He was drinking too much, and way too eager to join me in our imaginary chase, that led to a hospital bed with beeping machines keeping him alive. If he did come around, an if, despite the positive prognosis, it'll be another trauma he'll have to deal with, in a place without a lot of healthy coping mechanisms. Thanks to me, Desmond had a taste of the real monster of East Hook, and a taste was usually too much. I could still help them though; I was seeing things more clearly.

Thankfully, Mr. Sinclair was buried closer to the road than Cadie, so everyone who came to his burial wouldn't have stood behind Cadie's grave, able to see the tag a few probably would have recognized. I still didn't know if anyone else had seen it yet. It was funny, how the blinking neon arrow that sent me down my path was mostly invisible to everyone else. It could still serve as a beacon to me though.

The wind picked up and I put my head down and closed my eyes, listening for Cadie or absent her, Mr. Sinclair. Instead of one of them speaking Yeats to me, this time I whispered a passage to myself, about greater beings than us living a clearer, fiercer life because of our quiet.

It was just me and the wind, for the moment. I was expecting company. I was wearing the same uncomfortable dark suit I wore to the funeral, never changing when I walked away from the church and spent the afternoon back at the shops. My thermos was matte blue and I bought black gloves to wear while I sipped it. The grass of the cemetery was probably fifteen feet from me, down a slight grade, with a smattering of trees and branches blocking me from view.

From where I was I could see the back of Cadie's grave unobstructed. The blue E and yellow H barely visible in this light, the darkness robbing the paint of its true color. It looked more like a botched engraving that a defacement. I was tempted to shine my flashlight on the stone. I had done it once or twice since I'd been there, just to re-confirm its presence, confirm that while whatever I'd started was based on almost nothing, there was something real there.

I had been wondering what kind of calls I was missing on my actual phone since the Quebecois took it. I imagined a few voicemails from my mother, maybe a message from Desmond. I know Guardado and Ivy both tried to reach me because they sent emails. I was able to access my school account from the burner phone. Guardado's message was from Thursday, telling me he had to submit all final grades by Saturday at midnight. Thinking of it had me checking my watch, realizing that was in less than three hours. He also said despite knowing he was going to fail me, he planned on waiting until the very last minute to submit my grade. I understood, for the first time, that he had been trying to help me the whole time, the whole semester.

Ivy also wrote to me, telling me to check in because she was worried about me. Hers was from Thursday night, right around the time I was being marched at gunpoint on the Big Hook bridge. Her instincts were so sharp. I decided to shine a light on Cadie's tombstone one more time, that stupid tag that drove Ivy away. I could have used those instincts the last

317

few days.

Before I could even reach for my torch, I heard a car come up to the cemetery and slow down. I saw the headlights a few seconds later, then saw them shut off. The cabin light flashed, illuminating the passenger opening the door and getting out, as the driver sat still behind the wheel. Once the door shut again, everything was back in darkness. I put my head down again and closed my eyes, not to listen for ghosts, but ghouls. I heard the cautious crunch of footsteps, stopping every few steps, probably to check that the road was clear.

I opened my eyes on the other grave my vantage point had a clear view of through the trees, Mr. Sinclair's, and saw the shadowy figure emerge under the park light.

His walk was cautious, all his movements were cautious as he located the tombstone, knelt behind it while swinging his backpack over his shoulder to access what was inside. He first pulled out a stencil, resting it on the back of the stone, then pulled out two cans of spray paint.

I heard a car drive by and so did he, and he got into a sitting position behind Mr. Sinclair's grave and sat perfectly still as the headlights passed. He didn't need to, the road ran perpendicular to the tombstones, so no one's headlight would ever point into the cemetery. The one light on the grounds pointed back toward the road anyway, so even if someone were stopped on the road, they could only make out the stone outlines.

If you were sitting behind the cemetery though, that same light illuminates everything not blocked by the grave markers, including late night vandals. The car passed and he put the stencil up on the tombstone, shook the first spray can, and made a solid, but not fully steady E. He put down the stencil to admire his handiwork, flipped it and grabbed the other can. His H was worse, he moved the stencil too far left and the middle line started to the left of the vertical one, removing the symmetry of the letters that I always thought was the whole point of the tag.

If anyone else had a right to change it up though, it was him. After he finished the H, HK calmly put the stencil and cans back in his bag and darted behind the tombstones back to the car.

# Photorealism

A few things the Quebecois said to me during our sit-down hadn't make sense. How they thought I skimmed from their stash box in the bay, when Rocco and I found it totally empty, except for some painting photocopies. At first I had chalked it up to leakage, infecting the lobsters and poisoning the area, but it didn't fit. The group that was too careful to actually touch and carry their product would have been tracking it closely enough to know how much was left out there down to the hour, much less the day. We hadn't even seen empty bags or evidence of drugs. Whatever had been in there when they last checked had been removed by someone before we got there. And removed by someone they weren't expecting. It was probably the same someone who was out there just before us, cutting traps in the bay.

When the detective told me they all had alibis for both the night the lighthouses were vandalized and the morning traps got cut, it broke my reality. It had me turning to supernatural and ancient causes, even looking for ways I could have done it and forgot, when really it was the simplest reality: they just didn't do it. Sinclair obviously couldn't have done it alone; he could barely stand up unassisted when I last saw him. So someone else had to be involved.

While I was working as their prisoner on the sheet tentacles, I kept waiting for the otherwise pragmatic group to come to their senses and scrap the whole thing. The whole concept came to me when I was desperate to survive, under inhuman pressure and probably recovering from a concussion; it was totally half-baked. They could have kept the attention on the water with a body much better than with a bridge prank.

The only reason they initially agreed was because the one by the door, the one whose English was just a little less accented, must have convinced them it of the idea's merits. He must have kept privately pushing the idea as we were working, to make sure they never pulled the plug. I had him pegged as a man of taste, but really he was just a traitor, seeing a way he could use me to get one over on his mates.

The few sleepless hours I spent in the jail cell had me fixated around my terrible luck. How I had found the one house in East Hook with a perimeter alarm system, the one house I had ever even heard of that had one. After I hopped the gate, I didn't see any green or red lights signifying a motion detector. When I canvassed the outside, I didn't see any of the telltale signs the house even had an alarm. There were no spotlights, wires near the door, even any lights on inside. There were no stickers or warnings, the place seemed deserted. It wasn't an alarm that drew Officer Methot, the cop that happened to be on the Quebecois payroll, to the property for a routine check.

It was a phone call, from the only person who knew I was going there, HK.

I struggled with why for a bit, knowing I knew truly little, but at least knowing that nothing HK had asked me to do was in some way helping the Quebecois. He was clearly trying to bring them down, but still blocking me at key points. I considered that he felt I had found all I could with my investigation, and tipping off the cops to my break-in would provide enough probable cause for a search of the new property, one that would unearth that key evidence the detective was talking about, something that would stick. If he had thought that, his assumption would have been wrong. It would have been beyond cruel to his high school friend, but it would have been less cruel than what he really did. He didn't call the police, he called his mole within the Quebecois, the traitor who stood by the door, and kept me alive.

HK wasn't looking to bust the Quebecois, he was looking to steal from them, or at least steal more than he already had. He could combine everything he heard from his man on the inside with everything he heard from me, an unknowing spy driven desperate enough to go sprinting head down in every direction he pointed me in. He worked with Sinclair the whole time, helping him bust the lighthouses, helping him cut the traps, and helping him frame me and bait me, with the stencil he always had. If his place really was broken into the night before I got there, then it was because the Quebecois was looking for something he stole from them.

His co-conspirator, the traitor Quebecois by the door, had helped him steal from the trap in the bay, and had told him about the new shipment coming in. He also most likely did help with the vandalism and trap lines, too. With the way everyone in town grouped the Quebecois together, as an indistinct mass of other, he could have joined in on their alibi without actually being with them. That night, for the first time, I regretted that I never learned his name.

I guessed the Quebecois hadn't really got involved until

Methot picked me up at the manor house. HK tipped his guy off, and instead of keeping it between them, maybe monitoring the situation, he told the whole team. They had no choice but to dispatch their muscle, able to keep it above board as a trespassing arrest. Having me there must have spooked them enough that when a surely hammered Rocco confronted them and ran his mouth, they tried to kill him, staying, while the moment still suited it, in theme with sea monsters. I guessed they then confronted Sinclair about his plans almost bringing everything down and stuck him with too much heroin or gave him a bad dose. They then went to stick Desmond, the only other person they knew I was working with, to draw me out and see what I knew before they got rid of the last loose end, that they knew about.

That told me a lot, the one thing that finally drew them out of their over-protective bubble, was someone going to the manor. I wondered what could possibly be there, to spook them so completely that they go after four people in two days.

They were right to have been spooked after all. I had their whole summer supply. I replaced it in the box with something out of their own playbook, a new waypoint, a sketched version of one of my paintings corresponding to a location, but with a scribbled note on the back, instead of my tag. It was the Medusa, the one that hung behind the counter at my mother's salon. On the back was my temporary cell number, below that Saturday 10PM, and below that $10,000.

I had to go to the cemetery to see how my little stunt affected all the plans, especially the ones that had me taking the fall. I had to know where I stood with HK. The other night he had given me clothes, money and his car without asking any questions. Seeing him ride up in a car with the Quebecois told me he knew what I had but didn't know that I knew he knew. Seeing him spray the grave told me he was still going to pin everything on me, not the Quebecois.

Thirty minutes after I saw him, I texted him a picture of his trunk with the drugs center framed. And told him we finally had the leverage we need.

He tried calling me a few times, but I never answered, saying I needed to keep my voice down. Really I just didn't trust myself to lie to him over the phone. The way he'd played me over the last week, He was a different class of liar than I was.

I told him they were coming to my mother's salon at ten, which he must have already known. I asked him if he had a gun, and to bring it if he did, that we'd get the drop on them. He kept calling, but eventually just agreed to show up at the salon before ten. He wanted to meet earlier, but I knew better than that. He'd bring his gun to an earlier meeting, and most likely use it, relieving me of the stash with no fuss, leaving my body in the woods, the trash, or the water. I told him the truth, that I had some last-minute preparations to make, and wouldn't be there too far before ten, but that it was all ok because I knew the area so well and had a plan.

I checked the time on my phone, nine fifty-eight pm. The Quebecois were probably just about to barge through the front door, or the back one. I wondered if all four of them and Methot had come for me. I wondered how many of them had guns. I wondered if the traitor had a gun and walked behind the others. It was possible they brought some money, planning to play it friendly while they made sure I really was alone. Maybe Methot would come in his squad car, taking me in for vandalism while they searched the shop and the car for contraband. Maybe some brought canvas bags and lead pipes, wanting me to suffer a little, make it slow for all the trouble. I bet at least one of them had a needle they were ultimately going to stick me with, my first and last taste of heroin. Chasing the dragon into the deep.

Maybe HK was coming in the other door, holding his own gun with his own plan. Maybe he was just up the road ready to jump them on their way back, after they dealt with me, their traitor finally revealing himself. There weren't too many maybes that didn't involve a bloodbath.

I wasn't afraid of anyone outside my mom's shop. Not of their guns, their needles, their badges, their plans. Everyone's got to go sometime, and the last few days had cemented what little future there really is for anybody, not just art students. It could be noble to die along with my town.

But really I wasn't afraid because I wasn't at my mother's salon. I was in Lincoln Head, on the Manor grounds, opening the gate from the inside so I could drive HK's car into the inner driveway. I didn't need the car close because I expected I'd need a quick getaway, but because his trunk was full of fireworks and a couple plastic tubs of gasoline. I also had a flare gun with a couple sets of marine flares that rode up front with me. Once I was in and the gate started closing behind me, I honked the horn a few times, looking for motion in the windows or any shouts from neighbors. The lights stayed off, the surrounding houses stayed dark and silent. I parked just fifty yards from the house, grabbed the flare gun and started to circle the property, double-checking the compound was as empty as I was expecting. I figured I had at least twenty minutes. It just needed to not rain.

Satisfied I was alone on the property. I unloaded the

goods from my trunk. I tried to avoid the louder banging firecrackers, focusing instead on the ones that spread sparks out the farthest. I tried to be careful, buying supplies at three different stores and three different gas stations, but as I got closer to the house, I felt like it was something I shouldn't hide. If I had a flamethrower I would have brought it.

I looked around the driveway for a rock and finding one a little bigger than my fist, hoisted it, carried it over to the window by the door and threw it through. No audible alarm. I brushed the glass off the frame with my sweatshirt sleeve and twisted the doorknob to let myself in.

The house was dark, but my eyes started getting used to it. The fog diffused the moonlight, giving the windows, especially the bank facing the water, a blank gray glow that helped me keep my bearings. I still had to feel my way along the wall for a light switch, walking a long way into the apparently huge room before I found one. When I turned it on, I confirmed the place was almost entirely empty.

No art hung from the walls and no carpets lay on the floor. The foyer, a grand, high-ceilinged room with three wide arched doorways and a winding staircase, had only a single chair, and there was nothing grand about it. It was a simple straight-backed wooden chair with cloth padding on the seat. I spotted a door underneath the stairs, most likely leading to the basement. Thinking I needed a plan to canvas a place this big, I should start at the bottom, so I walked over to it and grabbed the knob. It was locked. The door itself was heavy, maybe too heavy to be wood, and had no budge when I pressed my elbow then my whole shoulder into it. A heavy locked door in an empty house. I guessed I had solved another mystery, but I wasn't playing detective anymore. I was an artist again. I adjusted my plan to start the canvas from the ground level.

I stayed against the wall, keeping my hand on it as I walked through the arched doorway into what probably was supposed to the be the dining room, also empty, without even a chair to match the foyer. My shoes squeaked on the hardwood floor. If anyone were home they would know I was there, even if they were all the way on the top floor where I thought I had seen the light three nights earlier. I stopped in the middle of the room, half lit from the light in the foyer, and listened for any movement, inside the house or outside. Like in Sinclair's house, I could only hear my heart, but the increased rate wasn't from fear, it was excitement.

Once I turned on the light in the kitchen though, the spike was because of fear, when I saw used dishes piled in the sink. As I approached I noticed the same coffee cup I had seen on the deck the last time I was there was in with the plates. Someone either was there earlier that night, had been in the house since, was in the house with me, or coming back at some point. I leaned over the sink and looked at the dinnerware, picking up one of the plates. It was plastic, cheap, not a really a match with the rest of the place. I wondered if whoever had been there was squatting. There was apparently no alarm, why not try?

The kitchen space shared the wall of windows with what must have been designed as a living space, sunken, four steps down from the kitchen. The windows were at least twelve feet tall and functioned as mirrors with the interior lights on. I saw my reflection, standing near the sink, flare-gun in hand and took a mental snapshot in case I'd want to paint it someday. The way the reflection faded in the panes further from the light was a cool effect, one I hadn't seen. I had done reflections in glass, but never at night. With no lights visible on the outside, there wasn't a clear fade-through to distinguish where mirror turned back into window, I supposed it would make a more compelling work, albeit a more confusing one. The man I saw looking back had confused everyone who cared about him in the last week and had hopefully confused a few who really didn't.

I walked closer, watching the reflection solidify in the pane I was walking toward, and fade in the others surrounding it. My paintings had never confused people, you could always tell what the fog was hiding, you always knew. I turned from the reflection and the artist there, walked back across the kitchen and turned off the light. The windows showed fog, so impenetrable it's all they showed. I couldn't even see a glimpse of wood from the deck just on the other side. Someone could be out there, something could be out there, and that night, in honor of my father, maybe because I finally understood him, I was thankful I didn't have to know.

I had already seen the sunken living room, so I moved back through the dining room to the stairs and went up. The collection of rooms on the second level were all empty, all barely lit by the ghostly glow in the windows. While a few had bathrooms attached, they were all so open and spacious that I never had to worry about something hiding in a corner. If anything were, I would have heard it and the echo. I kept going up.

The third level was clearly designed to be a master suite and was not empty. A crumpled sleeping bag lay in the middle of the floor with a pillow next to it, both had the same flimsy, cheap, temporary feel of the plates in the kitchen. I flicked the light on, listening for any reactive movement, then checked out the master bath.

A roll of paper towels sat on the marble counter, between two sinks, one of which had a bar of soap near the rim. I edged open a closet door to find a toilet and one half-used roll of toilet paper on the floor in front of it. The glass shower with a massive square head above it was clean, but I saw a glint on the edge of the jacuzzi bath, something reflecting light from the bedroom. It was a champagne flute, plastic, with remnants of something crusting the bottom. Another mystery, to be sure, and another one I had the good fortune not to give a shit about. I padded back out of the room, down both flights of stairs then out to HK's car.

I popped the trunk, and grabbed the drugs first, the four bags surprisingly easy to carry, given their value, and even more surprisingly easy to part with, as I dropped them on top of the padded chair in the foyer. I went back out for my other supplies.

I made a full loop of all three floors, spreading the gasoline as I went, making sure to splash all the built-in wood features, like bookshelves, desks and intricate moldings. I left an unbroken trail as I went, so the flame would snake through the entire house, no matter where it caught. In every corner of each room, I placed a different gas-soaked firework. When I completed the circuit, I was basically out of fuel, so I took the can and put it in the sink on top of the dirty plates. I wriggled the coffee mug out from under it and filled it with tap water. The oven was gas, six burners under a matte range, so I flicked them all on high and doused each flame with water, leaving the gas running but not burning, and made my way out. This time I went a little faster.

Unburdened of everything but my flare gun, I stepped a few paces from the house, aimed, and because *my head was full fire*, shot a flare right through the front door. It pinged off the bottom of the stairs and into what was either designed as a sitting room or office, catching the gasoline at every hit. The walls caught before the floor, but the fire spread with the gasoline into all the rooms. I could tell more from the amount of smoke than the light, which was flickering and small. I was still able to follow it into the kitchen, and hear the blast of it catch the gas, blowing out four of the windows and letting a lot more oxygen in to feed it. Smoke was pouring out, opaque against the fire, but disappearing into the sky, darker and thicker, but still fog. People would notice the smell before they saw the flame.

I heard the telltale pops of the fireworks and felt another blast of hot air come through the door at me. I looked up and saw the second-floor windows were glowing. But instead of the cool, unknowable gray, they were glowing with an angry orange. The fire had caught, and was going to go for a while, it was time to get out of there. I just had one more flammable item I had to get out of HK's car.

I retrieved it, shook it, used it, and got halfway down the driveway before I stopped to turn around.

The fire was brighter than I thought it could be, flames were coming out of the roof. The whole house was going down. I could see the heat pushing the fog farther and farther from the structure, burning it off the property. I wondered if the lawn would catch too, and the altar. The smell was growing stronger, and the hot wind from the house more intense. I took my phone out of my pocket, turned it sideways, and framed the house and the trees and the mist.

In the lower left corner of the picture, on the driveway, spray-painted in perfect white block letters, almost as if they'd been stenciled, read "HERE BE MONSTERS."

I emailed the picture to Guardado, put the phone back in my pocket, and hopped the gate, hitting the ground running.

# Afterword

He had to walk practically the full length of the top deck just to find a free chair with an awning over it. Lots of people were trying not to get too much sun, but the deputy harbormaster was actively avoiding it. After the winter and a month of fog darker and scarier than any he'd remembered, this much sun just felt obscene. His skin, too callused for any rope to chafe and too thick for the cold to cut through, couldn't even put up a fight against it. It itched and bubbled and peeled on the day they set sail and hadn't improved any now that they were a few hours from home port. Who would have thought the sun was the problem with a Caribbean cruise.

The chair he found was angled differently from all the surrounding loungers, almost perpendicular to them. He looked in the direction of the sun, then his watch, to get his bearings before calculating that while most chairs were facing North by Northwest, his was facing North by Northeast. The deputy harbormaster was sure whoever had it last had just dragged it out of place, but instead of dragging it back into conforming, he nodded to himself. He was fine with standing out, his view was better looking sternwards.

There was no table next to the chair, so he had to be careful how he settled himself. He checked his hands before deciding. His right hand was holding a pina colada, the absolute best he'd ever had. Since the first day, they were all he drank, morning to night, and he intended to have at least one more before he disembarked. In the dining room, they had a big vat of it with a spigot anyone could access any time. At a few of the events he would order it from an actual bartender and try to watch them like hawks as they made it. He even asked one about the recipe and the guy shrugged and said it was pre-mixed. He intended to ask someone at check-out if they could give him the recipe.

His left hand held a book of word scramble puzzles he picked up in the airport before his flight down. It was a long habit of his to try the scramble every time he had access to a paper, and he almost always solved them. Down at the Porpoise, they would sometimes save it for him or would try it themselves and get stumped, then bring it to him with their tail between their legs for his help. The puzzles in this book were a little harder than the newspaper ones, he had only solved three full puzzles, but he was getting into a rhythm and wanted to get to five before he got back to East Hook.

In the front pocket of his Hawaiian shirt was a pencil, in his bathing suit pocket was a pencil sharpener, reading glasses and his room key. He threw the puzzle book down on the chair and took care sitting and settling into the chair, so as not to tip the drink over. He knew if he left to refill it, someone else would take this prime spot before he came back.

He left his Crokies attached to his sunglasses, even though they dug into the back of his neck through the pillow. As careless as he'd been with his skin, he wasn't taking any risks with his eyes. His sunglasses stayed on, even most of time indoors. He recently concluded that his eyes were the best thing about him. Aside from up close reading, they'd never let him down.

333

Back in May, it was his eyes that kicked off the two weeks of terror and destruction back home, piercing the thickest fog of the year to spot that poor O'Reilly girl in the bay. He couldn't remember exactly, but he suspected it was the third consecutive night shift out on the water, after the lobster boat got torn apart but before the house burned down, that he decided to book this vacation. Bobbing out there blinded, waiting for something to attack from below, came damn near making him permanently forget everything he loved about being on the water. He needed to get back out on his own terms, on calm seas in warm weather, with someone else driving, and his eyes further out towards a horizon he could clearly see.

This was mostly doing the trick, a ship this big didn't bob, and even the mornings were crystal clear, at least by nine AM. He made it a point to not rise before then.

He got into a pattern while he sat in the shady chair. He'd work on a scramble puzzle until he got stumped, then he'd make a point to gaze out at the big blue through his shades, almost immediately forgetting the frustration the puzzle was causing him. Sometimes he'd get fed up and look at the answers in the back, and his frustration would double, as he didn't recognize half the words they used, if they were even in English. No matter what trick the book was trying to pull, a minute or two overlooking the water calmed him down. Seeing so much of it, and nothing in it was like therapy.

With his setup, there wasn't much to see on the deck either. Occasionally people would walk by, and he'd scope them out as best as he could. He liked watching people behind his sunglasses, sometimes he tilted his head down, pulled his hat down low to make it look like he was sleeping, then look up through his shades and take in everything. He never did it to be a creep, though he doubted he could convince anyone of that. It was more about plausible deniability. Eyes like his sometimes saw too much, and he was on vacation. With the shades, he didn't even have to look the other way, no one could prove he was ever looking at all.

The people who passed weren't proving to be as interesting as the water, or the scramble puzzle. He didn't even need to look to know it would probably be an older person, wearing a button down shirt and shorts or a sarong covering a swimsuit, walking slowly in loafers or flip flops, with a drink in their hand, hardly ever looking out at the water. When he couldn't see them, they all smelled the same, like sunblock, and sounded the same. Walking with slow, easy gaits, their feet landing softly.

That's how he noticed her first, from the sound of her footsteps. The speed wasn't different, but the tone was. Those feet were walking with a purpose, and the way they were hitting the ground suggested some real tension, something he hadn't seen in anyone else since day two. The deputy harbormaster slouched in his chair, pulled his hat down low, and looked up out of his shades waiting for the owner of the footsteps to walk past.

What he saw walk past didn't match anything he'd seen to that point. She was young, she couldn't have been more than twenty-five. About Cadie O'Reilly's age, he couldn't help thinking to himself, as he did for every girl he saw or read about since that night in the fog. She was barefoot, which could have explained the different sound the steps were making. On the ship they recommended against going barefoot, there was a fungus they had ninety-five percent contained. There was no drink in her hand, which could have explained the tension. Looking at her walk though, he saw it, the straight-backed posture and how she held her head perfectly still as she walked. Her pants were dark, form-fitting and shiny, and she had a tank top that showed off some patches of suntanned skin.

The first time he saw her move her head it was in his general direction, but like him, she was wearing big sunglasses so he couldn't pinpoint the exact target of her gaze. He hoped it wasn't him, but stayed perfectly still just in case, even inhaling slowly so his stomach would go up, to complete the illusion he was sleeping. He kept his eyes on her, trying to take in the details of her face. Her sunglasses, the big, cheap plastic ones you buy in the ship convenience stores, stretched across too much of her face for him to be able to make out her features. He saw she had a strong jawline, at least the way she was holding her head, but he couldn't tell anything about her nose and cheekbones. A thicket of wavy black hair tumbled down around her ears and over her shoulders, some strands caught by the breeze sprayed towards him.

She didn't look his way for long, moving her head back into that same locked position as she strode forward. He kept his eyes on her after she passed him, watched her continue her walk to the back of the boat, and from the new angle, learned a little more. She was wearing a backpack, but a strange one, black and sleek and shiny like her pants. It didn't look like it had any zippers. On her left shoulder, set against the bronzed skin, was a tattoo of weird fish or shark.

The way she was walking he could tell she wasn't looking back, so he came up out of his slouch and leaned forward, so his view wasn't blocked by the fabric of his chair's awning.

She was the most interesting thing he'd seen so far, and he was planning on watching her until she gave him a reason not to. The lean forward only bought the deputy harbormaster another ten seconds or so. He was ready to stand up and walk just to see where she led him.

He was sure she'd lead to some overly muscled, overly groomed, or overly moneyed boyfriend, but he stood up just the same, walking to the railing to look straight down the ship at her. He let her out of his sight briefly to scan the other hundred and eighty degrees on the ship, seeing if anyone else was looking where he was. He imagined a few husbands whose wives were up getting a drink might risk it but didn't see anyone. The way the deck chairs were arranged, almost everyone else was pointed in the opposite direction, so he probably was the only one, an intimacy he enjoyed as he started strolling sternwards.

Not too long after he started walking, she stopped. The deputy harbormaster was sure she heard his footsteps, and leaned back against the railing, pointing his body and most of his head away from her, keeping her in the corner of his vision through his shades. His shoddy attempt at nonchalance was thankfully unnecessary, as she didn't turn towards him, instead turning out toward the water. She put both hands on the railing.

He saw her looking out at the water, wondering what she was looking at and wondering what he could pull from the encyclopedia of maritime knowledge he had in his brain that would impress her most, or make her laugh. While he dug through the archives, he noticed her lean over the railing, almost leaving her feet to get a good look at the side of the ship and the water churning directly below. She was brave, his knees almost got weak when just leaned against the railing. Looking down at the water immediately outside the boat had lost all its appeal since May. Conscious of the railing now, he took a step away from it, creating a buffer zone as he kept walking towards her.

With more proof she was interested in the water, the deputy harbormaster's confidence grew. If he just talked to her, made her laugh, it would probably be the best memory he took home from the trip. She started touching her backpack, making sure the straps were the right length. The tension he noticed even before he saw her was more evident, all her muscles looked clenched. She took her sunglasses off and laid them carefully on the deck beside her. She stood back up and moved her upper body from side to side, trying to loosen up her back. She hopped up and down a few times on the balls of her feet, like she was getting ready to do something.

Based on her lack of footwear, he would have guessed yoga, and she could have used it, with how tightly wound she looked. She moved again to the railing, looking down at the water again then back towards the stern, gripping the railing tight enough that he could almost make out the blood leaving her knuckles. He was still forty feet away and she hadn't noticed him.

He stopped, not wanting to be noticed, and not knowing what to say if he was. He didn't lean back on the railing or even try to look nonchalant, he just stood there. She took her hands off the rail but didn't step back. She fiddled with her watch and touched her backpack again. She tilted her head all the way back until she was looking at the sky, and kept it there, long enough to take two deep breaths, and he saw the tension leave her body. First it left the shoulders and her arms just hung down, then her chin fell and back slumped a bit. Her knees bent slightly, and she was back on her heels.

Tension found its way into his muscles as he watched her put her hands on the railing one more time, take a giant step up to put her right foot just inside her right hand on that railing, then pull her left foot up too. She crouched there, balanced like a spider for four fast beats of the deputy harbormaster's heart. In one graceful and powerful motion, her hands let go of the railing and she sprung herself away from the boat and into the air, above *the murderous innocence of the sea.*

# The End

# Acknowledgments

While the idea for Fathoms has been with me for some time, this book is really a pandemic baby. Its development provided some order to those long monotonous days. But you need more than order to survive, so my first thank you is to Victoria, who provided the joy as my new wife during that time, and keeps providing it every day, hour, minute, and second we're together. Maybe if I keep writing long enough I'll be able properly express your effect on me, but I doubt it. Until then you'll just have to be content that I love you more than I can express.

A massive thanks to my early beta readers: Clarkie, Jesse, Jack, Ellen, John, Cilla, Chip, Charlie & Turner. Your questions and feedback helped shape the story and gave me the confidence to share this more widely. Thank you to Ken for proofreading. And thank you last to my publishing grumble: Emrick, Bella & Truffles.

A lot of media influenced the creation of Fathoms, but nothing more than the documentary Heroin: Cape Cod, USA. Seeing what is really churning and wriggling beneath even the most idyllic surfaces helped me rethink the world I was actually seeing. Sometimes if the coat of paint is pretty and fresh enough, it can cover up a lot of rotted wood.

If you are struggling with substance abuse there are resources nearby. Look for Narcotics Anomymous local and virtual meetings and see other resources at <u>na.org</u>. No matter who is trying to make you invisible, we see you.

Thanks for reading! Be sure to visit kjmcquade.com for information on all my writing and everything going on with me. You can also stay up to date on my work and thoughts by signing up for my newsletter.